BLACK RIVER

Tales of the North Country

MARK A. CLARKE

KIRKUS
REVIEWS

TITLE INFORMATION

BLACK RIVER
Tales of the North Country
Mark A. Clarke
CCE Publishing (240 pp.)
ISBN: 9781737301745

BOOK REVIEW

Clarke's short story collection details characters and communities surrounding a river in the northeastern U.S.

Black River, running through the Adirondack Mountains, is a place the author knows well-Clarke's grandfather founded the Dade's Inn motel in the region in the 1930s, and his father and mother took over the business in the late 1950s and ran it until the early 1960s. The author's focus on community is conveyed through 31 loosely connected short stories, based on his father's tales of the "rugged backwoods" in the Black River area, all united by people who are a "robust group with character." The stories celebrate both the remarkable and the mundane, including a bar fight begun by a Dade's Inn regular called Harold ("Harold"), the terrifying appearance of a bear behind the Inn ("The Bear"), and an examination of local Christmas traditions ("The Magic of Christmas"). Clarke's ability to evoke the transcendent qualities in ordinary moments is a hallmark of the collection; one of the standout stories is devoted to Clarke's memories of churning homemade blackberry ice cream with his grandpa Dade, told so sweetly that the reader can almost taste the frozen treat: "The finest gift we can give to one another is our time." Human connection is a central thread throughout, and descriptions of the locale affirm Clarke's strong sense of place. His prose is simultaneously immersive and matter-of-fact ("Trying to distinguish the facts is like taking a stroll in the Hundred Acre Wood. The stories have taken on a life of their own"), drawing some of the more disparate stories together as the author jumps between people and time periods, from the Second World War to contemporary exchanges between a husband and wife. Clarke's stories celebrate this unique area and those living in it, immortalizing the comical, the quotidian, and the extraordinary in equal measure.

An entertaining set of vignettes chronicling an endearing, close-knit community.

ALSO BY MARK A. CLARKE

Columbia: Those Who Honorably Served, June 2021
Harriet's Egg, December 2021
Digger Digger Digger, October 2022

Photograph by Lenny Hall (artist and title of the painting unkown)

BLACK RIVER

Tales of the North Country

MARK A. CLARKE

Published by
CCE PUBLISHING
Edgewater, Florida

This is a work of creative nonfiction. While all the stories in this book are mostly true, no doubt some embellishments have been added through the years. Also, some names and identifying details have been changed to protect the privacy of the people involved.

Copyright ©2023 Mark A. Clarke
All rights reserved

No portion of this book may be reproduced or used in any form, or by any means, without prior written permission of the author.

Cover, author images: Lenny Hall Photography
Cover, book design: Cindy Casey

Published by
CCE PUBLISHING
Edgewater, Florida

Printed in the United States of America

Paperback ISBN: 978-1-7373017-3-8
Hardback ISBN: 978-1-7373017-4-5

Mark A. Clarke

DEDICATION

To Shannon and Ryan

TABLE OF CONTENTS

Otter Creek 145

White Lake 171

Acknowledgements...............239

About the Author...............240

Introduction

Rivers have long been a popular subject in text and art. Because life emerged along riverbanks, the river represents the passage of time and offers a message about life. In the Bible, the river is the source of life as with the Garden of Eden or the baptism in the River Jordan. It is a metaphor for a spiritual journey in *Siddhartha* by Herman Hesse and a symbol of freedom in *The Adventures of Huckleberry Finn* by Mark Twain. It is the central theme in the series of paintings by Thomas Cole titled *The Voyage of Life*. The Hudson River artist gives a visual portrayal of man coursing through life starting at birth and ending in death.

Black River is a collection of stories about people, their lives, and the river that passes through their small corner of the world.

Black River gets its name from the tannic acid that naturally darkens its waters. Beginning its journey at North Lake, it runs northwest between the Adirondack Mountains and the Tug Hill Plateau, emptying into Lake Ontario. Along its path are small hamlets with names like Steuben Corners, Holland Patent, Alder Creek, Forestport, Port Lyden and Boonville. For generations, my ancestors drank the waters and breathed the woodland air.

My father was a good storyteller, and these stories reflect those hardy, resilient individuals who filtered out of the rugged backwoods in the Adirondacks. They were a robust group with character. You might call them fibbers, frauds, fakes or fabricators. Some were just outright liars, but they had flare and were some of the most creative and talented storytellers the North County had to offer.

The names and events that appear in these stories have been altered. The people (for the most part) as well as the actual events have faded with their retelling. These stories are like Winnie-the-Pooh wondering the Hundred Acre Wood. Pooh stumbles upon a set of tracks, then there are two sets of tracks, and then three and then again four.

So, too, are the stories in *Black River*. Simple and straightforward, they began as chronicles of a time and its people, but with the telling and retelling over time they have entered into the realm of fiction. Trying to distinguish the facts is like taking a stroll in the Hundred Acre Wood. The stories have taken on a life of their own. It is what I call the creative and evolutionary process of storytelling.

Take the story "The Magic of Christmas." Mildred, the main character, was modeled after my maternal grandmother. The events at the tavern, Bastogne and the café in that story actually occurred. The characters were altered, and the dialogue fashioned. The story "Night Visitor," another example, was conveyed to me by a high school classmate and the song "Pony Boy" was a tune sung by my mother-in-law to her grandchildren.

In many stories the events occurred. My dad shot a bear and the bag of peanuts off the backbar, my brother broke an inn window(s), someone knocked over the honey jar, my grandfather's beagle ate two pies, and sadly the septic tank story is also true. "A Day With Dad," "Log Jam's Mutt," "First Deer," and "Dead Eye" were stories told to me as well as other episodes that are found in other stories. I was the altar boy in "Monsignor," I was witness to the classroom incident in "School Yard" and the GTO was one hot muscle car owned by a dear friend of mine. Herman was German, Joe was Russian and most of the characters in the stories are composites with their names changed or the events slightly altered.

I used the Mary Shelley classic Frankenstein as my approach to writing Black River. I pieced the stories together and allowed them to take on a life of their own. First I began with an event and location, then included a time and a set of characters. Primarily this made up the "body" of my story. I then "stitched" them all together in a narrative, being careful to include a moderate seasoning of humor as with a Thurber, a Twain or perhaps some musings of say a Will Rogers. I included a catch ending with some stories to satisfy the O. Henry in me.

As I wrote, the characters and the events took on a slightly different appearance. I discovered that truth can be subjective and whimsical; it is a convenience in the hands of a storyteller-writer. Like the Pooh Bear, truth was a difficult path to follow for it is a winged creature that leaves no tracks.

Mark Twain could appreciate that. He understood that the purpose of a story is for amusement and entertainment. Mark Twain has been credited with saying, "Never let the truth get in the way of a good story." Some dispute the claim. They attribute the quote to a Celtic saying, "That's my story and if there's a lie, so be it, for it wasn't me who first composed it."

Someone once said there are two types of lies. There are lies and then there are damn lies. There is a third type called fiction. It is the kinder and more benign form.

Black River is a collection of stories about a people, their lives, and the river that passes through their corner of the world. It is best clarified in the story "Googer."

"They are those who overcame adversity and left their mark on those who pass(ed) . . . a shaft of light softly filtering through the forest canopy shedding light along the path. Unheralded, . . . directed us along the way."

I hope the reader finds some measure of enjoyment in their story.

SECTION 1

~~~

WOODHULL CREEK

~~~

HAROLD

The sign over the backbar read "There's Always Harmony Here." It was an advertisement by Carstairs Blended Whiskey. It rang true, most of the time.

Harold was one of the more colorful patrons of Dade's Inn. He lived down the road several miles next to the old Forestport ball diamond tucked into an opening of poplar trees. Harold worked with heavy equipment and had bulldozed the ball diamond for the local town to play hardball shortly after the Japanese surrendered and many of the men were coming back from the war. It was a way for "our boys" to blow off some steam on summer weekends over a beer or two.

The automobile had become not only an item of familial status, but a growing necessity. Auto factories during the second war were retooled to make war machines. Coupled with shortages of supplies like rubber for tires and engine parts, folks had to make do with what they had.

Harold was too young for one war and too old for the other. During the Second World War the need for Harold's mechanical skills increased with demand. His tinkering with automobiles was honed to a desired and indispensable skill. Once he attached skis to the front wheels of his Model A. This enable it to glide over the snow packed roads of the Adirondacks. Its novelty was a wonder to all and his handicraft was as refreshing as well water. His skills were admired and much appreciated by friends and neighbors.

He boastfully exclaimed, "If you want the easiest way of doing somethin', find the laziest man on the job, ME!"

The validity of this axiom wasn't a universal proof, but it struck a chord of common sense and Harold had mined a good deal of life's sum and substance over the coursing years.

Harold never was one to embrace falsehoods; however, he was known to massage the truth once in a while. You see, Harold had become quite a celebrity in the community because of his expertise. He was showered with numerous accolades to the point that he began to view himself as the favored son. Add a touch of rye whiskey and Harold's boasting would transform into harmless bravado.

It was at these times the locals wouldn't pay him too much attention for Harold was inoffensive, all 5 feet 5 ½ inches of him – when massaged of course. Another aspect of Harold was he rarely conformed to time. He felt he would not be a prisoner of it. Timeliness was reserved for weddings, child birth and, of course, death (unless avoidable).

And then there was one other; that was five o'clock, Friday afternoon at Dade's Inn – the weekly cocktail hour. The local riff-raff looked forward to it. They could expect at five on Friday that Harold would burst into the tap-room, hike up his britches, set his work cap at a rakish tilt and with fisted arms akimbo, exclaim in his most menacing voice, "I'm the toughest sona-bitch in this place and there ain't a goddamn one of you can KICK MY ASS!"

Napoleon could not have delivered it any better. Leveling a threatening stare from one end of the bar to the other, he silently dared anyone to take up the challenge at the risk of their own peril. He would then enjoy their reaction.

"Aw shut up Harold . . . Can't one drink in peace. . . What a pain in my royal ass."

Pausing for effect, he would adjust his pants and swagger to the bar; all the while looking left and next right to see if there was a belated challenge. Pause again for effect, he would then order a shot and a beer. Good humor would abound and harmony returned.

It was always the same scenario, like a Greek Tragedy. You knew the play's ending; however, you paid the price of admission to enjoy the performance. The audience would then return to the mundane topics that are so consequential to simple country folk, but befuddling to the cultured urbane. Thus went the performance: weekly, monthly, and seasonally. It was unfailing. You could set your watch by it.

Some say there are two seasons in the Adirondacks – July and winter. At the beginning of the warmer weather the woodlands seem to release men.

Most of them are lumbermen who toil in the craft until the lack of snow makes it difficult to skid logs or the black flies and horse flies induce derangement. It is at this time that these solitary men drifted into the lowlands to find a vacant stool in some out of the way section of a favored tavern. Unaccustomed to the ways of lowlanders, they are contented with the company of a frosty beer or two.

It was a Friday afternoon at five o'clock sometime in late May that Harold made his expected appearance. Harold burst into the taproom. Raising himself up to the full 5 feet 5 ½ inches, he hiked up his britches then set his green work cap at a rakish tilt. With fisted arms akimbo he exclaimed menacingly, "I'm the toughest sonofabitch in this place and there ain't a goddamn ONE of you can kick my ass!"

In the short moment of silence required to savor this impressive public display, a lone figure rose from the shadows of the corner bar stool, took two steps Harold's way and mumbled, "I think I can." A fist, about the size of a toaster caught Harold between the eyes sending him sailing over a table and sliding into the corner. Unperturbed, the stranger sauntered back to his stool and continued to nurse his frothy beer.

For that brief moment the harmony was disrupted. Somehow this Greek Tragedy had a fresh ending. The outlander was unaccustomed to the Friday entertainment and had naturally taken up with the open invitation. There was no ill will intended. It was simply "fact of the mater." No one blamed the woodlander. His action was understandable and without malice. What was one to expect?

Harold somehow departed the taproom unnoticed and not a word was heard from him in the following days. When someone called on him at his home, no one answered the door. A neighbor thought they saw what appeared to be raccoon eyes peering from behind a slightly drawn curtain.

The next Friday five o'clock came and went. After the six, seven and eight o'clock hours passed the legion of onlookers gave up hope that Harold would make a showing. Even the stranger seemed noticeably disappointed. On into the evening hours the festivities resumed, but there seemed to be something missing – Harold.

The following Friday frivolous conversation was bantered about the bar.

Harmony hummed. As the hour of five approached there would be one or two furtive glances in the direction of the door. When the hour of five struck there was no Harold. About five minutes later when the door creaked open there was disappointment when the outlander appeared. He gave a friendly nod to the crowd and took a stool in the far corner of the bar.

Shortly thereafter there was a click and the door partially opened. It was just ajar enough to see an eye peering in. It gazed throughout the room until it remained fixed on the lone figure sipping a beer in the corner. The door immediately shut. There are times like this that it is difficult to discern the mind of man. What is it that makes one the person he is or likely to become?

In a flash, a lone figure plunged into the room. All eyes were glued to the man who stood in the doorway like a colossus, all 5 feet 5 ½ inches of himself. It was Harold glaring back at the crowd through yellowed raccoon-like eyes. Hiking up his pants, he adjusted his work cap wildly to one side.

Fist resting on his hip and elbows turned outward he bellowed, "I'm the toughest sonabitch in this place and there ain't a goddamn ONE OF YOU CAN KICK MY ASS!"

Before anyone could say a word he pointed a flexed index finger at the stranger in the corner adding, "Except that big sonabitch OVER THERE!"

Good-naturedly the big fellow directed Harold to the bar stool next to his and bought him the first drink. All the while there were comments of, "Aw shut up Harold . . . Can't one drink in peace . . . What a pain in my royal ass."

It wasn't necessary, but Harold left the door open just in case it required a swift egress from the premises. And as the sign read, "There's Always Harmony Here" . . . mostly.

THE INN

One of my earliest memories was the sign advertising Carstairs Blended Whiskey. It read, "There's always harmony here" and it hung prominently over the cash register on the back bar in Dade's Inn.

When I was a toddler, my family relocated from the western part of the New York state. We found temporary lodging in the garret of the inn; a log cabin structure named after my grandfather, Dade. With the aid of two lumberjacks, he built it and a motel in the 1930s to serve the locals and seasonal lumbermen as Prohibition came to an end. My father and mother took over the business in the late 50s and ran it until the early 60s.

Two large hardwood doors served as an entrance to the inn. They were designed by a skilled local craftsman and hung with hand-hewed wrought iron hinges. One door opened to the main area which served as a dining area. It had a scattering of tables and chairs. Beyond, was a solid mahogany bar with wooden stools.

Patrons picked their preferred station to savor a few wet ones. The bar would seat a dozen people or three times that many standing when business flourished. Overhead, wainscoting rested on top several exposed spruce logs that served as the tavern's ceiling. It extended the width and breadth of the taproom. Timeworn and rich with decade old tobacco stains, the coarse interior had a manly discoloration. Retaining a stale barroom odor, the taproom was poorly lit. It held a fitting ambiance for the rough-hewn, care-free characters who frequented the inn. The solid interior offered a rustic durability with a warm, sociable feel where cheerfulness thrived.

Two pale-green restroom doors were located at the north end of the main room. Some nameless, run-of-the-mill artisan skillfully painted the renderings of two deer heads on the doors. They denoted gender - buck for male, doe for female. Inevitably, some buck would blunder into doe territory which would result in a high-pitched shriek followed by some hoots, howls and theatrical laughter. Generally, misunderstandings were a result of a sudden natural urge or the fallout of too much whiskey. However, juvenile silliness accounted for the other incursions.

Between the restrooms was a bulbous jute box that attempted to brighten up the flat interior. Appearing like a B-rated sci-fi robot, it played an array of tunes popular in the day. When nature called, a queue of females formed next to it, each patiently waiting their turn outside the one-stall ladies room. As the line lengthened, some clown would insert a coin in the jute box and play a popular Patty Paige crowd pleaser while his associates would devilishly sing along.

"Please release me, let me gooooo ..." It was instantly enjoyed by all except those with a bloated bladder waiting in line.

Frustrated, the afflicted eased their discomfort by swaying slightly back and forth, knees fused together. The Svengali-like tempo added to the anguish of those suffering. Displaying obvious discomfort, they shifted occasionally from one foot to the other and back again. These tormented souls endured their difficulty until their agony presented additional sport for the rogue gallery. Gleefully, the scoundrels emphasized the word "GO" with each chorus. It electrified the horde, sending many into a paroxysm of delight. Predictably, someone shouted:

"Hey honey, you want to dance?"

As if on cue, some joker followed with:

"While you're up that way, here's a quarter for the jute box. You seem to take a liking to that tune."

The increased laughter provoked the unladylike response:

"Hope you get yours stuck in a zipper, you neanderthal."

The men winced and the women applauded. The rude exchange introduced a silent truce until a lively tune struck up on the jute box and geniality resumed.

The native log interior was like a second home to those residing in the surrounding woodland communities like Forestport, Woodgate or Alder Creek. Centered on the back bar was an ancient black cash register that divided an inventory of fortifying spirits. A wooden billy club was accessible under the bar for cracking ice or the skull of those ruffians who "failed to get with the program." It served a necessary purpose but was applied sparingly. A window at both ends framed the back bar like bookends.

Unlike European bars, an American bar is long and stretched out like a boardwalk. The bar at Dade's Inn was dubbed Mahogany Ridge and extended the length of the main room.

In England, pubs were places to "take a pint" and discuss literature, politics and issues of the day. Darts were the preferred recreational sport. American bars were built for consumption and plenty of it. Bragging developed into a science and lying became an art.

Adirondack legends, lore and mountain mysteries could trace their roots back to Mahogany Ridge. You can be certain Paul Bunyan and Babe the Blue Ox was conceived in a barroom somewhere in the backwoods of the Adirondacks Mountains – no doubt a product of a jug of apple jack or a barrel of O' Be Joyful.

It is ironic that the sign that hung prominently in Dade's Inn that advertised whiskey contributed to the promotion of harmony - of a sort. In this case it was Harmony's dysfunctional stepbrother, Disharmony.

Adjoining the main room was a porch-like area with a separate entrance which catered to small parties or discrete lovers. It had benches and serving tables designed and built by Seward, a skilled carpenter who enjoyed the outdoors and Thoreau-like existence. Like Henry David, his scholarship was a resourceful mind. Seward harvested trunks of small white birch trees and decorated the space with his resourcefulness. The ivory saplings extended from the floor to the ceiling, which gave the room a trace of the Adirondacks and quaint woodland flair. Tastefully, their snow-white trunks appeared growing through the porch, past the ceiling into the beyond.

Bright neon beer signs glowed and hummed in the windows. They advertised local beers, Utica Club and Genesee Ale. These signs were the modern version of the Homeric Sirens from ancient times. Covertly, they tempted the parched traveler as might a Parisian Street walker to a listing sailor.

Tastefully, pictures of attractive, half-clad ballet dancers by Edgar Degas hung on the walls. These sensual dancers were witness to and testament of the North Country's proud recognition of classic art. Gazing at these fine prints for some time, one local mossback and connoisseur of the Police Gazette rightly expressed the common sentiments held by those in his "neck of the woods."

"Now that's REAL art. 'Specially thems that ain't got much clinging to 'em."

Adjoining the taproom was an entrance to the kitchen. It consisted of a cooking area for the preparation of food (stove, refrigerator, deep fryer, etc.) and a cleaning area (sink/dishwasher) for washing dishes and general cleanup. Beyond was a large walk-in cooler, an area for dry good storage and an exit door that led outback.

On one of the shelves was a plain, unadorned cookie jar but hardly so to one so young. It was dear to my heart, the jewel of our possessions that came with us to the Adirondacks. This cookie jar prompted a second childhood memory. Unlike most cookie jars, this one was not so ordinary. This one had special meaning and fond memories.

Children know cookie jars possess secrets and speaks to them in a language of its own. Cookie jars are viewed with awe and wonderment. They are blessed with hope and promise; cookie jars house youthful dreams of possibilities.

To a child, it is like venturing into a confectionary rabbit hole. It whispers tenderly to toddlers with feelings of sweet exploration. These containers concealed flavorful riches like ginger snaps, chocolate-chip, or oatmeal raisin and . . . ah yes . . . pecan cookies – my favorite. Cookie jars embody the true spirit of childhood.

Anything worth pursuing requires a certain element of risk-taking. To a child in pursuit of the tempting and the tantalizing, it is a risk well worth taking.

I came to learn an important lesson. It is that all true stories end in tragedy. And it is unavoidable. Tragedy, the shadowy silhouette of disaster, came in the form of an adult who loomed supreme and omnipresent in a child's life. The parent suddenly appeared unexpectedly, and tragedy struck like a serpent. Then came the rhetorical question.

"Did I say you could have a cookie?"

Heartbreak followed misfortune. The crestfallen received a scolding and then condemned to isolation.

"Now go to your room."

It is said that wisdom, unlike knowledge, is obtained with experience.

This is the role of the adult, and this is the fate the child.

Grown-ups are beings who have lost their sense of wonderment with the passage of time in the accumulating years. The ceramic receptacle that once held the wellspring of youthful enchantment, would eventually lead to a tragic end. It was reassigned. Transformed, if you wish, by that grownup notion they innocently called repurposed.

My cookie jar was converted into a common, sordid, lack-lustered, unappreciated receptacle known as a honey jar. For those unfamiliar with the term, it is the polite name for a chamber pot. My cookie jar was relegated to that dreadful station of what the average peons would commonly pee into or what is pejoratively referred to as the common commode. A treasure had been transformed into tribulation. It was like converting Aladdin's Lamp into a Pandora's Box.

It is with that cold sense of adult expediency that misfortune snatched the pecan cookie jar with all of its charm and departed with my youthful desires. Repurposing became the indifferent stepfather to the orphaned twins, Wonder and Delight.

So was the fate of my cookie jar. But as destiny would have it, this would not be the end of it. This launched into a third childhood memory. One not soon forgotten.

The move from Rochester to Forestport was a challenge for the five children. Our transition, like my cookie jar, would become permanent and took some adjustment. Lodging was a priority and short term. The garret over Dade's Inn became our temporary quarters and a room in my Grandpa Dade's motel was utilized for bathing and such things.

Ascending into the loft above the taproom became a nightly ritual and a form of evening entertainment for the regulars. Climbing onto the bar, each of us would wiggle a grasp onto the lip of the rectangular hole that served as an entrance to the loft. Placing a foot into Dad's palm, he would give us a "leg up" by shot-putting us upward into the arms of an older sibling who had ascended before us.

Army cots arranged in the loft served as our beds. Once safely aloft, Mom would tuck us in for the night. A metal grill was fitted securely over the ceiling entrance to ensure that nightly roving didn't result in disaster. We were forbidden to venture near the hole for fear of falling through and injuring ourselves, but we would quietly crawl to the opening and sneak a peek at the activity below.

As with all children, the nighttime pleas for the use of the bathroom were to be expected. This made running an inn difficult and disruptive, not to mention very annoying. My father solved that problem.

In the 19th century outhouses and chamber pots were common and served Americans well. Many parts of the United States still didn't have indoor plumbing until the early part of the 20th century and even then, indoor plumbing in rural America was not universally acknowledged or assured. Chamber pots were common and served inhabitants well. Located under the bed, these white porcelain receptacles were practical, not to mention convenient. On cold nights instead of traipsing through rain, sleet or snow to the outhouse known as the "the forty-yarder" in the Adirondacks, our forebearers found a simple solution, the chamber pot. So why reinvent the wheel was the thinking of my father. Enter the cookie jar/chamber pot.

Should we require the use of the bathroom at night, we were instructed to pee in the improvised receptacle. It was good-bye to the cookie jar, hello honey jar.

The honey jar would serve as our interim potty, privy, lavatory, or loo, if you wish. Necessity became the mother of invention at the expense of my cookie jar. By paternal decree, field testing was skipped and it went directly into utilization. As expected, a glitch or two would develop and one night it did.

With an occasional Patsy Cline or Nat King Cole tune playing, the evening droned on with the humming of idle conversation like the steady buzzing of a beehive. When you are young, sleep can come swiftly. It can and it did. It was sometime later that evening that a rainstorm came suddenly upon us. Thunderstorms swiftly and abruptly appear out of nowhere in the Adirondacks. They bring with them a deluge of water that can rush forth unexpectedly with a torrential drenching much like a waterfall and then, just as suddenly, fade away. Such was the thunderhead that suddenly appeared.

There was a window in the loft that remained opened in the summer evenings to let in fresh air. Without warning a storm approached from the west. It announced its arrival with the flicker of light and was followed by a series of low rumbling. Caught in the brief natural light was the shape of a child near the honey jar answering nature's call.

Whether it was the sudden flash of lightning, a child's drowsiness or a combination of both that caused the incident, what occurred next became fodder for the mysterious case of whodunit in the years that followed.

But what wasn't so mysterious was the honey jar had tipped over spilling its contents all over the floor. Combined with the now surging sheets of lashing rain blowing through the open window, there appeared a localized flood the likes rarely seen since Noah, or so one thought.

Be that as it may, a small tsunami of yellow liquid quickly fanned out. Luckily, the volume of "honey" was initially distributed away from the entrance of the loft. A large quantity of amber fluid formed an enormous puddle in the center of the floor. That was fortunate, for had it gone in the opposite direction it would have created a sizable waterfall through the loft entrance. On the other hand, the floor had either not been constructed quite evenly or the passage of time had pressed the beams at an angle, causing the floor to slightly tilt, thus gradually slanting in the direction of the opening. Slowly the liquid contents were drawn by the forces of gravity in its direction.

Simultaneously, here and there the ceiling above the taproom gradually began to sweat. If there was the slightest crack, droplets of the liquid honey found it. Aided by gravity, it began to ooze and notably drip one drop here, and then one drop there with no particular pattern. It was late in the evening, and everyone appeared to be too deep in their cups and fixed in conversation to take notice.

The first to become aware was Walter Feller. Walter was in his usual posture leaning over his beer with head tilted to the side taking note of those around him. Retired, he had taken up the hobby of social voyeurism or what he called a sociological adventure. If anyone were to take notice it would be Walter.

Feeling a drip on the back of his neck, he raised a brow, detecting something seemed amiss. With the force of nature and the irregular ceiling, the liquid honey appeared at the garret entrance. Ever so slightly a rivulet trickled down from the loft entrance. The unusual event intrigued Walter enough to remark,

"Passable and nice but the falls at Forestport are more presentable."

By this time, the rafters went from sweat to bleed. It was followed by a constant drip . . .drip . . . drip here and a gradual drip . . . drip . . . drip there.

Art, a patron and one of the inn's nightly fixtures was the first victim. His 10-gallon Stetson hat caught and captured all in his immediate vicinity. Small puddles began to form pools along the outer brim.

Two young lovers, embraced in their spellbound romance, were next. Oblivious to all but each other, they continued to dance in the center of the room as if they were strolling in the morning mist of an April rain.

One notable trickle of fluid dribbled onto Harold's shoulder. Harold, who was always sensitive to any slight or imagined hostility, spun quickly around like the pint-sized fire-breather that he was and snorted,

"There ain't a one of you can kick my ass."

Quickly looked left and right for the phantom culprit who dare challenge him, he was too lost in his self-importance and remained ignorant of the storm brewing overhead.

The trickling gradually increased. It advanced to drizzles and then again some more. It drooled into small gentle rivulets of human honey descending on the bar.

Glancing to his left again Walt mumbled to no one in particular, "That's a marked improvement but the Forestport falls still has you beat by a long shot."

Kaiser, Herman the German's hunting dog, raised his head and sniffed the air. Sensing that all standards governing civility had been set aside, lifted his leg and peed on the B-rated sci-fi robot jute box. It suddenly luminated and began playing the Patsy Cline favorite, "Please release me, let me goooooo."

And so it was with the parade of others, who, at that late hour were blinded by drink, balderdash, bluster or bravado. It finally came to the attention of my parents. Mom quickly scurried aloft and discovered the problem. She hissed through the garret entrance the need for towels. In the minutes that followed she and dad seemed to stem the tide – so to speak - and sop up the remaining pools on the bar with bar towels.

All inquiries were hastily met with, "The loft window was open . . . the rain came flooding in. Let me get you another it's coming down real good outside."

Quickly and quietly he and Mom removed the bar glasses and sopped up the puddles with bar towels. They replaced all their drinks with fresh ones – "no charge" with a bar chip indicating that the next one was on the house.

All the while Dad cussed under his breath. One could naturally assume he was upset because of the open window and the sudden cloud burst that put a damper on the festivities. In reality it was the loss of revenue brought on by the lack of foresight. Serves him right, a cookie jar was intended for pecans and not to be used as a pee can.

Tommy Two Trees, a proud member of the Lakota tribe and visiting his cousin Seward, dipped his finger into a small pool that had been overlooked on the bar. Raising it to his nose, he smelled it and then placed his fingertip in his mouth.

"Minne Tanka," he mumbled.

Tommy Two Trees then bent low for a better examination. He breathed in long and deep until satisfied. With his discerning sense of smell, he raised his head and nodded, "Minne Tanka."

Without uttering another word, he turned and quietly departed. Mom watched and winched as she quickly wiped up the remnants she had missed.

"What's that he says?" Harold asked.

"Minne Tanka" chimed in Walter, who was an astute social observer and knew everything about anything, "is Indian for water of the Great Spirit. Minne means water like Minnesota, the land of the lakes. Tanka means great like them big hairy beast that roamed the plains. Sioux called the buffalo Tanka. An Indian's life centers on the buffalo."

"Yeah, I know. I watch Bonanza and the Lone Ranger," Harold huffed.

Walter now had an audience and was getting warmed up.

"Tanka was powerful medicine to the Indian. They call the Great Spirit Wanka Tanka. Wanka means sacred, Tanka means great like the buffalo. Put it all together and there you have water of the Great Spirit."

As if on cue Walter lifted his glass, emptied its contents, and slid his glass forward indication he'd have another for his throat was dry from the lengthy explanation.

"Oh, how nice," someone remarked.

Nudging Seward, another patron asked, "Hey, Seward. Ain't, you got native blood in you? Is that what it means?"

"It might. That all depends on the inflection of the word Tanka. Minni tanka is a term reservation Indians use for the whiskey sold in bars just outside the reservation. It could mean water from the Great Spirit or what they call weak whiskey. Walter noticed Kaiser was lifting his leg, ready to give the jute box another complimentary squirt.

Seward continued as he pointed to the dog, "What it literally means is buffalo ..."

"Prairie water," my father quickly chimed in. "It means pure, fresh, prairie water. Now drink up and have another."

Herman's pooch was about to launch another volley at the jute box when Dad turned to the German and snapped, "Herman, get that G-d d—n dog out of here. We run a respectable business. Next thing you know they will want to take our liquor license away thinking the place isn't fit for the public. And then where will you take your next drink . . . in the men's room?"

Ordinary objects withhold secrets. As in the classic movie, Citizen Kane, a young boy's sled named Rosebud had a story to be told. The cookie jar, in a sense, was my Rosebud. Viewed with childhood awe, my cookie jar was a receptacle for pecan cookies, those delicious and delectable treats so sought after in my youth. However, the container became a victim with a dark past. This jar went from pecan to pee can, a receptacle commonly known in the Adirondacks as a honey jar.

I look back fondly recalling those earlier days. It was an age of innocence, when Carstairs Blended Whiskey was devoted to the promotion of harmony and a common cookie jar captured a child's imagination.

EDDY AND THE GERMAN

When the war came in 1941 it seemed everyone joined some branch of the service. However, when the war ended and the "boys" returned home, there were two who were really affected by their war experience. One was Eddy Steiner and the other was my father. Both of them had been prisoners of war in Nazi Germany.

It was some time after the war had ended that Eddy was having a few beers at the White Lake Inn. It was common knowledge that he was a decorated soldier during the war and as a POW, the Nazis had treated him severely. He never discussed his war experiences and no one brought the subject up. He, like all of the young men who went to war, only wished to find a job, get married, buy a house and raise lots of kids.

On this particular evening Eddy sat on the corner stool of the bar, pensive and alone. Herman, a former German POW commonly referred locally as Herman the German, walked in.

Herman had been in the Luftwaffe and he along with his unit was taken prisoner in North Africa early in the war. His involvement in the war effort was inconsequential. Working as a crew member for the Luftwaffe, he saw no combat. In fact, he was just assigned to the unit when they were overrun and taken captive by the swift moving allies. Unaccomplished, he was shipped to the states and lived a rather comfortable existence as a German POW in the Adirondack Mountains located in upstate New York.

He grew to like the Americans and was quite taken by his host country. While his countrymen were desperately seeking shelter from the lethal payloads of the B-17s packing the Aryan skies with lethal loads or scrounging for morsels of dwindling sustenance, Herman was enjoying the comforts of Yankee hospitality. At the end of the war Herman was repatriated to what was left of war torn Germany. Comfort had become a constant companion during his stay in America, so after a few years of nomadic existence in his devastated homeland, he ambled back to the Adirondacks, a land of abundance.

Herman slowly came to be known as a harmless prankster. The locals perked up when Herman made an appearance. Loud and comical, he was a character, a local curiosity, genial and entertaining.

Herman came into my parent's inn one early winter day during hunting season. He was dressed in a scarlet woolen hat, matching hunting coat and flared pants. He had a pair of brown leather laced boots extending to just below his knees. Barreled chested, Herman was a large man with a commanding voice and manly presence.

As his custom, he entered in a bold Prussian fashion, strolling to a prominent opening located at the center of the bar. Looking briefly to his left and then his right measuring his audience to determine if he had attracted appropriate attention; he raised a massive meaty fist above his head and slammed it firmly on the bar announcing, "Daaay bee no EEESTAAH diese yeer!"

Conversations diminished quickly and everyone quietly looked toward Herman. Again he furtively glanced slowly to his left and then his right. He paused for effect and then proudly stated theatrically, "Daaay bee no EEESTAAH DIESE YEER!"

Bewildered someone asked, "Herman! What 'n hell you talking about? What's this about no Easter?

"I say, diese yeer, daaay be no EEESTAAH!"

With measured movement, Herman leveled a finger in one direction. "Foe YOOHS," to another, "Und YOOHS," and then to a third, "Und YOOHS!"

Waving his index finger he dramatically decreed, "None of YOOHS! ALLES KAPUT! AUSGESTORBEN!"

Raised up proudly, he adjusted his pants and ordered his usual shot and beer. In the stillness that followed there were a few muffled laughs, some chuckles as Herman the German waited pensive and patient.

Someone cleared their throat and probed further. "Herman, why are you saying there's t' be no Easter. You got a crystal ball or somthin?"

"Perhaps you spoke to the Pope and he gave you a heads up," prodded another.

Then spoke a third, "Is that it? I didn't know that you and the Almighty were that goddamn close."

Now there erupted thunderous laughter which gradually dwindled to an anticipatory hush.

"Besides, ain't you a Lutheran?"

The ball was now in Herman's court and all were waiting for his reply.

"I NO sprechen to de Poop. I NO sprechen to no one. I let Herr Parker sprechen for me."

And with that Herman downed the fiery liquid from his shot glass . . . winched . . . and then he took a long draught from his beer, reducing the temperament of the liquid fury. Turning with watery eyes, Herman hastened to the door and exited without another remark.

He reappeared shortly dragging a large dead jackrabbit in one hand and a double barreled Parker shotgun in the other. Kicking the door closed with one foot, he prominently paraded to the bar; placing both the shotgun and dead rabbit on top of the bar. The white furry creature was leaking red droplets on the smooth wooden surface.

Raising himself up to full stature, Herman announced to the assemblage in a deep baritone voice,

"DIS IST HERR PARKER . . . und DIESE IST HERR EEESTAAH BUNNY. "Und I MAKE HERR PARKER SPRECHEN TO HERR EEESTAAH BUNNY und HERR EEESTAAH BUNNY SPRECHEN NO MORE. EEESTAAH BUNNY IST KAPUT!'"

Picking up the rabbit by the hind legs, Herman proudly displayed it for all to observe (along with a string of rich red spittle oozing from the mouth of the very dead hare).

"I say I kilt de EEESTAH BUNNY und daaay bee NO EEESTAAH DIESE YEER!'"

With this Herman punctuated his last statement by slamming down his fleshy palm again on the wooden bar with a thunderous vibration that slopped some precious amber fluid from shot glasses and a few foamy mugs around.

The histrionics were classic Herman the German and the entertainment was well received. It ensured that his glass would remain full that evening and his wallet likewise.

It was a particular evening the weekend of the Fourth of July that Herman came striding boldly into the White Lake Inn not in his scarlet woolen hunting outfit, but a gray Nazi uniform adorned with the insignia of the Luftwaffe of the former Third Reich. It drew immediate attention by all, including Eddy. Both Herman the German and Eddy had been in their cups but that's where the similarities departed. Herman was social, jovial, engaging and Eddy was not.

Somewhere after Herman's entrance, the usual pause for effect, his striding to the bar and the ordering of whiskey and beer, Herman declared with flair, "DAAY BEE NO IN-DE-PENDENT DAY DIS YEAR. DAAY BEE NO FORT-AUF-JEW-LYE. I KILT ONKELSAM und DAY BEE NO ..."

Herman had hardly got the words out when Eddy bolted from his stool, pulling a knife from its sheath and plunged it firmly into the abdomen of Herman the German. Amid the confusion, someone wrestled Eddy to the floor and disarmed him before he could repeat the process.

Eddy was abruptly pulled away from the fracas all the while spitting and yelling about the "NO GOOD MURDEROUS NAZI SONS OF BITCHES" ... and the like. He was quickly hustled out of the premises and spirited into the night.

It was quickly ascertained that Herman, the now leaking German was in need of medical attention and quickly. Should Herman be taken to the local hospital it would take over an hour of precious time and a lot of uneasy questions would be asked to no one's benefit. It was agreed by those present that they should take Herman to a local retired doctor and see what he could do for him.

Arriving late in the evening, Herman was brought into the good doctor's home. After examining Herman, the doctor concluded that it was good that "the wound wasn't too deep" and nothing vital was "disturbed." Thankfully, Herman had been "boiled to the ass" and Eddy didn't have the opportunity to "improve on his work." Fate or luck interceded.

Giving Herman a tetanus shot, Doc cleaned the wound and closed it with an undetermined amount of stitches (in Herman's present condition a pain killer was not required). The mid-night service was deemed "on the house . . . consider it a community service." All present swore to remain mum on the unfortunate mishap. Herman agreed, especially when he was told should he not, "Eddy would finish the job."

The issue was never brought up and nothing ever came of the affair. The collective reasoning held that whatever punishment Eddy was due was already meted out years ago as a guest of the Third Reich.

In the years to come, the Fourth of July was energetically celebrated as is customary.

JOCK

His skin was the rich shade of chocolate and his deep bass voice resonated pleasingly. Jock was a jazz musician who played piano at my parent's restaurant in the Adirondacks. His partner, Danny, played a stringed bass. His skin was a lighter brown but not nearly as light as his Caucasian wife. A razor thin mustache and a front tooth framed in radiant yellow gold enhanced his luminous smile.

Jock was electric when he played. The piano was an extension of his soul. His large earthy hands danced about the keys with the dexterity of Bo Jangle. All the while his massive brogans lively drummed a rhythmic beat on the pedals and the floor.

Baby let me play with yo' yo-yo,

I'll let you play with MINE.

Baby let me play with yo' yo-yo,

I'll let you play with MINE.

With a slight southern accent and a naughty glint in his eye, Jock's smoky voice sang with a smooth cool richness. Jazz was pure freedom. It had the improvised pursuit of a butterfly in flight. Extemporaneous and risqué, Jock embraced the spontaneous rhythms like the August temperament of a Harlem night. A white handkerchief swiftly mopped the beads of sweat that dappled his brow. He continued,

Adam and Eve were sitting on a rock,

Eve told Adam I see your aaaaaahhhhhh!

Baby let me play with your yo-yo,

I'll let your play with mine.

Thump! Thump! Thump! His mighty heel beat to the rhythmic spirit that gave flesh to the song. Danny plucked on the bass strings in lively descent . . . doon, doon, doon, doon, doon. In tandem Jock added . . .

A baboon sitting on a Maltese cat,

she had a belly full of pussy and . . .

Abruptly the music stopped while Jock rose, placed one hand behind his head and thrust his hips vigorously forward , one, two, three times adding,

. . . taunt like that.

Baby let me play with your yo-yo,

I'll let you play with mine.

And on . . . and on . . . and on . . . went the song with a variety of bawdy lyrics sadly lost to the measure of time.

At the music break, Jock's burnt amber eyes drew the mute attention of the bartender. With a broad smile he gave a nod to the shot glass positioned on the corner of the upright piano.

"Gimme a touch, Billy," Jock said tapping a massive index finger beside the shot glass. "Just a touch." Then quoting Greta Garbo he added, "and don't be stingy."

The amber liquid disappeared with a flick of the wrist. Flushed with a spirited glow from within, the social scholar emerged in the person of an aged black musician. Dispensing his worldly wisdom, Jock began.

"Billy, I like you. I like you a lot. There are three great things in this life. That's Nerve! Bullshit! and Money! But there is one thing greater than 'em all."

He paused while tapping his shirt pocket.

"You'll find that right here behind your Lucky Strike pack. That's heart. If you ain't got heart, you ain't worth a damn. Billy, I like you. I like you a lot, but . . . you ain't worth a DAMN!"

Savoring a second shot of whiskey in a similar manner as the first, Jock laughed hardily and bellowed, "Billy, give me some SKIN!"

Good-naturedly the apprentice slapped palms with the savant. Chuckling with a smile, Jock closed his bulbous eyes and threw back his head crooning . . .

Five foot two eyes are blue,

oh what those fives could dooooo,

Has anybody seen my gal.

And his heels went, thump, thump, thump, as he tracked the beat.

She's got a turned up nose,

rolled down hose,

Flapper yes sir one of those,

Has anybody seen by gaaaaaaaaaaaaaal.

The day was young and lively and the night would prove to be promising and even livelier. The smoke from cigarettes created a gentle haze as glasses were filled. Modesty was unleashed and became unrestrained. Gradually the tamed inward nature of the patrons emerged unchecked. Impulsive lovers gyrated and swooned in shameless communion with the music. Swinging and swaying in a mingled mass, they bumped and ground their sweaty bodies in unholy fashion. It was good to be young. It was good to be alive. Jazz ruled the night.

Life on weekends in the Adirondack was bursting with a variety of jazz tunes. Compelling songs flourished full-bodied and shameless. They fractured the conventional and soothed the spirit. It was a realm where Jock governed supreme. The maestro and his music rejoiced in temporal existence which was limited merely by measure and melody.

Pausing occasionally in delight, Jock played on into the evening. The music tempo became the bread of life. Jazz had the ability to captivate, transform and transcend. It was the simple recognition of soul and self and life.

On this summer afternoon, a soft breeze filtered through open windows of the smoke filled inn. Outside, the fireflies danced on soft natural melodies. They were a part of the subtle mystery of life. As the evening drew to a close, Jock played one last tune.

This town is full of guys that think they're mighty wise

just because they know a thing or two

you can see them every day, strolling up and down Broadway

Telling of the wonders they can doooooooo.

When Jock engaged the piano keys, reason took a holiday...

They wear flashy ties and collars,

but where they get their dollars,

they've got an ace down in the hole.

For street wisdom was generously bestowed by the smoky voice of a black musician.

They will tell you of the trips,

that they intend to make,

from Florida right up to the old North Pole.

But their name would be mud just like a sucker playing stud,

if they lose that old ace down in the hole.

The applause was robust and sustained. In the silence that followed there was a tacit awareness that Jock's music had become a requiem to all that was temporal in life but eternal for an evening. Existence turned into wonderment. Soul was self.

The Canal

WARNING: *This contains discourtesy, offensive language and physical force. The author is not responsible for its contents.*

The three riffraff were significantly intoxicated before they entered the tavern.

"LOW BRIDGE! WATCH YER G-DDAMN HEAD," yelled one, slapping his buddy in the back of the skull.

To say that they were loud and obnoxious would be unwarranted. Drunk, dirty and disagreeable was customary. Embedded in their clothing were the accumulated stains, mostly the product from tobacco spittle. Their attire assumed a coarse shade of brown like the mules they drove on the tow path along the Black River Canal.

The Civil War had been over for the past dozen years or so. Soldiers had drifted back home, at least those who were capable. Some of them limped, others were assisted by crutches. Others simply rode on the back of a buckboard to their hometowns. Too many were permanent residents in places like Shiloh, Antietam, or Gettysburg.

But these three men were not counted among those returning. No, these three had never left the comfort of the local taproom.

In the ensuing years after the war, commerce increased along the Black River Canal. It transported the produce and raw materials from the Adirondacks south to the Erie Canal. It consisted of mostly farm produce like hay and potatoes or native logs hewn from the bountiful woodlands and milled into lumber. Shipped on barges to various places to the south and east; it nourished a mounting market that came with the influx of immigrants seeking a more promising future.

The three sought useful employment guiding mules that towed barges laden with goods to market. It was only temporary though. They worked just long enough to replenish their whiskey coffers. Ushering mules along the tow path was dull, tedious work. It held no promise and was without intrinsic value.

To break up the monotony, they stopped in small villages along the way and conducted periodic drinking bouts at "mahogany ridge." The aftermath resulted in an abiding hangover and their stumbling behind their ornery beasts with an occasional dragging. Their past was as obscure as the pedigree of the mules. Similar, they were one part horse, one part donkey but unmistakably 100 percent ass.

The trio treated everyone like the animals under their charge – sometimes worse. They would press a man hard until he started to sweat. Laying in wait for a misstep and without restrain, they would abuse him with their liquored tongues. Finally, after pummeling him into a heap, the threesome would take turns putting the boot to him after their victim laid collapsed in a morbid mound on the floor.

Fair was a foreign concept especially in a bar fight. The joining of the two words was redundant. The moment they entered a tavern a bar fight was inevitable. To the victors went the spoils they would say. Fair was a suitable term used only in reference to a warm summer day.

This was their world as they entered "Sudsy" McDonald's fine establishment, a mere walking distance from the Black River Canal. Sudsy catered to all types just as long as they had the fee for admissions. The sign behind the bar said it all – "Beer five cents. No Credit."

His clientele was mainly local lumberjacks and itinerant workers from the barge canal. But mostly they were those associated with the lumber trade.

Lumberjacks were a hardy group who found the wages low and the work hard – suited for Irishman. Lumbering hardened the body, yet softened the soul. It required individuals who weren't afraid to toil with their hands in the pursuit of a day's work.

Yes, hard work came natural and often to the Irish.

Some of them were adventurists from the "old sod." Others were driven by the potato famine from their native land. Both came to the Adirondacks with a hunger and were seeking a new home. What developed was a gradual appreciation of the solitude of nature in this untamed woodland called the Adirondacks.

They found oneness in life and a simple appreciation therein. Amid this vast newness were whispered uncertainties and muted challenges. It had the power to rouse the spirit of the cynic or charm those who viewed life with contempt. The great hunger of the past was forgotten. America restored the renewed approval for life.

America was a contest of survival. It retained the power to capture, command and control the imagination. It was a fervent land that was moved, manipulated and molded by the simple raw workings of the human hand and fertile mind.

Yes, this was a land well suited for the Irish.

Patrick Kelpy stood at the end of the bar sipping a beer. His family had previously left a crippled Ireland that was devastated by the potato famine. Sailing for North America, they were unable to pay the required entrance fee for the indigent Irish, so they landed in Canada.

He was one of three young boys who survived the hardships that took the lives of the rest of his family. Coming to live with distant relatives in the Adirondacks, he and a brother worked in the lumber industry. The youngest served with the army in places like Antietam, Bull Run and Fredericksburg. This came to an end when he was severely wounded at a small town called Gettysburg.

Patrick and his brother married sisters and began raising a large family in a hamlet unofficially known as Kelpytown. After a long week of hard work, he would stop at Sudsy's for a quick thirst quencher.

Patrick attracted the attention of the three as they entered. It seemed that everyone who worked on the barge canal had a nickname. The large fellow went by the name of Heft, the corpulent one was dubbed Gordo and the shortest of the three was nicknamed Pugs. While Gordo and Pugs continued with the angry stares, Heft, the big burly fellow, sent a fist crashing down on the bar. It commanded the attention of Patrick, the owner and his dog obscured by the shadows in the corner.

"Bar keep," he yelled. "Set 'em up. Whiskey all 'round. None of that panther piss worthy of imbeciles, idiots and Irishmen. Just the good stuff."

His companions ceased to glower and glunch as they tipped their heads back and gave a fair rendering of a wolf call,

"HOWOOOOOOOOOOooooooooooooooooooo!"

"Hey Heft," blurted the stouter of the three. "What do we have here? Can this be a Bog Jumper? You know a filthy bog trotting Patty O'Fool."

Just getting warmed up, Gordo went into his unbroken rendition of canal humor.

"A real fumblin' Dublin, shanty Irish, thick Mick. Yeah, a regular stinking Irish papist. A genuine clover pickin' Leprechaun."

Patrick looked up. His impassive stare inventoried the three – Bull, Oink and Stubby.

"I'm not here for a beer. Allow me to finish in peace and I'll be on my way."

"Peace he says. You mean in pieces," chimed in the bulky brute. "We don't care for dogs 'n Irish scum the likes of you. Drink up and then make peace with your God for your ass is mine you bog jumping, clover eating piece of fumblin' Dublin S—T."

With that Heft threw back his head and downed the amber contents from his shot glass. He would have continued with the diatribe but the fiery infusion momentarily deprived him of breath. Without missing a step Pugs, the short one continued with some whiskey wit.

"You're a bit hard on the bog trotter, ain't you, Heft," argued the sassy runt. "Leave the Mick alone. Can't you see he's just a simple Paddy making his way home to his shanty s—t hole he calls a home?"

"You mean outhouse," argued Heft?

"Is there a difference," hissed the short surly one?

Patrick finished his beer and was prepared to leave.

"Here, have another. It's on me," bellowed the portly one tossing a copper coin into a spittoon. Releasing a ripe wad of tobacco juice into the receptacle, Gordo kicked the spittoon in the direction of Patrick. "Fetch it yourself you filthy Mick. What's left you can drink as your chaser."

The roar of laughter from the three caused the lone dog to raise its head and give a low growl.

"See, Heft. Seems the damn dog don't care much for no cat-licks neither."

"If it's a fight you're after then step outside and come in one at a time. I'll do my best to accommodate you. Otherwise, step aside and let a man through."

"One at a time he says. We come in together and together we stay."

With that Patrick was bum rushed by the three. Heft came first. Side-stepping, Patrick shoved him headlong like a bull crashing into the near wall. Ducking the second he sent a solid blow to his midsection and Oink doubled over. But Stubby snuck in and landed one on Patrick's jaw sending him over a table and sliding into the corner with the growling dog. Now getting into the action, the growling dog latched onto Patrick's left calf.

"Pugs, yer losing your punch," Gordo panted catching his breath.

"Punch nothin'. Let him have a face full of this."

With that Pugs displayed a skinning knife. Watch me carve out an eye or two," he grinned.

Bar fights as a rule generally begin and end quickly. This was no exception. Patrick snatched the dog by the hind quarters that was latched on his leg and swung the snapping dog at the stub of a man who was lunging with the knife.

The dog striking Pugs' head sounded like an ax being buried into the trunk of an oak tree. Blood, hair and teeth went flying in every direction. It was unclear if it had belonged to the man or the dog. It was probably both. Pugs collapsed in a isolated heap.

Swinging the dog by the legs over his head, Patrick made another sickening sound when the dog came down on the cranium of the largest of the three. Quickly, Patrick turned to confront Gordo, but the fat little man was nowhere in sight. Something rushed past the front window. He was accelerating in a grade school pace in the direction of the barge canal. The fat little man hadn't reached that kind of velocity since the beginning of summer vacation on his last day of fifth grade.

The bartender stood unresponsive, motionless. He was too stunned to utter a word. Patrick looked at the dog limp in his hands. It had perished sometime during the unfortunate altercation.

Stepping forward, Patrick laid the now deceased dog on the bar. Gently petting the dead dog, he then reached into his pocket and took out a five-dollar gold piece, a week's wages. Placing it next to the lifeless dog, Patrick whispered, "I'm truly sorry about your dog."

As Patrick turned, he wiped the blood from his swollen lip. He then limped to the door and into what remained of a bright summer afternoon.

SAL

A large man entered the inn by a side door. He paused, examined the room and ordered a pack of Camels. Pitching a quarter on the bar, he unexpectedly poked his head into each restroom before leaving through a second exit.

Shortly, he and another man entered the tap room in unison. Each came by a different door. The hulking duo wore large woolen jackets that extended below their knees and a dark gray fedora set low on their brow just above their deep set eyes.

With a quick scan of the barroom, the first man exited a second time. The other placed a table and two chairs in the corner of the room and moved the remaining tables and chairs to one side. A young boy in his early teens slipped quietly from behind the bar and into the kitchen to get his father.

When the first man returned, he held the door open for a demonstratively smaller man with white hair and icy eyes, but similarly dressed. Although slighter of the two men, this serious man carried himself with a quiet sense of importance. His shadowy eyes made study of the room in a glance. He entered. It would have made Charles Darwin smile.

Walking to the solitary table secluded in the corner, he removed his overcoat and hat, handing them to the larger man and then sat down. Placing the coat and hat on wooden pegs located on the near wall, the meaty attendant resumed his place beside an entrance door.

An older gentleman appeared from the kitchen, spotted the seated man and smiled. The two larger men instinctively slid a hand into their overcoats. With a quick motion from the seated man, his two companions resumed their stoic poses.

"Sal. Salvadore Calzone. It is good to see you," the proprietor said cheerfully. "I see that you have brought your two daughters." He teased. "How nice of them to join you."

As if broken by a spell the seated man stood up and beamed, "Ha! Dade, yoo always make the jokes."

The humor was unappreciated by Sal's companions.

"How nice to see yoo. Look! Yoo rigazzo grasso. Fat Boy. Yoo make Mamma Calzone smile. No?"

"You should see me next week. I am putting linguini on the menu."

"You stick to potatoes and meat. Leave pasta to the Eye-talianos. Come, come, sit with me."

Dade warmly shook his hand and then took the seat facing Sal. Quietly standing at his father's elbow, his son attended to the seated guest first.

"Mr. Calzone, would you like something to drink?"

"Vichee," he responded politely.

The young man then turned to the man with angry eyes. "And you sir?" Scarcely audible he hissed, "Vicheeeeee."

The youth politely attended to the other associate whose narrow eyes stared menacingly beneath untamed brows. "And you sir? What would you like?"

"Vichee," he intoned quickly with lips barely moving.

Pleasantries were exchanged. The two talked at length about family, the weather and other subjects of passing insignificance. During the cordial exchanges there was an occasional chuckle, the product of common wit and humor.

After a comfortable interval Sal mused, "You know what they say about Sal Calzone? They say Sal Calzone … he kill three fingers Canigliari."

Sal touched his index finger to his thumb and continued uninterrupted.

"They say … Sal Calzone … he kill Rosario the Rat … and Ice Pick Tony."

He lightly touched two more fingers.

"They say … Sal Calzone … he kill Squeaky Stefano and Milwaukee Mike …"

He continued naming names until he ran out of fingers on both hands.

Lowering his voice to a whisper Sal continued, "Sal Calzone … he no kill … no one!"

Then leaning slightly forward with hunched shoulders and upturned palms, he rasped, "Sal Calzone … Sal Calzone , he no hurt a flyyyyeeeee."

And with that he gently sat back in his chair with arms crossed on his chest smugly grinning. Dade returned the smile.

As Sal stood up to leave they embraced. Their eyes momentarily fixed.

"Take care of yooself." It was less of an understanding and more of a command.

Looking up into the clouds Sal said, "It is cold in Herkimer today. Maybe for some, no?"

Sal's passing reference may have gone beyond the weather. Big Tony and Fat Frank from Herkimer were found stuffed down a well some time ago. Each was eventually found with a hole in the back of their heads.

It was rumored that a particular shipment of whiskey from up north didn't make it to Franco and Anthony's place of business. A visit was made locally by a couple of their associates on a Friday and they demanded the return of the merchandize by the upcoming Monday. It wasn't an allegation but rather a statement of fact. It was useless to deny any association to the missing cargo. Moreover, half of the spirits had already been sold or consumed locally.

"Sal …." Dade was cut off by a wave of Sal's hand. It seems Big Tony and Fat Frank's pursuits were getting too big for Herkimer and their dealings began spilling over into other areas. It proved to be an unfortunate business decision on their part.

"Let us not talk of business. No? "

One of his assistants opened the door allowing Sal to exit the inn followed by the tavern owner. He held the door for the young lad who carried a wooden box filled with unmarked bottles that pleasantly clinked.

"Please take this … a gift from … friends."

Sal made an attempt to graciously refuse but it was now Dade's turn to raise a hand and stop Sal. He motioned for his son to place the box in the automobile.

"Let us just say it is good business. But then again we should not be speaking about business . . . among friends. No?"

Sal nodded and then grinned. The three departed east in an enormous Buick to an out-of-the-way place somewhere secluded in the Adirondacks.

MARK A. CLARKE

THE SWITCH

Switch \'swich\ n: a slender, flexible shoot cut from a tree.

The switch was not conceived by my father, but in a brief time you could say he improved on it. In defense of my forefathers, they lacked inventiveness as well, however, it didn't keep them from exploiting it.

In the Adirondacks switching became a birthright, a kind of heritage that was handed down from one generation to the next. Like the beloved family Hawkins 50 caliber rifle, it became the modest inheritance of simple folk. My father received switching from his father. His father was heir to the switch from his father before him. Then again, his father's father was the beneficiary of the switch from his before him.

It went on like this for as far back as anyone could rightfully remember. In fact, the switch was so warmly received by consecutive generations that its charm and appeal never waned. My grandmother said its appreciation resulted in the loss of quite a few branches on the family tree.

An adage says that if you spare the rod, you will spoil the child. The rod referred to is more commonly known in my neck of the woods as the switch. I have it on good authority by one of those who study such things, that the switch finds its early origins traceable to the Adirondacks. For our urban cousins and those less worldly, the switch is a regional device handcrafted from an indigenous sapling, largely the type of hickory known by the Latin term, carya ovata.

A switch is about an arm's length in size that is formed from a tree branch that is devoid of any protruding leaves or twigs. It makes a distinct whistling sound when heartily sliced through the air. If properly applied, the switch is lashed about vigorously and then applied to the posterior of some unruly juvenile. Any supervising parent or custodian in possession of a valid driver's license (driving permit acceptable) or has recently voted in an election may participate. [Note: there was a local ordinance that extended participation to those who a) intend to take a driving exam or b) would consider voting. The second provision was scrapped because it caused a ruckus for same-day voter registration.]

Infractions requiring adjudication are typically dealt with promptly, however, time limits may be optional. "Wait until your father comes home" is sufficient. The "switchee" (delinquent) commonly referred the switching session by the colorful title of "an ass whipping" or just a plain old fashion north county "butt warmin.'" The practice was not universal but if your name ended in an E, and was preceded by a C, L, A, R, and a K, it was a customary practice.

A switching comes without the presumption of innocence. You can expect no trial by jury. However, the sentence will to be swift and exacting. I speak with the voice of experience. Promptness is to assure that those who are known to be light of foot are unlikely to quit the area in breakneck speed.

Experience is a preferred recommendation but not a prerequisite.

My ancestors have lived in the Adirondacks since it was considered a "frontier." That same "good authority" enlightened me that the switch did not derive its origins from the Native culture.

Indigenous folk viewed trees as useful camouflage in the pursuit of wild game. No Iroquois, foremost of the First Nation, would consider fashioning such an outrageous device. They may craft a prized bow with a sleek quiver full of arrows, yes. Construct a reliable tomahawk, which is true, or possibly shape an ornate coup stick to smite one's enemies, certainly.

But a switch? Not a chance. It would be beneath them to even consider such a shameful doohickie.

A warrior was to follow a noble path, roam the wild woods in search of game, fish the rushing streams that flow from rocky mountainsides or paddle along the passageways of a clear mountain lake. It was honorable to sit among peers around raging fires; to speak openly of the great things that they have done and then smile with admiration as they take note of their own self-importance. The switch was uncivilized, a blight upon The Nation. No, our noble native brethren would not devise such a monstrosity. The fountainhead of such folly requires additional consideration.

The switch, as you may have already suspected, is likely European in concept and more specifically British. It is sort of the mild version of The Cat of Nine Tails, which was frequently employed by the English on the high seas. When walking-the-plank or keelhauling were thought too heavy handed and a seadog required some immediate modification of behavior or perhaps a bit of fine-tuning in his attitude, a British captain might resort to a little "scratch of the cat." With all hands-on deck, the punishment was meted out to the rolling beat of the drum.

One English captain struck with indifference was noted to have said, "Splendid, quite splendid."

And then he dismissed the crew with a hardy, "Now get on with it ye galley gobs."

In a sense, flogging was to ensure the sun would never set on the British Empire. Sadly, it did for a host of those "galley gobs."

Constructing the Cat of Nine Tails was not an easy task for the novice. It was too elaborate for the unsophisticated colonial "land lubbers." Besides, King George must have had a patent on it. The ruler of the seven seas had an iron-fisted monopoly on its usage.

In those days King George cornered the market on anything significant like sugar, stamps, and tea. "For King and country," they would say. "The Cat" was a captain's duty. How was one to instill the proper management that was required to bear the burden of ruling the seven seas? Nay, the scurvy knave will bear it and like it as all good English subjects.

But in North America "The Cat" was received as being just plain un-American. What upright patriot would fashion a Cat of Nine Tails, whose design and relentless use was promoted by the "Bloody British"? It just wasn't respectable.

Americans fought a revolution against such cruel and oppressive despotism. Were a faithful American to get his "blood up" over some wayward, sassy, impudent lad, why he could just tear a branch from the limb of a sturdy hickory tree and "having at"? Not only was this convenient and easy to fashion, but it held promise. The woods were full of them. Besides, it was their right! Their duty! The switch was a true testament to the freedom of self-determination. Hear, hear!

Now there you have it. Yankee ingenuity was at work. Fathers across the Adirondacks were dutifully stating, "Down with the British. Up with self-rule. Now son, assume the position."

All the while they could be heard singing, "Yankee doodle went to town, riding on a pony. Tore a switch from an old oak tree, and wacked another fanny."

My father was not one to squander his inheritance or shirk a duty. My approach to dodging the switch was to simply lie. Lying was a plan that I thought was adaptable, achievable, had real potential. But if at first lying did not work, I would simply lie to cover for the lie.

Now that was a flexible plan and had boundless possibilities. I thought that if the first lie didn't do the trick, invent another and then so on. However, there was one small catch, while experimenting with the truth my mom informed me that she could always tell when I was lying. I argued that it really wasn't a lie but merely a fib.

But mom could see right through me. She countered it with, "A fib is really a lie dressed up in a fancy suit and tie. A fib," she reasoned, "was in fact a lie in disguise." Fib or no fib, Mom told me that all mothers could tell when their children were lying.

I found this earth shattering. The foundation of my childhood was disintegrating before me. In the years that would follow, I pondered this concept long and hard. Was it possible for a mother to tell if her child was lying or not? Whether this was true or not came with uncertainty, for my mom had me convinced of it.

In any event she planted the seed, and it had therefore become a self-fulfilling prophesy. Any attempt at lying, however small, skimpy, or paltry it may appear, resulted in nervousness that would cause me to sweat. I would immediately begin to tremble and to stutter. This was followed by light-head-edness, which prompted me to sway and wobble. The trembling, the stuttering, the swaying, and the wobbling got so bad that the unexpected occurred. Leakage. A simple glance at my trousers was proof enough. "Book 'em. He's lying."

Now if mom could sense I was lying, it was a given that dad would know as well. I had to rethink this whole approach over and come up with another strategy. Running away suddenly entered the picture, but that was only a temporary fix. I tried running away one time, but I only got hungry and end up slinking back home. I might try telling the truth. It is said that honesty is the best policy. However, one can bet the person who dreamt that up was a more convincing liar. In the years that followed I adopted the use of the six principles of good government.

Rule One – be a good boy.

Rule Two – if you cannot be a good boy, do not get caught.

Rule Three – if caught, admit mistakes were made and then direct the attention to someone more conspicuous, more outrageously bad or reprehensible (see Rule four).

Rule Four – blame it on him.

Rule Five – if Rules Three, Four and Five should fail; acknowledge one's faults, express remorse and ask forgiveness (three Hail Mary's and three Our Fathers help if you are Catholic).

Rule Six – if all else fails, fall on your sword, and become a martyr. Rule Two through Four seemed more worthwhile, and most suited to my wants.

My eldest brother helped to perpetuate the family use of the switch. He must have been partial to them because he had the uncanny tendency to promote the tradition. You could say it was habit forming. Trouble attracted him as naturally as bees to fields of buttercups.

His most egregious behavior of note was hurling rocks. At an early age he would throw a rock at practically anything that was moving or stationary for that matter: trees, birds, stray dogs, grazing cows, or passing cars. He was most dedicated to slinging rocks at propane tanks like the two located behind Dade's Inn.

"I like the way they sound when hit. They make a sweet twanging sound. There's nothing like a good ole TWAAAAAAAAAAAAAAAAANG to start the morning," he would say. That was unless the TWAAAAAAAAAAAAAAAAANG was instantly followed by a familiar tinkling sound. That ping-CRASH would be the unmistakable sound of a rock ricocheting off a propane tank and crashing through a windowpane. That tinkling sound was the full, jingling symphony of falling shards of glass. These sounds also suggested the onset of something rather alarming was afoot.

And that something "afoot" was usually my older brother who flashed by me seeking refuge in the woods. There left little doubt that trouble spelled with a capital T was soon to follow. And it would and it did.

You could hear my brother and my father somewhere in the back lot discussing matters. One was stating a position rather forcefully, "How many TIMES do I have to TELL you to STOP throwing ROCKS! With each emphasized word the switch was solidly planted somewhere on the buttocks. The other immediately responded with a plaintive HOWL in testimony that the switch had found its intended target.

One should have intervened and argued that "boys will be boys" or that the propane tank ought not to be positioned near windows. But that was too philosophical to a hostile and unsympathetic ear especially if it were armed with a switch. This was not the first time that something like this had happened. Nor was it the second, third, or even the fourth. This was an ongoing problem that needed to be resolved once and for all. This afternoon session would extend beyond the normal.

A conscience holds a good man to account. The lessons of the past just did not seem to be working for my father like it did for his predecessors. Currently, the only mark a good switching left was on the buttock, not on the behavior. Perhaps an innovative approach was in order. My father, a learned man, thought long and hard on the subject. There were preliminary inquiries, broad discussions until he happened upon the name of Dr. Benjamin Spock more and more. My father thought, "Just who is this Dr. Ben Spock anyway. Let me investigate this guy." And he did.

He found that Dr. Benjamin Spock was an American pediatrician, a notable expert on child-rearing who was influential on a generation of parents. He professed things like, "if you respect children, they grow up to be better people." That seemed clear enough. He professed that whether a parent is right or wrong, "inflicting physical punishment will lead to lasting resentment" . . . and "modifying behavior and not enduring enmity was the intended lesson."

But what really changed my father's approach was what Dr. Spock said about parenting. He said, "The child supplies the power, but the parents have to do the steering" and in so doing "each of us help to create a better world for our children."

Now that was something to sink your teeth into that he could support. Who doesn't want a better world for their children? It was up to my dad to seek a novel way forward, to assist my brother down a new pathway of becoming a better person and thus the betterment of the world. Times were changing, and he must change with them if his son and the world were to become a better place.

Advancing forward on this new approach to parenting, my father found himself tending an empty bar when a lone stranger came in for a beer. He ordered a cold bottle of Utica Club. While he settled in the two of them struck up a general conversation. Like most discussions the general state of things were bantered about. They soon found that they had certain things in common. They were both married. They both had children about the same age. After a second beer the general topic focused on the topic of child rearing and discipline. My father, the newly converted disciple of Dr. Spock took the lead.

"You know, I have had a devil of a time with my oldest son. At every turn he was getting into trouble. If it wasn't one thing, then it was another. Each time, after ample warning, I was compelled to take the switch the boy for some misdeed, but it had no lasting effect. Oh, he was always whole-heartedly sorry for his offense, but memory would fade, and he would be right back at it again in no time. I found myself exasperated and worn out just switching the boy. But this last time was the final straw. He had an appetite for throwing rocks. I don't know how many windows I've replaced by his foolishness. When he broke that last window, I said to myself that's it. I will teach him a real lesson this time. After that last switching, he promised me that he was through with throwing rocks. In fact, he would not throw another rock for as long as he lived. But he always says that.

"After talking to my wife and some friends, I had a change of heart. My approach was too . . . too . . . well . . . I decided to change my approach. If whipping the boy was not working maybe sound reasoning would find its mark. I sat down with the boy, and we had a good long talk. We spoke at length and before you know it two hours passed by. At the end of it all, we saw each other in a different light. We came to a mutual understanding that felt good and suited both of us.

"I am sold on the power of reasoning. It is a powerful tool, and more people should reach out and enjoy its rewards."

My father took an added step forward by using a broader scope.

"Nations would profit from it. In fact, not only would nations benefit, but future generations would be thankful!"

The man ordered another beer. Taking a sip, he added, "You say that problems in the world would be solved with following the working of Dr., what's his name?"

"Dr. Benjamin Spock."

"All that with just a simple couple of hours sitting down and chit-chatting with your son. Is that what you are saying?"

"That I do. Dr. Spock broke the child rearing barrier much like Chuck Yeager broke sound barrier."

"Now that's interesting."

"The proof is in the pudding. Do you see that window over there?"

My dad directed the attention of the stranger to corner window at the other end of the room. Turing on his stool, he pointed to the window where the silver propane tanks were situated outside next to the building.

"You mean that one?"

"You are correct. I've replaced that window time and time again. Every time my son would throw a rock through it, I would give him a switching with no lasting results. After the last time we had that talk, and the window has remained intact for over a month now. And do you want to know why? Reason, my friend. If more people would just resort to mutual understanding to resolve their issue, the world would ..."

Before my father could get the rest of the words out, there was a sound of a TWANG, PING-CRASH, and the tinkling of broken glass as it fell. A small, jagged rock slid across the barroom floor and came to rest under the stranger's bar stool.

Reaching down he picked it up and placed the rock on the bar. The two peered toward the now broken window and the last thing they saw was a young boy in a dead sprint disappearing into the undergrowth of the woods.

SECTION 2

~~~

LITTLE WOODHULL CREEK

~~~

BLACKBERRIES

Each season is enriched and prized for its rewards. July is the month of berry picking – blackberries in particular. Along the dusty roads in the backwoods of the Adirondacks one can occasionally happen upon a patch of ripe black caps.

To their delight, country youths are skillful in discovery. Without attentiveness to thorny brier, they wade headlong into the berry patch disregarding sharp thorns, bears, and other such concerns. When accompanied by a companion, it is tacitly understood that a heads up is not required. Rushing headlong into the shrubbery, one maintains a committed eye on the prize. Rich thumb sized berries, plump and juicy, become the early casualties. Eagerly, several clusters hastily find their way into the mouth.

Savoring is strictly an urban luxury and a waste of time to a young boy. The rural Law of Serendipity maintains that quantity prevails over quality. Only when several handfuls are ingested can one pause and appreciate the tender blessings of nature.

Alerted by your absence you can expect to be joined by companions in a throaty chorus of "ummms" and "ahhhhs." Eyes fixed, nodding in momentary fellowship, they are then attracted to new clusters. Dexterity is a honed skill. It is a talent well-suited for berry picking in the remote pathways in the Adirondacks.

Soon the first three fingers of both hands retain a permanent shade of deep purple-black. The tongue and lips are ghoulishly colored as well. Clothing becomes a casualty to the impulsive and the careless. Wiped and spattered with soiled hands, t-shirts take on the early renderings of a Jackson Pollock painting. Frayed jeans, stained with dirt and grass, complete the sincere picture of an age untroubled and carefree. It is a fleeting gesture to the whim and impulsiveness of youth.

Palms cupped with heaping mounds of berries, we move on with the last vestige of ripened harvest. In so doing we make note of the "patch" and its location to be certain of continued visitations. Upcoming incursions must be studiously planned for in a matter of days the remaining undeveloped berries will emerge succulent and attract both beast and fowl alike.

Like his father before him my grandfather grew up in the Adirondacks. He never lost the simple earthly pleasures considered important to childhood. With the wild forest as his backyard, Grandpa Dade seemed to intuitively know where and when the next crop of ripe berries would appear and where the best berry patch could be found.

After instructing my brother and me to get two bowls he would state, "Fill one and give it to Eunice (our grandmother)." And then add, "The other is for you."

He would then divulge where we could find the out of the way, elusive berry patch. Smiling and in a low voice he would caution, "Watch out for the bears."

If the bowl we picked for Grandpa Dade seemed to be the larger, let me just say it was to appease the Spirits of the Forest for having consumed the greater portion while picking.

Wild berries are ideal for making homemade muffins or pies. Once Eunice made two pies and placed them on the window sill to cool. Patsy, my grandfather's beagle, was attracted to them by their pleasant aroma. When Eunice went to check on the pies she found Patsy with two empty pie tins. A good scolding and the soubriquet "Patsy two Pies" was all that came of the affair.

Sometimes muffins were in the offering. Once while quietly whistling some unfamiliar tune (as usual), Grandpa Dade entered the inn through the rear door with a warm tray of muffins covered with a linen cloth. Just out of his oven, fresh and steaming, he tenderly removed several muffins. Breaking one in half he slathered it with golden butter and offered it to the nearest grandchild. Patiently the remaining siblings waited their turn. Our unveiled pleasure was sufficient reward for his labor.

But the more memorable time was when Grandpa Dade arrived one warm afternoon with a contraption that consisted of a wooden bucket and other oddities. There was a galvanized cylinder that was inserted into the wooden bucket. It was connected to a medal yoke that spanned the bucket from one side to the other. And when the handle was connected and turned, curved blades rotated inside the cylinder.

"What's that for?" we asked.

"You'll see," Grandpa Dade replied.

We curiously watched with fascination. With the cylinder firmly in place, he filled it with a combination of raw cow's milk heavy with natural cream, granulated sugar and some vanilla extract. Assembling the remaining components that came with the contraption he packed ice between the wood bucket and the cylinder. As a final touch he added some rock salt which I later learned lowered the freezing point. He turned the handle to show us that it rotated the blades inside the galvanized container that held the mixture. The greater the effort the faster the blades turned.

"Here," he directed to the eldest. "Now you try."

Unaware that the process required steady turning for a significant amount of time, it became a challenge to see who could turn the handle the fastest for the longest period of time. One by one our arms began to ache and the rhythm was slowed to a near halt. That was when a fresh arm would take up the cause. Time passed slowly and seemed like hours before the contents thickened. When the task appeared almost complete, Grandpa Dade opened the lid and added a couple of hand full of wild berries into the white creamy mixture. It became evident this was ICE CREAM. The only question was how long it would take before it would be ready.

Grandpa Dade completed the now demanding task. Lifting the metal container from the wooden bucket, immediately the hard cold exterior began to frost over. After taking off the lid Grandpa Dade used a wooden spoon to separate the creamy mixture from the blades within. Winking to the youngest, he sampled the velvety mixture himself.

Teasing he would state, "Yuck, this tastes terrible. By Golly, I think we will have to throw this whole batch out and start again."

In unison we pleaded, "NO, NO, NO! We will eat it!"

In childlike animation we eagerly danced about with enthusiasm as several bowls and spoons somehow appeared. The unspoken question now loomed. Will I be first? Please . . . Me, Me, Me! But it was not to be. Those of us who were older brooded as Grandpa Dade handed the first bowl to the youngest and then the next and so forth.

Anxiety governed inner emotions for we had our doubts that there might not be enough. When it came my turn my mood changed from a doubtful disposition to one of glowing gratitude as a generous potion was scooped out and handed to me.

Never was there a more jubilant gathering assembled. Even the beagle got to lick the ice cream from the blades of the mixer. Sing-song we remembered our manners. "Thank You, Grandpa Dade."

In the passing years amid the divisions and discords of our youth, soothing memories rise like cream in raw milk. For me, important lessons come from that time when my grandfather made a batch of homemade ice cream.

Are not the more meaningful things in life the products of simple events? Things that are foremost in my life often come with spontaneity and are events I happened upon like a patch of wild blackberries. I have profited from the lesson of staying power and hard labor like the churning of raw milk into ice cream.

Perhaps the thing of greater value is shared time. The finest gift we can give to one another is our time like that of a grandfather to his grandchildren.

We are held hostage to our own wander lust. Metaphorically, we climb mountains, sail uncharted waters and explore distant lands in search of the meaning of life. But perhaps, like Dorothy, we need only to pause and realize that the meaning that we seek is right there before us.

The meaning of life is life itself.

The Bear

A black bear attacked one of our horses. It was a Pinto mare named Patches. I call them our horses because they were pastured on land next to our inn.

Patches had broken through the barbed wire fencing and had claw marks made by a bear on her hind quarter. The bear must have received the full force of both hooves before it was all over. Nonetheless, the bear made a hasty retreat. The young Pinto bolted through the barbed fence and in the process sustained a nasty wound near her hind fetlock.

Blood was oozing pretty good when we found her and got her calmed down. The claw wound to her hind quarter was superficial but the barbed injury to her fetlock was notable. She would require the attention of a veterinarian. It was the weekend and the local vet was out on another call. Promising that he would get there as soon as he could, it still would take a fair amount of time.

There happened to be an old army veteran by the name Jess Warren who had trained with the cavalry during the Spanish American War. He was at the Inn sipping a beer when he heard the news. He offered to take a look at the mare.

Old Mr. Warren stood in front of the horse for a length of time sizing things up. He gently extended his hand, palm up, to the mare. He made a friendly nickering sound. Cautiously the mare sniffed his hand. Drawing in a deep breath, she let it out in a slow, steady sigh.

Gradually Mr. Warren slid his hand down her neck, lightly patting her shoulder as he explored. All the while Mr. Warren spoke in a low soothing voice explaining his intentions.

"Steady, girl. I'll be alright. Just let Ole Jess Warren take a quick look-see at your leg."

He ran both hands down her barrel; one on her back and the other along her ribcage. He lightly patted her as he proceeded. She neighed. He paused and responded with a nicker in a low, soothing voice – horse-like.

Each time he spoke, he stroked her lightly.

"It's ok, girl. I see you're upset." He looked at the claw wound. "Stumbled into a bit of bad luck, I see. Don't give it a thought. That ole bear will get his comeuppance in its good time. Mr. Jess Winfield Warren will fix you right up. Good as new. You can bet on that like your holdin' aces full."

The mare drew in several deep breaths and slowly exhaled. She was taking a liking to Mr. Warren.

"That's it. You take your time and I'll take mine," he said reassuringly.

Mr. Warren proceeded thoughtfully and deliberately. He conducted himself as if the injury was his. Taking his time, he guardedly approached the hind quarter. He conducted himself with tenderness and care, the kind that comes with years of experience. He massaged the gaskin and cannon, which is located just below the mare's knee. Guardedly, he approached the wound, taking his time.

"It's not that bad," he said down-playing its significance. "Ole Jess'll make you as good as new. You'll see."

Turning, he issued an appraisal. "She's gonna need a vet. She will have need of stitches and some medication to fend off infection. Has anybody contacted a vet?"

"He's in Lowville on call and won't make it here 'til sometime this afternoon."

"Well the bleeding needs to be tended to. The best method would be a large puff ball or some cobwebs."

"Puff balls or cobwebs," someone questioned?

"The powder in the puff balls is an old Indian cure; it coagulates the blood. Cobwebs will do the same thing and act as a temporary bandage if you can locate enough of them. Do you have an old barn or shed around here," he said looking around? "If so, use a stick and wrap cobwebs around it nice like a loose ball of yarn. Bring it here and I'll take care of the rest. It should do until a vet can give her the proper attention.

"Oh, bring a clump of that Adirondack moss when you come. You know that green hairy stuff that looks like little spruce trees growing in the woods. We'll need some fresh hay and a bucket with a scoop or two of grain. And be quick about it. She might not be so agreeable for too much longer.

My brother and I bolted, snapping a willow stick off as we ran. My other brother sprinted into the woods in search of moss. We made several stops probing the dark dusty corners of the barn and sheds. We had to shoo away a good many spiders that resided in the webs. The spider webs rolled nicely into a ball like cotton candy. We were pleased and much surprised with the accumulation of the soft fibers. Sprinting back, Mr. Warren looked over the soft silky bundle and he grunted his approval.

"That'll do. Yes, that'll do just fine."

My brother arrived with enough moss rolled up in his shirt to stuff a pillow. Mr. Warren chuckled to himself stating, "That's first rate."

The mare had been mildly distracted by the loose sections of hay. Patches chewed passively away; occasionally stopping to glance to the side; perking her ears and then continued with her chewing.

Mr. Warren approached the mare with the bucket of oats, sweetened with molasses. He let out a couple of deep sighs and a nicker. Reaching into the bucket, he scooped out a pinch of grain, placed it into his mouth and chewed. Blowing the sweet scent of molasses towards the mare, he attracted her attention. Bobbing her head up and down, she took a few short step towards the old man.

"Here you go, girl. Look what good ole Jesse Warren brought you."

He shook the bucket making the kernels of glazed oats click along the sides. Flaring her nostrils, the Pinto raised her head and drew in a chest full of the sweet aroma. She gave a snort and then pawed the ground with a hoof. The syrupy mixture was Ambrosia to a horse. It served to distract her like honey to a bee.

Setting the bucket before Patches, Mr. Warren waited for her to take pleasure in her good fortune. Leisurely, his focus returned to the maimed limb. Tenderly he raised and curled the offended leg into a curve like a fiddle head fern.

Smoothly he worked; dabbing the blood away from the gash with a white t-shirt someone had provided. As he did so, he lightly unwound the spider webbing around the laceration. Over and over again, he rotated the stick about the wound. Around and around the webbing unraveled; the soft sturdy mesh trapped the rich red blood into its network. Again and again and then again the stick twirled about the limb until there was a tangled web of congealed blood and finally the bleeding stopped.

"Give her some water, but not too much. That'll hold her until the vet comes."

Having finished with the grain, Patches grasped a section of hay between her teeth and gave it a shake from side to side. The hay blossomed and fell to the ground, allowing her to access a more manageable portion to eat. Stroking Patches along her neckline, Mr. Warren whispered something to her as she continued to chew. Turning he nodded to my dad and returned to his orphaned beer.

The vet came early that afternoon. He unbound the bandage and stood back scratching his head. "Is that moss I see?"

Then when he removed the layer of moss he seemed even more puzzled.

"Is that spider webbing? I thought I saw just about everything. Who wrapped the wound like that?"

When it was explained that Mr. Warren had taken emergency measures to stop the bleeding, the vet announced,

"NOW, I've seen it all. They never taught us anything like that at Cornell. This Mr. Warren knows his way around horse flesh. He did a commendable job and I think I'll tell him so."

But he didn't get a chance to express his sentiments for Mr. Warren had finished his warm beer and was long gone before anyone noticed.

An ad hock stable was made for Patches in the wooden building we called the barn. It was a more secure area and better for her recovery. It was doubtful that the bear would return anytime soon, what with the licking it took from the hooves of the mare. However, the black bear was still lurking somewhere in the area.

Summer nights were a time of leisure in the North Country. Adult beverages flowed abundantly at the inn and were most heartily consumed. It was on one of these cheerful, yet raucous evenings that a four hundred pound black bear appeared from out of the wooded darkness.

Bears by nature are loners and stay to themselves. Unless you suddenly come upon one in the wild or venture too close to a mother with her cubs. Bears avoid human contact and their communities.

This inherent behavior was altered with the introduction of man. Bears, like man, are partial to a free lunch. Open dumps become the bear's version of McDonalds and attracts them like ants to a picnic. Stupid people trek to the local dumps as if it were the local zoo and feed them. When this occurs people tend to get hurt.

As one seasoned woodsman put it, "Extra stupid things happen to remind us that we do extra stupid things."

Attracted by the scent of human food, bears will venture into inhabited areas looking for a free meal.

This was one of those evenings and the usual crowd was being especially festive. Mom had served numerous dinners from the kitchen – mostly steak, salad and fries.

Preparing to close the kitchen, she exited the back door of the inn in an effort to close the kitchen window that vented the oily smoke from the deep frier. As she has done numerous times, she reached up to remove a wooden stick that held open the hinged window. In doing so, from behind her she heard a strange throaty growl. I was immediately followed by the more familiar growl of Tammy, our mixed breed dog.

In the shadows was a large black bear. When confronted by Tammy it raised up on its hind legs, all seven-feet, four-inches into a threatening and menacing pose.

Tammy darted to the side and then behind snapping at its legs. She lunged in and out, and then retreated out of its immediate reach. This created a distraction that allowed my mother to dash into the inn. Quickly, she sought out my father, who was slinging beer and engaging in some lively conversation.

To avoid a potential panic, she whispered in his ear but the noise was too loud for him to make out the words. She spoke a little louder, "Bill, there's a bear out back."

He whispered back, "Sure there is, honey. Can I pour you another drink?"

"No, Bill," she said a little louder. "I'm not kidding. There's a huge black bear out back."

This caught the attention of those in the immediate vicinity.

"What did she say," someone asked? "Did she say a bear?"

"What? There's a bear? Where?"

"She said there was a bear. Out back somewhere. That's what she said."

Like a stone tossed into a pond the news quickly surged outward, flowing from one person to another across the room.

"What? . . . Can't be, I just came from outside. . . How big? . . . Nothing can be that big. . . . I heard they can reach as big. . . Naw, she must have seen a cow or somethin.' . . Hey Red, can a bear be as big as a . . . ?

Dad never heard the increasing chatter for he grabbed the thirty-ought-six Savage from behind the bar and rushed through the kitchen and out the back door.

It took a moment for his eyes to adjust to the darkness but the snarling and snapping of Tammy and the bear captivated his immediate attention. The two had been propelled, dodging and surging one way and another into a grove of pines.

Amid the snapping tooth and slashing claw, Tammy held her own. She rushed in, latched onto a clump of hair, gave it a shake or two and then retreated out of the reach of the befuddled beast. Again, she noticed an opening and then lunged low to the ground making a strike and dashed out; all the while avoiding the inevitable counter thrust.

Raising the rifle to his shoulder, my father let three shots ring out almost simultaneously: BangBangBang. If military training had taught him anything, it was to shoot quickly, be accurate and aim slightly low in the dark. The flashes momentarily lit up the night. All three found their mark.

The bear tumbled over, momentarily thrashing about, flinching as it fought to fend off the inevitable grip of death. Then it sighed and lay still.

All the while, the dog darted in and out; latching onto some fur and then shaking left and right in a frenzy. Satisfied, she scurried out with a mouth full of hair. Tammy made a last lunge, clamping onto the limp neck of the dead bear. She wrenched violently from side to side. Wide-eyed and almost in a trance, she emitted a deep growl that had previously remained dormant and nearly forgotten of her ancestral past.

The local paper of record stated:

"According to Clarke, his wife, Phyllis, went to the rear of the establishment to close a window and walked into the path of the bear. Clarke's dog came between the animal which was 7-feet, 4-inches tall and the woman.

"Clarke, meanwhile hearing the commotion and seeing his wife running grabbed a 306 Savage and with the assistance of Dennis Green, Boonville, and Vic Martin, Waterville, went looking for the animal ..."

What wasn't reported was the following.

A loud raucous drinking fest carried on late into the evening and ended sometime in the early morning when someone suggested that the old mangy black bear be transported to Bourgeois' gas station in the center of B'ville and stuffed into the station's lone doorway as a gift. Someone suggested that a cigar ought to be stuck in its kisser in honor of the occasion. Another offered to prop a full (to a certain extent) can of Utica Club beer in its paw in the spirit of the celebration. An old ball cap with white lettering that read "Forestport" was placed on its massive head as an afterthought.

The paper also didn't record the reaction of the game warden when he gathered in the strange and surreal scene. For beneath this masquerade of madness there lay a dead wild animal that had been shot and killed out of season. The first words out of his mouth were, "Has anyone see Billy Clarke?"

His dubious reputation of being a celebrated huckster had preceded him.

WHEN LILACS BY THE OUTHOUSE BLOOM'D

'The septic tank is the greatest innovation in America," claimed Odell Seward before bracing himself with the fiery elixir commonly known as the "boilermaker." Throwing back a stiff shot of high-octane, low-grade whiskey and a soothing beer chaser, Odell added, "It lessened the burden placed upon humanity and pioneered the dawning of the modern man."

This bold claim went unchallenged by his bar buddies who were gently getting boiled themselves.

Tapping a stained fingernail on the timeworn bar, Odell ordered another set up. He looked about him with goading eyes, found no takers and then nodded a self-satisfying approval.

Who better to make such a brazen claim than Odell Seward, the community plumber and septic steward? When it came to plumbery and other issues of sanitation, the masses were inclined to concede to the wisdom of experience.

Mary, my mother-in-law, was known to occasionally vent her mindset on general subjects. She once affectionately broached the subject by stating, "The scent of lilacs always reminds me of Pulver Station."

Pulver Station, septic tanks, lilacs?

Pulver Station was a railroad stop hardly worthy of an empty glance from a passing train. However, it sported a splendid one room schoolhouse that Mary held in high esteem. The scent of lilacs revived youthful memories of her days spent in primary school. The rustic clapboard schoolhouse captured her childhood affections as well as those of children from the surrounding dairy farms.

Sadly, this ancient relic went the way of the milkman, paperboy and the telephone party line. When I pressed why lilacs reminded her of a one room schoolhouse at Pulver Station, she responded matter-of-factly, "Why . . . the outhouse, of course."

Ordinary people from that period possessed a notable amount of common sense. Simple problems required simple solutions. Schoolteachers found there was a direct correlation between student learning and the distance measured downwind from the outhouse.

Lilacs were commonsensical. They were planted around the outhouse to suppress the unpleasantness associated with rural plumbing or lack thereof. Therefore, the drone of education required that distraction be kept at a minimum. With its radiant scent, the soft murmur of rote education was permitted to drone unencumbered on a soft, mellow breeze. This was nature's remedy for such a crucial, yet fundamental task.

Outhouses were common in the not-so-distant past. Mid-century, outhouses would commonly be found scattered throughout the Adirondacks. In some remote areas, outhouses were still utilized into the latter part of the twentieth century.

Folks referred to them as "Forty-yarders" because outhouses were ordinarily situated forty yards away from the residence. Its placement was of prime importance. Prevailing winds played a decisive role in the planning and the posting of these structures. The female head of the household would designate a location, usually as far away from the kitchen as was discreetly possible. Her suggestion was more befitted an order rather than a request because the solitude and sanity of the residents were held in delicate balance.

The State of Government may be regulated by men but the State of the Household was ruled by women. There is a clever mantra from those days and it remains true even today – Happy wife, No strife.

Hence, the outhouse was relocated as directed.

The supplies were simple. Toilet tissue was in the form of a Sears and Roebuck catalogue – one page, single ply. Sanitation resided in a simple sack of lime. A liberal sprinkling of the white alkaline powder in "the pit," made the fly population manageable. Our forefathers used good sense when it came to these kinds of matters.

Lilacs were a practical solution to a perplexing problem. Good judgment was simple and ... common ... in those days

The evolution of toiletry made the outhouse ephemeral. Detritus: the Science of, unlocked the mystery to the septic system. And like a Biblical heralder, Odell Seward became a messenger of glad tidings.

He and others sent forth a cry proclaiming the good news, "Here comes Johnny." And to the delight of the masses, septic systems appeared in countless dwellings throughout rural hamlets. Even houses of worship join in proselytizing the good word.

Hallelujah! Mankind had found salvation from the denegation, the grunge and the offensive odors from the muck of mortal man. Indoor plumbing saved mankind by flushing away our filth and granted us Divine Grace unsoiled with human grime. The evils associated with the outhouse were in the past. Salvation was at hand. Mankind was saved from the savagery, the soil and the stench of human existence.

Old Scratch's handiwork would no longer plague Sunday worship and religious instruction with flies and befouled air. Cleansing water would flow like milk and honey through white porcelain fonts to underground cisterns, washing away our iniquities.

"Hallelujah, brothers and sisters. We are saved!"

That is the kind of testimony that could provoke Odell Seward to raise his glass and state with conviction, "To progress. Cheers!"

However, advancement to "new fangled" contraptions was slow to develop in the Adirondacks; progress was received like a drizzle on an overcast day. Although septic systems were becoming fashionable; they were looked upon by some as the newest snake oil accessible to the masses. They weren't immediately embraced by all. There were skeptics.

It was like when the Pet Rock was first introduced to Omar and Gertrude Thurston. Omar, the typical progressive, joyfully ushered his wife, the skeptic, to their rear window. Ecstatically, Omar gazed into their backyard consisted of rocky rubble and gamely informed his wife, "Gertrude we've struck the mother lode. We're RICH!"

Not sharing in his delight Gertrude muttered dryly, "If rocks were of value, the government would have taken them a long time ago."

Progress paused for a holiday.

Innovation came with a price and it had its share of setbacks. Why even the Wright brothers experienced a minor crash or two. And like the "Age of Flight" so too was "The Septic Age". My grandfather became an early martyr.

The family business, Dade's Inn, was built by my grandfather early in the first quarter of the last century. Built of logs, it was converted into a public house with indoor plumbing, bathrooms for each gender. Sloping sewer lines found their way to a septic tank located behind the inn.

The system was underground and self contained. Excess waste water from the bar, kitchen and two bathrooms was channeled into a large metal tank, where microbes did their thing. After breaking down the waste material in the tank, drainage lines directed the corrupted water into a leach field and then filtered it into sandy soil. What remained was a soupy odiferous sledge that required the services of Mr. Odell Seward for removal. Mr. Seward would transfer the waste to a remote, distant location. Very distant.

It was getting late one evening as my dad was immersed in a heated debate over some insignificant element about baseball. Dade, his father, had just paid for a round of drinks and placed a large wad of bills that he was accustomed to carry in his back pocket. With a general good-bye he made a quiet exit through the kitchen and out the back door to his motel next door.

Some minutes passed and dad thought he heard a voice in distress coming from the rear of the inn. He listened carefully. Barely audible, he heard the plea again.

"Help me, help me, and help me."

It sounded like the subdued voice of his father. Thinking that his father had stumbled upon a black bear, Dad grabbed the .303 Savage off the back-bar and ran to the rear of the inn. Remembering that the back light was on the fritz, he quickly grabbed a flashlight.

He shot a beam of light out the back door but didn't notice any movement at first. There it was again.

"Help me, help me, someone help me!"

Here was an urgent cry for help and it definitely belonged to his father.

Oddly, Bill saw no one.

The voice earnestly pleaded for assistance a third time.

Directing the flashlight to ground level where the voice emerged, Dad saw to his alarm and dismay that his father had become trapped in the middle of the inn's septic tank. Awaiting a visit from Mr. Odell Seward, someone had mistakenly left the lid off of the tank and Grandpa Dade was now lodged up to his chin in human sludge.

"Bill that you? Help me, son," his dad urgently pleaded, unmistakably overcome by the sea of septic gumbo.

After the initial shock of seeing his father neck deep in a tank of the putrid pooh, he gasped, "What do you want me to do?"

The response was immediate, "Give me your hand."

It came as natural as might come from anyone of us found in a similar situation. He looked at his father's extended arm dripping with a morass of Spanish moss-like smelly muck, and found himself in a dilemma. What could possibly be more revolting or repelling than perhaps finding himself encased in the muck of human excrement?

Bill lowered himself into a squatting position, clasping his arms about his knees.

Me, he thought. You want ME to give YOU my hand? The moment was monumental. It is like seeing Haley's Comet. It comes but once in a lifetime.

"Taking a midnight dip, Dad? A bit late for that wouldn't you say?

Humorless, the ire of indignation built like a seething storm until his temper erupted.

"BILL GET ME THE HELL OUT OF HERE DAMN IT AND I MEAN NOW."

Boiling with rage his fury sent the slimy surface rippling.

"Don't make any sudden movements. It'll make matters worse."

The ring of the septic waste rippling outward splashed against the sides of the tank and headed back in Dade's direction. He craned upward on his tippy toes, all five-feet, five-inches of himself.

A wooden ladder leaning against the side of the building was slid into the tank with the encouragement, "Whatever you do, don't swallow."

Had someone peered into that moonless night behind Dade's Inn, they would have observed something unseen by modern man. There lumbered what appeared to be a man from the chin up but below emerged something reptilian and primordial in nature. Primitive and prehistoric, it appeared to be some swamp creature from a bygone era.

Clinging to and oozing from was the accrued detritus of human waste. It bore the stench, the disgust, the desecration and debris of the miasmic muck of mankind. A new species had been revealed. Homo-vomitus.

Slowly it made its way to water, as all wounded animals will. It finally came to a secluded place where the Little Woodhull tributary converges with the Woodhull. There, a small curtain of water formed a waterfall that flowed over the crest of solid rock. The rush of water was aerated and created a natural frothy whirlpool that would eventually flow to the Black River.

Local lore claimed that the Little Woodhull had curative powers. Residents in the area, who normally heard the soft warble of the whippoorwill or the whistling hoot of the boreal owl, detected a plaintive cry. It was a cross between the snarl of a rabid bobcat and the howl of a wounded coyote.

Days passed before Dade was seen again. Someone thought they saw him disappear behind his motel with a shovel in one hand and a paper bag at arm's length in the other. In the weeks that followed no one spoke openly about the rumored mishap.

Seen blowing freely in the wind was a row of dollar bills fastened to a clothesline behind Dade's Motel. It imparted what one likened to the scent of soiled diapers and gave life to the local tittle-tattle. Nothing really came of the affair, but Aqua Velva was in short supply and the price of aftershave increased at the local pharmacy.

In the aftermath, there was unexpectedly an abundance of caddis flies, mayflies and midges found along Woodhull. Down river rainbow trout were in abundance and fishing met with renewed vigor. Below the Forestport dam, prize trout were in abundance and was harvested the likes of which had not been seen in recent times.

The wooden ladder was burned on a pile of yard debris, never to be seen again. Wherever Grandpa Dade went, the distinct scent of shaving tonic preceded him. He was known to furrow his brow whenever his grandson and namesake would cause mischief and his mother would call him "a little stinker."

Behind the motel where Dade was last seen with a shovel, there appeared a remarkable young cluster of white, violet and lavender lilacs that following spring. The assortment emitted an uncommon fragrance.

Father George, the local parish priest, was overheard to comment, "It smells like the aroma of the saints. Yes indeed, the scent of heaven."

Surely, Mary would approve.

When Lilacs last by the Dooryard Bloom'd by Walt Whitman

MOTHERED

My mother claimed that she got pregnant every time my dad placed his shoes under the bed. Together there were enough children to field a baseball team and then some. I suspect her reasoning was partially true. Using the baseball metaphor, it was more likely because dad was a pretty good pitcher, but mom was a better catcher.

With eleven kids it was a guarantee that one or more of the Irish horde got up on the wrong side of the bed and were destined to make for a very bad day. Someone once referred to us as savages. Mom smiled and politely thanked them. Had they been subjected to the constant onslaught she faced on a daily basis, they might have considered it a compliment, too.

Once, a well intended neighbor informed her that her children were eating mud pies in the yard.

"That's ok. It won't kill 'em," she announced unflinchingly. "Besides they need to eat at least a peck of dirt before they die."

Mom's role as mother consisted of a series of constant scuffles. Mother's weren't supposed to have bad days, however, we tried our best daily to prove that a misleading notion.

Each morning the battle would begin anew. Out of sheer exasperation Mom threatened to take us all down to Woodhull Creek and drown the "whole lot of us." Naturally this outburst might raise questions about the state of her mental stability. I never took the monition too seriously because she only made the threat a mere dozen times or so and, moreover, I could out run most of my brothers and all of my sisters.

If Mom had written an autobiography, she might have called it "My Struggle," but that title was already taken decades earlier by an awful Austrian writer.

With all the children accumulated, a simple trip in an automobile became quite a challenge. Like being held in custody at Marcy State Psychiatric Hospital, a simple excursion became a comic calamity; a theatrical farce of pure bedlam.

As a rule the slapstick pandemonium was piercing and riotous. Taunting, poking and jabbing led to anarchy and sheer savagery. These unpleasantries would result in some slapping and kicking which led to more slapping and kicking. To rein in the beastly hoard under normal circumstances was a daunting task, but to do it while driving a car was futile.

Mom made an attempt to maintain control with promises and pleading. When that didn't go well she resorted to harsher methods – the threat.

"Knock it off.

"Do you want me to stop this car?

"You're asking for it and you're going to get it."

With her zone of authority beginning to crumble and the power of persuasion becoming muted; she was compelled to resort to some more effective method.

The only remaining option left to her was the lunging sweep across the back seat with her right arm while firmly clasping onto the steering wheel with the other. Down the road we caromed between guardrails in break neck speeds. We were now being chauffeured by an unhinged mother transformed into Cruella De Ville.

Having already been served notice, the rightful culprits were now alerted and anticipating her next move. They simultaneously ducked below the seats just as the "KILL 'EM ALL AND LET GOD SORT 'EM OUT" parental arm-swoop was launched.

The fountainhead of her frustration usually found some mark. More likely it was some blameless victim like my younger brother Brian who was innocently counting cows in the passing fields. This docile exercise was unexpectedly substituted with a high-pitched howling and a torrent of tears. Revitalized and oblivious to her blunder she sneered a fresh warning,

"Keep it up and there's more where that came from."

The mayhem would temporarily fizzle to a stir, except for the lingering whimper and snivel of the wounded party.

Seasons are ushered in with foreseeable certainties. With winter there came woolen scarves and mittens; spring meant Keds sneakers and light jackets; summer resulted in cut off shorts and buzz cuts; and with fall there was the dreaded purge of stewed prunes, castor oil and Vaporub.

Flu season arrived with the return of Standard Time, the unofficial start of fall. No childhood in the post war years could possibly be complete without their mother purging the pestilence of irregularity that seemed to inevitably converge with the flu season.

Like most mothers of that period, Mom was fixated on bowel movements. If you weren't regular then the prevention of ill health required the conventional remedy – stewed prunes. If that didn't do the trick, it was the old reliable cure – castor oil.

Castor oil treatment would come suddenly and unexpected. Castor oil is natural oil extracted from the castor bean. It was the 20th century version of snake oil, a Marquee cure-all for practically everything from wrinkles, hangnails, fungal infections, joint pain, anti-inflammatory, lumbago, nightmares and constipation. The only thing it didn't seem to work on was lying.

Taking me aside, Mom would say something like, "Come here and have a seat; this won't take long."

If I had been the wiser, I would have heard a voice from the west forewarning, "Come here my pretty and bring your little dog, too. Hee, Hee, Hee!"

I expected a session of ear wax extraction from Mom using one of her hair pin and toilet tissue. Many times that was how it began. But when I was ready to leap off the stool she would throw in, "Sit still. Just one more thing."

Turning away she would load up a hidden tablespoon with castor oil. Turning toward me, with the finesse of a snickering Snidely Whiplash, she entreated me warmly, "Now open wide."

I was fool enough to keep my eyes opened and the suddenness of it all was paralyzing. It had the effect of Boris Karloff as the Mummy (in this case my mummy) ambling toward you with a spoonful of the foul, ill-tasting liquid Castor oil. Facial expressions varied from frowns to grimaces to glowers. It was similar to the twisted contortion created by sucking a lemon. YUCK!

A second dose might be prescribed which would require the assistance of my older brother who would clamp me in a bear-hug while I was force fed the evil elixir. And this was only part one of the autumn purge.

When the neighborhood became a long series of sneezes and coughs it was time for part two of the purge. It began with hot baths. Camouflaged in soap suds and plastic toys, we were urged to soak in a tub of hot water.

Like the story of Noah's Ark, we bathed in twos which resulted in a biblical size flooding. Dried and placed in pajamas, I was ushered into Mom's bedroom where she had a ceramic bowl, bath towel, a jar of Vaporub and a tablespoon. At the sight of the tablespoon I experienced a brief panic attack. A gagging fear of phase one surfaced. Relieved to find that the bottle of Castor oil wasn't in the offerings, Mom gestured for me to sit in a chair next to her cedar chest. On the chest was a large steaming bowl of water.

Smiling, Mom scooped out a gob of thick, slightly sticky substance from the jar with the tablespoon. It instantly gave off this strong pungent smell that permeated the room with its vapors as it melted into an oily patch.

All the while in a soothing voice, Mom instructed, "Lean over the bowl. Be sure to close your eyes and breathe deeply."

At first I was compliant. That was until I leaned over the steaming bowl steeped in Vaporub and become trapped under a bath towel. My eyes began to sting. My lungs began to burn. I could hardly breathe.

Amid watering eyes and fits of gagging and coughing, I heard as if in a far away voice my mom urging, "Breathe in honey. That's it. Keep breathing. Now breathe deeply."

If madness were a virtue, Mom struck the mother lode. I must have begun to hallucinate for my loving, nurturing mother morphed into this cold and calloused Cruella De Ville, again. When I lifted my head (a natural near death reaction), she placed a hand gently on the back of my neck and held it securely over the bowl.

"Breathe deeply . . . Breathe deeply . . . . That's a good boy. Breathe deeply."

Being a good or bad boy was irrelevant. What I favored most at that time was not being a dead boy. I much preferred being a live bad boy then becoming a dead good boy.

"Breathe in deeply until I say stop," was the last I heard before I bolted and neither my sisters nor any of my brothers could catch me. I spent the night hidden under the bed.

In the coming years it became harder and harder to gather us together for the autumn purge. It was like getting our annual visits to Doc Smith's office. All went well until the nurse entered with a tray of syringes. It then became a bounding bunny rodeo roundup. Yee Hah!

It was in later years I found out that Ricin, a byproduct naturally found in castor beans is a poison and can cause injury. Vaporub contains camphor which is toxic if swallowed or absorbed into the body. It has been known to cause inflammation in the eyes, mental status changes, lung inflammation, liver damage, constriction of airways and allergic reactions. The castor oil and vaporub treatment ended with my generation.

If mom was ever charged with infanticide by accident or design, I am convinced that she would be cleared of the charges. A competent lawyer would surely pack the jury with mothers who ran households with no less than a half dozen children in ages ranging from toddler to teenager. Upon examining all of the evidence very carefully and after a protracted period of several minutes, the jury would return with the verdict of not guilty.

"Mothers of the jury what is your verdict," the judge might say.

"Your honor … We, the jury find this poor mother's actions to be justifiable and we have found her to be not guilty."

"Case dismissed Mrs. Clarke," the judge might say banging the gavel. "You are free to go, "and adding, "You know I once had a mother who mothered, too."

Outside on the courthouse steps her lawyer might reveal, "This is the innocent case of a mother who so loved her children … that they were mothered in the first degree. This will stand as a landmark case and a warning to all you little savage tikes out there who feel like they can run amuck. The law will always stand firmly behind motherhood. The unmanageable will be managed. The ungoverned will be governed. The unruly will rule no more.

In a parting word on the subject, in the immortal words of that great

German philosopher Friedrich Nietzsche,

"That, which does not kill us, makes us stronger; especially when you eat a peck of dirt."

FIRST DEER

Deer hunting is a rite of passage in the Adirondacks. The first deer can be a real ordeal for the beginner. The cold, wet weather and hours of tedious monotony will produce an entrenched weariness that exploits the weaknesses of the common man. When one has not become disoriented, wondering in circles and getting lost, hunting is the true testament for patience and endurance. Competence requires a specialized skill set that evolves with years of experience.

Success may require capable supervision and support. Dejected, the tenderfoot will often falter and then fade into the shadows of society. A newcomer's focus is generally sidetracked with delusions of frost-bitten feet or some imaginary creature from Baum's haunted forest in the Land of Oz, drooling and skulking in pursuit of certain cruelty, inflicting unimaginable harm.

In the notable words of one obscure Adirondack guide, "Track and you shall advance. Seek and you shall attain. Aim straight and you shall slay the silly old bugger."

My brother, who was the first born and heir to our family honor and humble riches, required for this first hunt careful reflection with prudent planning. My father reasoned that his first born must achieve no less that a six-point buck thus causing a bit of effort.

Included in this challenge were a whole set of state laws that imposed untenable limitations like mandatory licenses and fixed seasons. The old adage that one should never make a law that can't be enforced, reared its ugly head.

In this wild and remote region of the Adirondacks, a license to hunt may be required but was not viewed as a necessity. The state may have an established season for hunting, but it wasn't practical because realistically it would not be honored by locals and could not be enforced by the authorities.

During the Depression, hunting went from sport to survival. For those whose livelihood was fixed to the forest, it has remained unchanged ever since.

These huntsmen possess a keen eye, steady nerve and woodland savvy. Unlike the urban bookworm, the Adirondack youth are schooled in independence, common sense and native survival. When America calls, they fill the ranks, fight well and make first-rate soldiers. A game warden's ability to duck and weave is useful for it becomes difficult to hit a moving target. What's more, they would be more apt to catch a hummingbird in their hands as to nab a poacher in their natural setting.

It is said that when buying diamonds, you don't consult a plumber. You seek the advice of experience, an expert in the field. Therefore, it was central that my father sought the services of Art Allen, an old friend, who was raised in the remote backwoods with a fixed set of skills unfettered by administrative regulations and management.

Art was the patriarch of the Allen's clan from Woodgate. They were regularly schooled in drinking, fighting and romancing all in the same outing - that is when they weren't hunting. These festivities usually commenced on a Friday and were curtailed late Sunday evening, although they were not opposed to extending the revelry beyond perhaps the middle of the month of August. The holiday season that followed was altogether a different story. This is where the band was truly deserving of the merit for their merriment.

If there was one talent that the Allen's were noted for and could not be excelled in, was hunting. There was no critter that walked, crawled, swam, flew or slithered that didn't attract their attention or pursuit from one time or another.

With a family as large as theirs it was a constant challenge to secure provisions for their platoon-sized feasts. They had a family recipe for each and every species in critterdom that could be shot, trapped, snared or out-witted in the Adirondacks.

Nothing was overlooked. Deer (which they specialized in), rabbits, ducks, woodchuck, turkey, possum, squirrel, porcupine, beaver or trout were regular guests at their table. Skunk was not out of the realm of probability, however, experience had proven that the meal preparation for skunk was too burdensome and time-consuming. Let's face it, who really wanted to prepare a meal that required holding a smelly polecat under water? Phew!

The Allens had lived in the Adirondacks for as long as anyone could remember. Local lore alleged that the Allens had established their name when the Adirondacks were part of the frontier. Some seemed to think they may have ventured over from Vermont and was somehow related to the famous Ethan Allen. But that is strictly conjecture. However, their ability to navigate the woods with stealth lent credence to the conviction that native blood, perhaps Oneida or Seneca, found its way coursing through their veins.

When it came to marksmanship, there were those who were perhaps their equal but none better. Even Goldie Donegal, who was known to have killed three running deer in one outing, couldn't best the Allens at the local turkey or ham shoot.

It was a common fact that Goldie was a "sure shot" with anything that moved, but when it came to a stationary target he failed miserably. He was known to whistle at a still deer just to get them in motion for a decent shot.

Goldie was once overheard lamenting about an upcoming tournament.

"I might have a shadow of a chance if that damn target grew legs and could lope around a bit," he groused.

There was a time when no one would enter a shoot unless there was an understanding that a person could win but one prize per tournament. That left the Allens sulking.

This was the kind of experience that gave my father confidence.

"You won't see a mule running at the Kentucky Derby," he often said.

What he required was someone with an Adirondack blood line dating back to the earliest of times whose skills were tried and true and pestered with such insignificance like a license or fixed season.

With this in mind, it was quite natural that Dad sought the services of Art Allen. It proved not to be a complicated mission for Art had squatter's rights at the end of his bar at Dade's Inn and any afternoon would be a suitable time and place for negotiations. Securing the deal required several hearty and robust rounds of his finest inventory. The time was finally agreed upon for the upcoming Saturday.

"Anytime you kin git thar . . ." Art garbled in a voice heavy with whiskey and they settled on that.

That Saturday Dad and my brother rose before first light to go hunting. It had snowed and nothing can instill delight like fall's first snow.

Winter arrived early that year, cold and white. That frosty morning an undulating coat of thick creamy whiteness had shrouded the spacious landscape. It was sculpted by the mystifying hand of the Divine with a gracefulness that brought delight. The day would be blessed.

Fortified with a filling breakfast of flap jacks, bacon, juice and strong hot coffee, the two checked their equipment to make sure all was in order – twice. Cloaked in a cave-like darkness they glided gently through the freshly fallen snow; two beams of yellow light guiding their way.

Freshly fallen snow softens sound. Pleasingly muffled, it takes on the characteristics of a muted instrument in the hands of a skilled musician. Robert Frost (aptly named) captured the moment best in the line, "The woods are lovely dark and deep . . ." Tracking would be gratifying.

When the two arrived at the Allen homestead, the scattered dwellings of gray clapboard remained unlit and appeared deserted. Walking through the downy snow near the first residence, a long throaty growl came from somewhere in the wintery darkness. My father reached for a stick of fire wood about the size of a small ax handle stacked on the porch.

"What's that for Dad?" asked my brother.

"Art's dog can't be trusted."

"Will he bite?"

"Unpredictable. But if he latches on . . . he won't stay long."

The first couple of knocks on the door brought no response. It was followed by two more solid raps. Nothing stirred. Peeking through the frosted window was like looking into a frozen rain barrel. The two were about to leave when the door slightly opened revealing a lone eye peering from within. The rattling of a chain promptly revealed Art's denture-less wife, Ellie, grinning broadly.

"C'mon in," she chuckled. "You'll catch your death out there."

Following Ellie inside, she bellowed, "Art we got company."

On the sofa, stretched the stationary figure of Art or what was left of his massive earthly remains. From woolen socks to his fuzzy bald pate, lay Art – all six-foot-four, three hundred and forty-seven motionless pounds of him. These were the remnants of what accounted for a lively outing that previous evening.

Captivated, the two visitors gazed curiously at the gray silhouette lying inert on the couch. Art was snoring in gagging fits of snarls and snorts, which were followed by deep throated moans and groans resonating sonorously. This revelation culminated in a troublesome drawn-out silence. The soft irregular smacking of his lips produced a spontaneous interruption of this temporarily episode. The command performance was repeated again and again with a slight variation in degree and duration.

Raising Lazarus would have been a less demanding task, but after several attempts Ellie finally managed to stir her husband from his deep death-like slumber. Somewhere in the course of the unnatural snorting, wheezing and whooshing of air, Art opened an eyelid. Sitting up and rubbing his red rimmed eyes, he acquired better display of his surroundings.

Grinning he bid them, "Welcome. Welcome."

Addressing his wife he followed with, "Look Honey, it's- Bill."

Art proceeded to shake his head from side to side in an attempt to clear his brain of the lingering fog fashioned by merriment the night before.

"What brings you here so early this morning?" Now grasping the clearer picture he added, "Oh yeah hunting. That's right. You want a deer for the boy. Have a seat." And in his usual genial manner he added, "It ain't much but we call it home."

Meanwhile, with her dentures retrieved, Ellie busied herself with breakfast. Turning on the kitchen light she lifted the circular disk of the cast iron stove and stirred the old ashes. Adding some newspaper and dry kindling to the embers she started the fire anew. Placing a cold cast iron skillet over the heat, several days of hard white grease fastened to the bottom of the pan began to liquefy and then sizzle. While spurting and spattering, Ellie added several strips of thick bacon to the liquid. The familiar scent of its frying prompted a scratching at the door.

Setting a second black skillet next to the first, the hard white lard gradually dissolved likewise within. Ellie cracked several eggs and plopped them one by one into the now simmering mixture. She paused momentarily and in a natural motion adjusted a flaccid breast to a more comfortable position under her worn house coat. Turning toward the living room she inquired, "How many eggs you boys want? Three? Four? Speak up, don't be bashful. Half dozen if you wish. The girls have been working hard this week."

"We've eaten already, Ellie, but thank you just the same."

"Suit yourself."

Not to be left out Art inquired, "How 'bout me? Where's my breakfast?"

"Yours is comin' right up."

With that said, Ellie opened the refrigerator door and reached inside. Walking over to Art she handed him a can of beer, which he immediately opened with an abrupt pssssssshhh! Taking a long draught, he emitted in a prolonged deep-chested belch that impressively vibrated throughout the room. He wiped his chin stubble with his forearm and added in a scholarly manner, "They say breakfast is the most important meal of the day. Sure, I can't git yoo somethin'? How about a beer Bill? No?"

And with a playful grin Art added, "What about the boy?"

The aroma from the kitchen prompted the old Red Bone hound on the porch to whimper and scratch a second time. My father opened the front door as the canine gave a low growl and scurried quickly past him, seeking shelter behind the couch. With head protruding, he showed his teeth. Art made a swiping motion with his free hand and sent the submissive hound deeper into the dark sanctuary behind the couch.

"Look around," Art began philosophically. "It might not seem like much, but here everyone's welcomed."

He drew another long steady draught from his beer, pausing for a belch and then continued.

"Bill, there's nothing ashamed at being poor."

He finished his beer and then happily requested another. Opening the can of Utica Club without delay, he then added, "It's just a minor inconvenience."

The conversation woke Stanley, Art's younger brother and boon companion, who was sleeping in a side bedroom. With hair in disarray, he sociably nodded to the invited guests and quietly walked into the kitchen. Ellie had plated several eggs on a platter with a mound of bacon and a stack of buttered toast. It was topped off with a heavy brown mug steaming with strong black coffee.

Stanley was quite a character. He once came home with fifty sizeable bull frogs in a bucket. He had overheard a "Frenchy" speaking about the high merits and enviable quality of fried frog legs. Stanley decided he might "give 'em a try." Sure enough, they were "Some Good!" But he concluded that it would take "the whole of Tupper Lake to track down and put together an honest meal."

On another occasion this same French Canadian expounded at length on the superiority of rattle snake meat.

"What's it taste like," Stanley inquired delving deeper into the more practical aspects of the subject.

"It tastes like . . ." the Canuck paused reflecting. "Well, it tastes like . . . sorta like . . . chicken!"

Satisfied Stanley went traipsing off around the region in pursuit of the elusive and friendless reptile. Finally, he located a host of native rattlers den up in the rocky timber region somewhere near Whiteface Mountain. The ordeal became a test of patience and agility, which required a hardy measure of inherited enterprise.

Stanley managed to distract the snakes' attention using the glint of the sun off the blade of his hunting knife. He bagged several good sized timber rattlers by decapitating them one by one using his razor sharp knife and the flick of his wrist.

Placing the skinned carcasses in a skillet with a few wild mushrooms and some salt pork he found the meal to be "measurably agreeable." He concluded that rattle snake meat indeed tasted like chicken, but reasoned that "lopping off their heads" was "right challenging" and without a doubt "worthy of the hunt."

Moreover, the skins made "right handsome hat bands." He decided that he was done with the experiment. Simply put, the effort to "locate and fix the temperamental critters was a waste of his time."

In the future if his preference was chicken, he "would just pluck a fat hen out of the chicken coop. But on this cold winter morning it wouldn't be frog legs or rattler meat. Stanley was attracted to Ellie's breakfast special.

My brother's initial instruction began with a narrative by Art, the master on the subject of hunting. There was no rhyme or reason to his discourse. His ramblings were whatever came to him that suited his fancy.

"There was this fellow by the name of Stretch Fuller," Art began. "People called him Stretch because he was the most notable liar in these parts. He stretched the truth a bit so we called him Stretch. He claimed to be a champion bulldogger from Billings, Montana. He claimed steers were as big as rhinos in them parts. When cattle weren't handy, he'd practice on moose, caribou, elk and the like.

"Once he came upon a twelve-point mule deer with its horns caught in wire fencing on the high plains. Being the Christian fellow that he was he decided to unloose the buck from its embarrassment. Grabbing the beast by the horns, he tussled with it freeing him of his predicament. Before he could hog tie it and stow it in his truck bed for his friends to see, it lunged through the barbed wire and loped off onto the plains. 'I was left with a handful of buck hairs watching his white tail flash off into the distance,' he said.

"That left me a bit suspect.

"I told him that that reminded me of a time that I spent fishing. It began to get dark, so I lit the kerosene lamp to make my way home. As I was taking in my fish line, I felt a tremendous tug on the pole. Out of the water leaped a huge brook trout as long as your forearm. It took me a bit of time to land it and in all the excitement I had kicked the lantern into the river wedging itself in some rocks. I decided to retrieve the lamp in the morning when there was more light. The following morning, I came back to my fishing hole and to my surprise as I lifted the lamp out of the water it was still lit. Stretch said it was far-fetched and barely credible.

"'You don't say. Tell you what,' I said. 'When you drag that deer back through the fence, I'll put a flame out in that lantern.' Stretch got the horse laugh and I didn't see him for a long while."

Glancing toward a window, Dad noticed that the morning was displaying a hint of gray light. He didn't want to appear rude but it was getting light out and they needed to locate a promising spot in the woods.

Art sensed his impatience and inquired, "Stanley how are we doing?"

Using his shirt sleeve, Stanley rubbed a circular area on the frosted windowpane and peered out.

"There's some does, a spike, no two, a four, and a six."

"Bill, you think the boy would like a six-pointer."

Flabbergasted he responded, "Sure, Art. A six-point buck would do nicely." He stood up and started to collect his gear.

"Where are you going?" Art asked. "We're not finished yet. There's time."

Just then an earsplitting blast from a rifle came from the kitchen. It sent my father and brother leaping from their chairs. Stanley had quietly raised the kitchen window, aimed his 30-30 Winchester at a six-point buck about 50 yards away at the edge of the woods.

Dad stood up and rushed to the window and just caught a glimpse of several deer bounding into the wood line while one lay on the ground kicking its legs in the final throws of death. Stanley ambled to the front door, slipped on his unlaced boots, grabbed his hunting knife, and disappeared loping into the freshly fallen snow.

Experienced hunters knew there were several things that attracted deer. They liked acorns, apples, alfalfa, corn and salt licks. This morning the doe were attracted to the acorns and apples underneath Art's oak and apple trees as well as his heifer's salt lick in a nearby pasture. The bucks were understandably attracted to all of the above, but especially the does.

Several minutes passed and Stanley reappeared dragging a six-point buck by the horns through the freshly fallen snow. There was a streak of red trailing from the exit wound of the chest cavity where the bullet had exited the buck. In no time Stanley had field-gutted the deer, placing the heart and liver in a pot that Ellie handed to him out the door. With red-soiled hands,

Stanley handed the back straps or tenderloin to Ellie. This, she immediately cut into strips which began to sizzle with the bacon.

Art continued undisturbed with hunting tales. There was the city fellow who was stopped at a road check and found that the black bear draped over the hood of his Buick was a farmer's Black Angus steer that had been roaming in a pasture.

In the intervening time, Stanley tied the spread hind legs to a single tree hitch for a buggy and looped the rope in a pulley attached to their porch ceiling. Raising the buck aloft the antler slightly touched the porch floor while a small portion of blood drained in a crimson pool in the white drifting snow.

Art recalled a lowlander who had such a serious case of buck fever that every time his country cousin shot at a lone buck, he thought that he had discharged his own and would eject a shell. The urbanite began to tag the deer when they noted that there were several unspent shells where he had been standing. He was still insistent that it was his buck.

Without saying a word, Stanley entered the house with two strips of raw liver. He handed one to my brother and the other he placed in his mouth and began to chew.

It is an old native custom in these parts that you eat a part of the liver of a freshly killed deer. It is as much of a symbol as it is a tradition. Life is a mystery and considered sacred. Life begets life and one honors the passing by eating the flesh of the newly fallen. Life is passed on anew, a representation of the sacred cycle of life.

That is not what my brother got from the stern, silent look from my father. That would have to be explained later.

What he did read in his eyes was, "This will be a supreme insult to Art, his family and this house. If you don't graciously accept the offer, you will not sit comfortably on your tender ass for a week."

He took the strip of liver and slowly chewed it all the while deceptively smiling and thinking it was chicken.

It was mid-morning when Art had exhausted his stock of tales. When Dad and my brother finally left, Stanley had secured the freshly killed buck over the trunk of the car. As they were saying their good-byes, Ellie handed them a plastic bag with "camp meat." Inside were the rest of the deer liver and the heart.

That coming Christmas Eve, as was the tradition, Dad served red wine (Chianti), thinly sliced wedges of sharp cheese and pickled deer heart – marinated in a gallon jar of white vinegar and spices for the last two months.

Like the adage credited to Napoleon that history was a set of lies agreed upon, my brother was credited with the six-point buck. Napoleon never won that war so I suspect the quote attributed to him is also a lie.

But one thing is true, and I can speak with conviction, is that my brother had a lifelong loathing of liver. He acquired a sixth sense when it came to liver being served at the Clarke household and found a way to stay at a friend's house for dinner.

He likes to recount to his friends about eating raw deer liver. When asked by his friends what deer liver tasted like? He would pause and in his worldly way saying, "It tastes like . . . Well, it tastes like . . . sorta like . . . chicken!"

EINE KLEINE NACHT MUSIK
(A LITTLE NIGHT MUSIC)

It was the beginning a typical evening. The taproom was dark and deserted and the nighttime revelry ended with last call. Undetected, a small creature scurried across the floor. The scent of stale beer lingered like the foul, fusty smell of old neglected sneakers.

A faint glow of the crescent moon shone through the window casement behind the backbar. It revealed an untidy taproom whose contents: chairs, tables, bar stools were casually distributed about in random disarray. An assortment of used glasses painted a lifeless picture in the gray morning light.

Earlier a patron had unburdened himself of his loose change and played "The Little Brown Mouse" several times in succession with his departure. Softly, the tune continued to play in the background.

"It was a Saturday Night about 12 o'clock,

And the bar was closed for the night,

and from out of his hole came a little brown mouse,

and he sat in the pale moonlight . . ."

Like a petty mosquito bite, it was intended to irritate those who remained behind. And it did.

It is not the monumental things in life that thrusts one into the emotional chasm of recklessness. No, this hazardous journey begins with the unimportant things in life. These are those insignificant matters that slowly eat away at us little by little, day in and day out.

These petty detriments de jour build, and gradually we begin to lose our sense of what grandmother called, "the God-given sense you were born with."

Like a Chinese water torture, that slow irregular pattern of the cold water dripping on the forehead, the accumulated effect of anticipation eventually drives one mad. The ability to maintain common sense and reason is reduced to the irrational and the absurd. So it was with my dad that one unfortunate evening. He reached critical mass over a bag of Planter's Peanuts and a common country mouse.

It was very late that evening. Dad had decided to play, what some of the locals liked to call "chamber music." It wasn't the kind of chamber music for the musically refined. But for those who are, might refer to the evening's entertainment as a concerto for technically the melody was a piece written for a single type of instrument.

In my father's case, that single instrument was a Parker shotgun, and he would utilize both chambers nearly instantaneously. Some may be tempted to identify it as a dirge, a lament, a reel, or a cannon. All these musical types would be fitting and appropriate. Nonetheless for our purpose we shall refer to the evening performance merely as chamber music.

Being raised in the Adirondacks, my father had been knowledgeable with the use of firearms since his youth. This Parker was a beautifully crafted 12-gauge double barrel shotgun, a family heirloom. A hinge pin located on the bridge of the handle allowed for a quick opening and loading. A flick of the wrist quickly closed the shotgun, and you were ready … to play some rather dissonant music.

Dad ran an inn that sold an assortment of food, plenty of cold beer and if you could keep your temperament, whiskey. There were other small items like gum, candy, an assortment of chips, pretzels, popcorn and packets of peanuts that were on display on the backbar. They could be purchased for a small fee.

During the depression, sandwiches and snacks were placed on the bar without charge for paying customers. Bowls of peanuts were standard. Proprietors believed that salted peanuts made customers thirsty and would result in increased beer sales. As times improved the handouts ended and bagged peanuts were sold instead. It was a sad day for those who liked to fill their pockets to snack on later.

Those always looking for something free were "&%#@! freeloaders." The one thing that Dad held in low esteem was a &%#@! freeloader.

"These moochers spend most of their waking hours malingering and scrounging. If they found something for free, they'd want it delivered," he said.

These were social parasites. They came in all shapes and sizes, and they did not conform to any one economic group. In fact, he said, "Those with more want more. There's a whole crew of 'em mixed up in government."

Scrounging was not limited to humans. There were pigeons, crows, and squirrels. But the biggest offender was the typical tavern mouse. It was a malingering, scrounging, shirking, sneakthief.

Yes, this marauder-mooch, this burglar-bandit, this night-raider led this detestable pack. Detestable was lacking in strength. Combine it with repugnant, vile, and revolting, then add loathsome, abominable, and abhorrent and you might have a passing understanding of my father's proper sentiment.

What could possible prompt such enmity one would ask? It was Planter's Peanuts.

Bags of peanuts displayed on the backbar sold for a mere five cents. Recently, when the bar was closed at night, something scaled the backbar. Locating the Planter's Peanuts display, chew a hole in a bag and stole off with its contents. It became a regular nightly modus operandi.

On a good night, the bandit might make off with the contents of a couple of bags. After deliberating with his friend Jack Daniels, Dad believed that the culprit was a mouse, although it was possible, he had an accomplice. Noticing some mice dropping at the crime scene, he concluded that indeed the filthy little filcher was a mouse. His next move was to formulate a plan. Dad was always ... usually a good planner.

A trap naturally came to mind. All he had to do was simply buy a mouse trap, bait it, and then wait for the little bugger to appear. Then "SNAP" problem solved. Things are never quite that easy. First, there were a variety of traps to choose from. As he made inquiries, each hardware store seemed to rave about their brand and found fault with the others.

If someone had a similar mouse trap, theirs was always better. The proprietor would argue that it was constructed with better material, therefore lasted longer and resulted (by inference) in a high body count. Additionally, it was made in the USA (patriotism suggested). One salesman upheld that his was at a bargain price. When confronted by another less expensive, he countered, "I'll match the price!"

So, on and on and so forth. Finding the right trap was as big a problem as getting rid of the mouse.

Next was selecting the proper bait. Dad quizzed the milkman as he made a delivery. Naturally, he suggested cheese. A local dog owner advocated dog food.

The windfall of cat lovers was adamant that their brand of cat food was the best. One unwavering tabby owner suggested tuna fish, "Be sure to buy Chicken of the Sea." Miss Isabel Wendell thought if she were a mouse, she should prefer chocolate.

Dad politely thanked her for her trouble and gave her a Hershey bar. Promptly she raised it to her nose, closed her eyes and smelled it. Unwrapping it carefully, Miss Isabel Wendell broke off a small piece and again with her eyes closed, let it melt in her mouth and murmured "Ummm." She repeated the practiced ritual until the entire candy bar was gone. Pausing, she stared longingly back as if expecting another but finally thanked Dad with a smiled.

Cheese? Dog food? Cat food? Chocolate? Flustered, Dad pursued the advice of one skilled in the art of hunting, Herman the German.

"Vas do zee maus eat?" Herman asked with his thick German accent.

"Eat? Well, it likes peanuts," dad responded.

"Vell, den give 'em pee nutt."

With a quizzical look dad asked, "How do you put a peanut on a mouse trap."

"No PEE nutt. pee nutt BOOTER!" He followed with a guttural mumble that sounded something like dumpfkoff.

Then "pee nutt BOOTER" it was. So, for a dollar ninety-nine dad selected the top-of-the-line, genuine-rodent-ridding mouse trap. It was named of all things - SNAP. Dad loaded "SNAP" with a dollop of Skippy peanut butter for bait. It took him only three attempts (along with a mouthful of profanities) to set the trap. The taproom lights were extinguished, awaiting the following day.

The next morning, he noticed the trap sprung. Both the mouse and the bait were gone. He set the trap and baited it a second time. Arriving early the following day, he blundered upon the same results. Tuesday came, snap . . . nothing. There was Wednesday, snap . . . nothing. And Thursday, snap . . . nothing. This trend continued for the remainder of the week. SNAP, SNAP, SNAP . . . nothing . . . nothing . . . nothing.

Evidently Dad had been out outwitted by a small ignorant mouse. Nothing could be more irritating than being bested by some stupid little creature who hadn't even earned a bachelor's degree. The one thing going for it was home court advantage, but it didn't even hold the mortgage.

Dad sought other traps currently on the market. He solicited old timers for their insight. What trap was the best? Was peanut butter the best bait? Where should you locate the trap? What were the best times to catch a mouse? Nothing seemed to work.

He decided to try his luck with a cat. It turned out that the cat was a bigger freeloader than the mouse. The only time that he saw the cat was at mealtimes and then it would saunter off somewhere to sleep. The mouse continued to make its nightly appearance and the caper of the missing peanuts persisted. The cat eventually got under foot once too often, causing Dad to spill an entire tray of drinks. That was it. The cat was dispatched to the tuna fish lady's delight. Dad would need to revisit the subject but in the interim, he had a business to run.

It was that fateful Saturday afternoon when dad grabbed a pack of peanuts and tossed them to Willy the Poacher. Some of the peanuts scattered helter-skelter across the bar.

"Hey Bill, what's the going price for a half bag of peanuts," Willy the Poacher jokingly probed?

"What?" Dad noticed Willy T's bag was spilling peanuts from one chewed corner. "That @&%# mouse! "Nothing, it's on the house," he fumed without explanation.

"That was it," Dad thought, "It is the last straw."

That mouse was about to get more than he had bargained for.

"Just wait 'til closing. Your little rodent ass is MINE."

That evening Dad found himself brooding on a barstool in the shadows. Before him was a half-bottle of Jameson whiskey and a bar glass with three fingers of Ireland's finest that he replenished from time to time. Across the bar lay a shotgun. The Parker was loaded with buckshot and braced with some good Irish whiskey; Dad appeared to be nicely maintained himself. As a second thought, he stuffed a handful of peanuts into each barrel as a bonus.

Late in the evening when constricted by spirits and fatigue the mind tends to wander. Clutching the Parker shotgun, dad began to gradually nod off. His mind strayed to an earlier time . . . 1944 . . . Italy . . . silhouettes of war. He had been on the front lines for an extended period. Life was a constant struggle: poor diet, insects, marching in the rain, the mud, trench foot, dysentery, sleeping in the open and without cover. He was in pursuit of the Germans or them him.

This one patrol ended late in the afternoon. He was bone tired as he entered a deserted Italian village. His squad found shelter in an abandon building in the center of town. Removing his socks and rubbing his sore feet, he became distracted by a window sign across the way. It read "Vino e Liquori." He didn't understand Italian, but any red-blooded American understood that that meant booze.

Laying claim to an area in the corner of one room, he slipped out a side door, unnoticed. In the waning light the store sign stated boldly, "Vino e Liquori." Conveniently, the door was ajar. Once inside he glanced around and noted that the place had been plundered. But in their haste they overlooked a large wicker basket hidden behind some discarded boards; it held a large glass jug of red wine.

With a furtive glance he uncorked it, took a discerning sniff, and licked his lips. Raising the opening to his parched lips, he took a long wholesome draught of the contents, "Ah, Chianti." The sweet red liquid was refreshing. It went down smoothly and registered a smile.

"Mama Mia," he thought, "The milk of a Roman goddess, nectar of the gods." It lifted his spirits, fortified his soul.

Again, closing his eyes he took a second, longer pull on the jug. It was somewhere between the third or fourth mouthful that he heard a not-too-distant echo of thunder. It had the familiar sound of German artillery. Some-one spontaneously yelled "IN COMING" as the deadly screeching approached.

Stunned, his adrenaline surging, the lethal missiles approached. Jerked by anticipation, he was abruptly thrust into the present-day. Clutching a shotgun, he discovered himself in a dimly lit room that smelled of stale beer and old discarded sneakers.

Wide-eyed and panting, he remained transfixed on the two beady eyes of a mouse perched on the barrel of the shotgun. With whisker's twitching, the mouse was passively gnawing on a peanut staring back at him not more than two feet away. Startled, his fingers yanked and created a brilliant flash as both barrels from the Parker shotgun were touched off.

"WA-WA-OOOOOOOOOOOOOOOMMMMMMMMMMM."

When the dust from the rafters settled, Dad lay sprawled on the floor out cold. The last thing he remembered was a slow-motion mixture of Chianti, German shelling, and one nasty little critter. In one arm he clenched the Parker shotgun and in the other he cradled an empty bottle of Irish whiskey. What spirits hadn't been consumed lay in a small dark pool beside him.

The scene left the impression that by proxy, the Parker shotgun had completed what the imagined German artillery had not. For blown clean through the window was the Planter Peanut display as well as everything else located on the end of the backbar. In an instant an untold quantity of peanuts now lay scattered helter-skelter everywhere about the parking lot along with shards of glass, splinters of window encasement, candy wrappers, shredded bags of pretzels, popcorn, and potato chips. Yet incredibly, the backbar remained intact, comparatively unscathed. A cleaner job could not have been done had he been stone cold sober.

The morning was greeted by a gentle breeze that played with the shredded window curtains through the jagged remnants of the empty window. Everything had remained as it was the night before except Dad was missing. He would remain incognito for the remainder of that day and part of the next. Just long enough for a disabling headache to run its course. It would take the ringing in his ears a little longer.

A technician was called because the jute box persisted on playing the scratched recording of "The Little Brown Mouse."

"He lapped up the liquor from the barroom floor,

and back on his haunches he sat,

for all night long you could hear his roar,

Bring on the g—damn cat."

The circumstances surrounding that evening drew general interest. Local lore swirled about, and it was often referred to harmlessly as the evening of "a little night music." A few of the rowdy regulars of Irish descent called the incident, "The Whiskey Rebellion." They would give a hardy toast to a mouse named Jameson and then sing a drunken rendition of "The Little Brown Mouse."

My grandfather, who was a second-generation Irish innkeeper, long advocated that whiskey was for selling and not for consumption. He held the final say on such matters. "Giving whiskey to a Clarke is like giving a loaded gun to a child."

His counsel in such matters were sound, sensible and correct.

SECTION 3

~~~

MOOSE RIVER

~~~

Mark A. Clarke

Monsignor

Civic responsibility was instilled in me at an early age the hard way. It came in the form of the 6 a.m. Catholic Mass. The early morning Catholic Mass was an earthly form of purgatory. Because of my constant faux pas as an altar boy I was damned and subsequently relegated to the earliest morning Mass on weekdays at six.

I was trained as an altar boy by the nuns at St. Joseph's in my hometown. I trained as best I could but realized that the whole sacrament was a mystery to me and at times could be an unsettling experience.

The nuns were aptly dressed in black and white, sort of the way that they viewed life. We were divided into two groups, boys and girls. Girls were considered to be sugar and spice and everything nice while boys were whales and snails and puppy dog tails. We were the black and they were the white.

Boys had two subgroups, good and bad. Most of the other boys were white like Moby Dick while I was the deep shade of road tar and, from the sentiments of a few of the nuns, should have been feathered along with the black sticky substance and run out of the vestibule on a rail.

Mass was completely incomprehensible to me. Most of the time the priest, in this case Monsignor, kept his back to the parishioners. You never knew just what he was up to because he rarely faced the people.

If this had been made clear by the nuns it remained as elusive and uncertain to me as Latin, the preferred language of the mantras used during Sunday service. At age thirteen I settled for the simple reasoning that is ordinary to all thirteen year olds. This must be something reserved exclusively for members only, those who are destined to wear black and white.

The duties of an altar boy begin with the preparation of the altar. They included lighting the candles, filling the cruets (one for wine and one for water) and placing them along with other items like a bowl and water for washing the priest's hands.

We were also charged with the responsibility for the communion plate and a set of bells, called the Sanctus Bells, used during the solemn ritual. But it was mandatory and of the greatest importance that all altar boys learn the Latin response to the dialogue given by the priest.

Latin was simply unmanageable. In school mastering proper English was a challenge but learning Latin was unworldly, a beast of a task. The undertaking could best be described by how Russia seemed to that great statesman, Winston Churchill. He described Russia as a "riddle, wrapped in a mystery, inside an enigma."

That aptly described my obvious disconnect with Latin. I found it to be all gibberish. The best that I could make out was substituting the equivalent in English, which sounded similar to the Latin phrase. "Dominus vobiscum," – the English equivalent of "the Lord be with you" –sounded like "Dominic go frisk him." One phrase sounded something like "my mama can beat your mama in dominoes." I managed as best as was earthly possible.

With my slow progress the nuns must have thought that any defect of mine would be overlooked by an elderly congregation who were set on salvation and were professionals seasoned in the art of the Latin mantras. The nuns may have reasoned that like the chorister who can't sing a lick, I would be drowned out by the ample and capable choir, that being the congregation.

I had been skilled at carrying on a lively tune in the school choir, but I was burdened and dreaded the thought of ably reciting the Latin mumbo jumbo in church. When it came to Latin, a dead language, I wanted to die. There was no intended disrespect when I suggested that perhaps we could use Pig Latin instead. This unwanted suggestion was returned with a cluster of cold, blank stares.

It was one weekday morning at six that I was assigned to assist Monsignor with a funeral mass. I suspect that this was punishment for having put out the Paschal candle on the previous Sunday after Mass. The usual procedure with any normal Mass was to extinguish the candles. But this I learned was not just any Mass.

The Paschal candle represents the flame of the sacred fire. It is the Light of Christ coming into the world. It represents the risen Christ, the symbol of light dispelling darkness or the symbol of life dispelling death. For a people who view the world in terms of black and white my transgression was a "nullus," a big "Uh Oh!" "No-No." But the Paschal candle was a part of that Catholic riddle, wrapped in a Catholic mystery, inside a Catholic enigma thing to this ignorant thirteen year old.

I was subsequently and promptly reassigned.

To an altar boy serving six a.m. Mass on a weekday is like being in the military and reassigned to a radar station somewhere out on the tip of the Aleutian Islands. This was not preferential duty. To make matters worse it was a funeral Mass.

In 1960 a funeral Mass was referred to as the Black Mass. Scary stuff. Imagine being thirteen years old, awaken before sun rise, called to serve a funeral Mass in a dark church with candles eerily flickering shadows along vaulted walls, in the company of Monsignor wearing a black and white cassock, mumbling a language you knew nothing about, over a very humble casket containing the impoverished body of a person; who had not one friend or family member to appear in this, the final act of his earthly existence.

It was as chilling as an arctic morn and difficult to imagine a sadder and more dismal picture. Not only was I unnerved, I was upset, unhappy and mad as hell. This may be one injustice among the numerous injustices in the world, but this was wrought upon ME, a young, ignorant, mystified thirteen year old who would have his due – mea culpa, mea culpa, mea maxima culpa.

On one particular morning I was assigned to serve the popular 10:30 Sunday Mass. It was well attended for it allowed the older congregation to sleep in a little longer. I had conducted all of my assigned duties as required and I joined the formal procession in my appointed position as we walked to the altar. When the time came to give a response, I did so in a timely manner in my ever so slightly altered mantra.

"My mama can beat your mama in dominoes."

Now the next part gets a bit tricky for those who are not well versed in the outdated Catholic Mass. Please bear with me.

Midway through the ceremony the Monsignor's hands are washed and dried with white linen. This purification is followed by delicately cupping the chalice in his hands with thumbs and index fingers joined together above the rim forming a figure eight. It is the recognized sign for eternity, a common symbol in science and math.

While holding the chalice in his cupped hands, the altar boy pours from the cruets first the wine and then the water through his fingers into the chalice. The water and wine is then taken to the altar where it is consecrated and transformed into the blood of Christ.

There are a few things worthy of mentioning. Monsignor enjoyed his wine. Unspoken and commonly known, Monsignor enjoyed the robust aroma, full body and flavor of wine. In short, he was quite fond of it. Another similarly known detail was that Monsignor detested watery wine.

When not conducting church affairs, Monsignor was partial to a martini or two. As a true loyalist of dry martinis, it was suggested that his bartender need only wave the unopened bottle of vermouth over his glass of gin. To the point, Monsignor did not like his martini tainted with dry vermouth and similarly his wine supplemented with water as well. However, when it came to Mass, he settled for the least amount of water that was ceremonially acceptable.

All altar boys were instructed (diplomatically) by the nuns that when Monsignor made an uplifting motion with his hands the altar boys were to stop pouring. The motion was a subtle message noticeable to the server but not the parishioners. We practiced pouring water over and over again to be sure that we had mastered the task.

When it came to the wine, the Monsignor's hands never moved so we emptied the entire contents of the wine cruet into the chalice. However the water was a different story. Even a drop seemed perhaps a bit too much. The process went something like this: wine, wine, wine, wine, wiiiiiiiiiiiiiine . . . h2 Oh No! Way too much.

This Sunday, the filled to capacity Mass, became the moment of vindication. As Monsignor approached me with his golden chalice, I poured the wine ever so slowly through his fingers that formed the eternity figure: wine . . . wine . . . wine . . . wine . . . wine. . . wine. . . wine. . . wine. . . . Monsignor's eyes were tacitly telling me to hurry up.

Next came the water. Instead of the H2 Oh No! It was Oh No! . . . H2 .

..H2…H2…. Monsignor's promptly raised his hands but it was too late. Like a running toilet it was H2…H2…H2…H2…H2…H2… By the time I had emptied the entire contents of water from the cruet into the chalice both he and I were on our tip toes. Just to make sure that there would be ample water, I had deliberately filled the cruet to the brim in preparation for the Mass.

Monsignor uttered not a word, but face to face and with both of our arms elevated, the unspoken meaning was unpleasantly clear. From his crimson face punctuated with glaring eyes the message read: "YOU WILL BE ASSIGNED TO THE NEXT 6 AM FUNERAL MASS AND BE ASSURED THAT IT MAY BE YOURS."

As the years passed I don't recall what transpired as a result of this unfortunate affair. It is significant to note that as a result of Vatican II (which came after my tenure as an altar boy) there were significant changes to the Mass. It was no longer spoken in Latin, women no longer had to cover their head in church and the more obvious change was that priests faced the parishioners while serving Mass. There was another less noticeable change. The priests poured their own wine and water into the chalice.

I like to believe that in a small way I assisted in this tender progression for change. I envision some becrazed older man slamming his fist on the table roaring,

"THE WINE IS THE SACRED BLOOD OF CHRIST AND NO SNOT-NOSED THIRTEEN YEAR OLD BOY OUGHT TO BE ALLOWED TO GET HIS DAMN HANDS ANYWHERE NEAR IT."

Requiescat in pace.

P. S. Dominic go frisk him.

MR. ARNOLD

He was small in stature but solid as a Florida live oak. Mr. Arnold walked in a quick pace with a ram rod straight posture beginning from his flat top buzz cut to his shiny brown Brogans.

Formerly, he had been a WWII drill sergeant in the United States Marine Corps. Many of those whom he trained for combat ended up in various atolls scattered across the central Pacific. Some of them never returned.

For him combat was an elusive mistress. Privately he resented the fact that he remained at Parris Island. Missing combat was like a muscle strain. It was an unseen ailment that persisted long after his discharge from the Marines.

His new profession turned out to be in public education. As vice principal he was aptly suited for the rural high school which was located in the foothills of the Adirondacks in the mid 60s. Or so he thought, but more importantly, so thought the village elders. The small town of Boonville consisted of the raw product of generations of scrappy lumbermen and difficult dairy farmers. There existed laws that governed the community but, save the major ones like murder or insurrection, most of them were often overlooked or put aside with the exception of deprived repeat offenders. Brawn existed as a law unto itself.

The principal of the school was a former math teacher, but his present position required that his focus be exclusively on the parent. It was tacitly understood that Mr. Arnold was the enforcer. Being a no-nonsense sort of person, he would latch hold of a brigand by the ear or the collar and drag you into his office. There were no formalities. His unyielding grasp was as good as an official indictment. A cuff or two to the back of the head quickly changed ones outlook on life and firmly established his own.

The recalcitrant usually stood dog hung before the orderly and immaculately arranged oak desk. Mr. Arnold, all 5-feet 5-inches, stood erect before the scalawag, notably front and center. One couldn't help to note his razor sharp creases extending down his khaki pants to the cuffs, which stylishly met his properly prepared shoes. At close inspection his glossy brown shoes reflected not only the likeness of the room but the rewarding role he shared with the "Old Breed" as well. Were one audacious enough to confront him, you would instantly notice a clean shave chin with two brown menacing eyes. It was the kind of face that guaranteed certain misfortune should you dare to interrupt his sober critique on proper decorum or were reckless enough to test his authority.

If you were bold enough to suggest that you would "get" your father, the former marine's response was quick and certain. After another cuff or two and a rough jostling he would instruct you to do just that. In fact he endorsed it enthusiastically stating, "Good, bring your ole man in to school. I'd like to tell him what a perfect failure he has been as a father. And if he gives me any trouble, I'll slap the snot out of him, too."

Mr. Arnold was a firm champion and mentor to the inexperienced teacher. "If education is to be administered properly there had to be order and discipline."

Any deviation from this tenet was handled privately. First and foremost, Mr. Arnold was not averse to lending instruction and guidance to the inexperienced. At the heart of being a good leader was supervision and leading by example. Lessons he had learned with the Corps.

Once there was an obstinate student who had become unruly in social studies. His classroom teacher, Mr. Westley, requested that the student, Henry, open his book to a certain page and follow the text while he read the passage.

Henry's response was an adamant "NO!"

Mr. Westley placed himself next to the headstrong's desk and again requested that he open his textbook and follow along with the passage. Henry, who had a noticeable nasal quality to his speech promptly responded, "I sa-head noh! An' hue kin go 'uck yerselve."

Mr. Westley's response was swift and certain. He latched onto the blasphemous youth by the scruff of the neck along with a few well-placed whacks to the crown of his head. Mr. Westley then hauled the flailing and kicking unruly offender off to Mr. Arnold's office.

Mr. Westley was not only a devout Catholic but a former combat veteran of the late Korean War. Blasphemy and disobedience was not to be tolerated. After a few solid thumps on the door he was let in by his impassive secretary, who was now used to these sorts of things. She then graciously invited the two to have a seat while she informed the vice principal.

Mr. Westley was called into the inner office first, all the while the teen fidgeted nervously in his chair. After a respectable interval, the student was escorted in. Henry slouched disapprovingly into the only available chair located in front of Mr. Arnold's desk. With measured intention he began, "Henry I understand that you and Mr. Westley had disagreement over an assignment, which led to an unfortunate confrontation."

"Yup."

"Now Mr. Westley," he began in stilted language. "Although Henry was offensive and disorderly in his conduct, you as an educator must maintain your composure at all times, despite the complexity of the immediate circumstances. I counsel you to restrain yourself and in the future, conduct yourself in a more professional manner. I recommend that you pull the student aside and use good sense and reason with the child. There may be perhaps an underlying factor which has prompted Henry to respond in this unfortunate manner."

Mr. Westley nodded in agreement.

"Now Henry. What do you have to say in your defense?"

Henry glanced at Mr. Arnold and then Mr. Westley. Drawing himself to an upright and vertical sitting position, he countered. "I tol 'em to go 'uck 'emselve."

It wasn't that he hadn't heard that kind of language. To be perfectly honest he had used the like from time to time as a drill instructor with raw troops. Yet, it took Mr. Arnold by surprise coming from one so undersized and bold.

"Henry, that will just be enough of that." Attempting reason, "We mustn't allow our emotions to get the better of the situation. . ."

Henry broke in, "I tol 'em to go 'uck 'emself and ewe kin go 'UCK EW-SELF 'OO!"

Henry barely got the "OO" out of his mouth before Mr. Arnold leaped over the desk and had Henry by the throat. His reaction was sudden and swift.

"To adapt, improvise and overcome" was the revered creed instilled in every Marine. And this credo became the foundation of the many fine traits he had retained from the old days in the Corps.

"YOU LITTLE BASTARD. YOU'LL NOT TALK TO ME THAT WAY!"

And had it not been for Mr. Westley's intervention, Mr. Arnold's displaced patience might have resulted in Henry becoming a patient under the capable care of Dr. Smith.

Following this episode when the proper time arrived Mr. Westley was granted tenure and the resulting outcome of this awkward affair was the termination of sermons by Mr. Arnold on professional behavior.

SCHOOL YARD

Owen was thirteen, unruly, and his behavior was septic. Mr. Graves placed him in quarantine in the back of the room.

"You let me know when you are prepared to join the rest of the class."

Owen stared out the window and wouldn't make eye contact. It was his juvenile way of telling the teacher to buzz off.

Mr. Graves was schooled in the philosophy that some people could use a good swift kick in the ass.

"It would do more good than harm," he was heard to say.

Billy the Kid in his assessment lack proper direction. Had someone placed a sizable boot in The Kid's backside, Pat Garrett wouldn't have found it necessary to come visit him with a Colt .45 Peacemaker.

Owen was a recalcitrant, but he wasn't a bad kid. Trouble just seemed to find him because, well . . . he was thirteen.

He had reached the age where no one could tell him anything because he had all the answers and was inclined to tell them so. Getting the last word in wasn't a duty, but a right.

There isn't much entertainment for a boy barely in his teens, isolated in the back of a middle school math class. Amusements were limited to whatever captivated his attention outside the window. Three trees, a stretch of lawn with a small driveway leading to the custodial area with a row of tall whatever-you-call-them hedges that block his view of what lay on the other side wasn't going to do it. Mr. Graves had painted him into a rather mind-numbing corner. He was left to his own devices. Like eighth grade math, this too would be a challenge for Owen. Inspiration went on an extended vacation in September and would remain so until June.

"I don't want to hear a peep out of you, Owen. Do you understand me?"

Owen crossed his arms on the desk and buried his head. That was a tacit way of saying "whatever."

When Mr. Graves continued with his lesson, Owen peeked over his arms and stared at the clock. He watched the second hand almost make a complete revolution before he finally gave up. He was miserable and would remain that way for the next thirty-seven and a half minutes.

Owen was suffering from a classic case of what the French call ennui. In English, it was called boredom. To Owen it was unrepeatable.

When Thomas Paine said, "These are the times that try men's souls," he wasn't talking about a middle school math class, but for Owen, he may well have been. When it came to crisis and tyranny, he was a living proof and his testimony spoke loudly from the last row, in the last seat next to the window.

Owen was placed in the unaccustomed position of having to think for himself. How could he possibly manage surviving the next torturous thirty-four minutes of Mr. Graves' math class?

What Owen needed was something entertaining to occupy his time and by chance it came – there was a fly crawling on the window.

Occasionally it would hum and dance about on the windowpane. It wasn't the kind of lively entertainment that Owen was wishing for, but he would make do. Owen first tried to anticipate in what direction the fly would go next. It was as hopeless as eighth grade math.

Owen watched the fly flit about while Mr. Graves droned on. Why, thought Owen, should a simple house fly enjoy the freedom that he lacked as a prisoner of Mr. Graves' mathematics? The thought caused him annoyance which led to irritation and finally ended in resentment.

"I'll fix that old fly. Let's see how he likes it."

Owen tried to catch the fly by making a swipe with an open hand. He earned an F as in failure, not even a lousy E for effort. He kept an eye on both Mr. Graves and the fly. Each time Mr. Graves faced the blackboard solving a math problem, Owen would take another swipe. Swish, a miss. Swish missed again. Owen received two more Fs.

The fly was now really getting to him. When Mr. Graves' back was to him again, Owen gently slid his open hand near the stationary fly and made a swipe. With his hand closed Owen couldn't tell if he captured the fly or not. Slowly he opened and took a peek. The fly slipped through his fingers and flew towards the window and resumed its buzzing and dancing about the windowpane.

Owen was more determined than ever to catch that fly. Waiting until Mr. Graves' back was to him while at the same time the fly remained motionless, Owen made his move.

In a flash his hand darted across the windowpane. Slowly, ever so slowly, he opened his fingers. There it was. The fly was trapped between his index and middle finger. With his other hand he grabbed the fly by a wing.

"I got you now you little bugger and you ain't goin' nowhere."

Owen thought long and hard what to do with the fly. He still had almost twenty minutes of class left. Holding the fly by a wing, he grabbed the other wing with his free hand. The fly hung suspended between Owen's thumb and index finger of each hand. Owen studied the fly.

It had a black body, two red eyes, six legs, two wings and a long thin nose. Ugly looking thing but it was interesting.

The fly, that was unaccustomed to being restrained, was a flurry of activity which caused one of its wings to become detached.

Owen set it down on the desk. It buzzed about in a circle, flipping over this way and that because it couldn't fly with only one wing. Now that was entertaining Owen thought.

To stop the fly from flitting about Owen pinned the other wing to the desktop. In no time this, too, became detached. Now the fly was limited to walking in circles.

Owen placed it on his palms and watching it walk around. It crawled through his fingers, on the back of his hand, then around to the palm again. Just when the fly was about to make another pass through his finger Owen was startled by,

"OWEN! GET UP HERE RIGHT NOW!"

Owen closed his hand and slowly walked to the front of the class. All eyes were now on Owen. He stood in front of Mr. Graves's desk with his hands closed in a fist behind him.

"Owen, let me see your hands." Owen tentatively held his closed hand in front of him.

"What do you have in your hands?"

"A fly."

'A fly? Open your hands and let me see."

Owen opened his hands to show Mr. Graves. The one was empty but the other held a wingless fly. Mr. Graves stared at the fly and then at Owen.

"That fly has no wings. Where are its wings.?"

Owen shrugged his shoulders.

He asked again. "Where are the fly's wings."

"They fell off."

"FELL OFF? WINGS DON'T JUST FALL OFF FLIES."

With that Mr. Graves reached behind him and grabbed the yardstick that was laying in the blackboard chalk holder.

Turning to Owen he raised the yard stick and said, "Extend your hands with palms down."

Bewildered, Owen did as he was ordered. When Mr. Graves raised the yardstick above Owen's outstretched hands, the entire class looked on in horror. If you were to take bets that day, everyone in the class would have wagered that the yardstick was intended just as a warning. Time became suspended with the yardstick. After what appeared to be forever.

WACK!

The yardstick came crashing down on Owen's knuckles. At first Owen winced and then he let out an unmistakable cry of pain.

"OWWWWWWWWWWWWWWWWWW!"

"If I catch you pulling the wings off of helpless flies again, there will be more where that came from."

Owen was ordered back to his seat where he remained whimpering until the end of class.

Saturday came and passed. Sunday as well. No one saw Owen nor Mr.

Graves anywhere in town. The following Monday, Mr. Graves was not in class nor was he for the rest of the week. Rumors whispered about and the odds were that Mr. Graves was fired. However, like the suspended yardstick, if you had placed a wager, you would have lost that bet too.

It turned out that Mr. Graves was not in school because of a death in the family. We felt sorry for his loss, everyone except maybe Owen.

Owen remained his old recalcitrant self. He didn't stop the hobby of catching flies but when he did, he no longer pulled off their wings, Mr. Graves made sure of that.

Instead, Owen started a new hobby. He would take the long strand of hair from the tail of a horse and carefully tie it around the body of a captured fly. Holding one end of the horsehair, the fly would buzz around in circles like an airplane.

It became an instant hit. Girls would donate a strand of their hair for Owen to use. This cultivated his social skills and a healthy following of admirers.

The other boys became jealous and tried to imitate Owen, but they could never figure out how to tie a length of hair around the body of a fly. Owen would never share that with them. It was a trade secret.

Owen became known as Andre by his friends as in Andre Delambre, the scientist played by Vincent Price in the classic science fiction movie, "The Fly."

Owen dressed as the human fly on Halloween. To the joyful approval of his close friends, Owen would walk unnoticed behind Mr. Graves down the hall like Vincent Price in the movie, "The Fly." His one atrophied arm would hang close to his chest while he took a step with one leg and slide the other behind him. He drooled for effect.

Owen never did take to book learning. On his seventeenth birthday he said goodbye to his faithful following and traveled with the circus. This became his calling and was the envy of all young boys who ever wanted to be just like Toby Tyler.

Someone once saw him selling tickets for a sideshow at the circus. Owen stood on a lectern in front of an exhibit called "The Human Fly."

He wore a straw hat, held a bamboo cane in one hand and a piece of horsehair tied to a fly buzzing around in the other. All the while he was encouraging fairgoers, "Come see the human fly. He will amaze you. Watch how he can crawl up walls and buzz around on a string like this little fellow here."

The folks were as amazed by the fly attached on a piece of hair as his former classmates were.

For a small fee, the rubes could watch someone, most likely Owen, dressed as a buzzing Vincent Price, scale walls like an acrobatic rock climber and swing about on a rope hung from the ceiling.

The last anyone heard of Owen he was running his own sideshow called "The Reptile Lady." He stood outside with similar straw hat, bamboo cane and in place of the fly he had a snake wrapped around his arm.

His spiel this time went, "Hear ye, Hear ye. Come see the Reptile Lady. She walks. She talks. She crawls on her belly like a reptile. Yours to see for only two bits, a quarter."

This, too, in reality was an exotic dancer, dressed in a green sequined outfit that made her (along with make-up) look something like a snake. She was skimpily clad in an attempt to placate and sway the more ardent skeptics.

It turns out that Owen married the Reptile Lady. Raised several children and live comfortably in retirement in Sarasota, Florida.

Looking back on it, his classmates never mention the incident of Owen, Mr. Graves and the fly when waxing eloquent about "the good ole days."

BEAVER

Beaver had developed a discerning taste for beer ever since his Army days during the war. He insisted that it "must to be wet and had to be cold."

As a paratrooper he jumped with the 101st Airborne Division into Holland as a part of Operation Market-Garden. Somewhere in the ensuing days, his war came to an ill-fated end. Beaver lost a leg from above the knee somewhere near Eindhoven.

"A German shell will do that to you."

He may have lost his limb, but he kept his life – barely. From then on, the only jumping he would do was on and off a bar stool.

A popular gray stone tavern, The Hulbert House, was located on Main Street and it was Beaver's preferred watering hole. The early 19th century landmark was built in 1812 and consisted of four large white pillars extending from its concrete steps to its wooden eaves. An airy balcony protruded from the second floor.

Every Friday Beaver entered the historic tavern through the front barroom entrance. It had a smooth hardwood floor with wide dark boards worn irregularly by generations of traffic which came and went with the centuries.

The walnut bar was curvaceous, extending around to the left and looped in a grand fashion towards the back stone wall. Ending abruptly, it provided a walkway between the wall and a service station. Dusty and timeworn, a large raven colored buffalo head oddly protruded from the western wall. It would have been more fittingly placed in a Deadwood saloon in the Black Hills of South Dakota.

When not serving himself, the bartender known locally as Joe the Russian would tended to the needs of customers – that being either a beer or whiskery or perhaps both if desired. Any departure from the bill of fare might warrant an irritable snap from the Russian.,

"If you want that other crap, go down the road."

Beaver liked the irascible Russian, but Beaver liked his beer better.

When an unfamiliar face rolled into town, Joe could be entertaining to a fault in an enterprising way. It usually began with a few bawdy jokes mixed in with some light laughter – just to break the ice.

In the predictable lull that followed Joe would inquire, "Would you like to see me make a half dollar disappear in a glass of water?"

Over a period of time Joe discovered that a half dollar was sufficient to tempt the curious without elevating concern. Joe made it a point to leave at least one fifty cent piece in the patron's bar change.

"Sure," was the typical response. "Why not?"

Without hesitation the Russian would fill up a water glass with tap water and place it in front of the mark.

"Got a half dollar?" he would ask.

The mark would slide the silver coin to Joe as he promptly presented a white handkerchief from his pocket. Rolling up his sleeves, he presented the coin to the unenlightened in the palm of his hand. For effect he would rotate the coin from heads to tails and then again. Now taking the half dollar between his index finger and thumbs, Joe placed the handkerchief over the coin and held both above the glass of water.

"Here squeeze it," he would offer.

Sometimes they would. With a bit of Russian razzle dazzle he then let the shrouded coin slip from his grasp into the glass of water. With a couple of taps of the glass he would remove the handkerchief and Presto! No coin.

"Pretty good huh!"

The fish was left staring into an empty glass of water. Joe would deposit the watery contents into the sink with a smile. "Would you like to see it again?" he cunningly suggested.

Either the appeal to curiosity or the assurance that one was in possession of a superior power of observation (or both) often motivated the smitten to provide (with the aid of the Russian) a second fifty cent piece. Joe would duplicate the procedure under the gaze and hyper vigilance of the groomed victim.

When the silver coin disappeared under the white cloak, Joe tempted the mark further with, "Here you can let it drop."

It didn't matter who released the coin, the results were always the same. The customer was out four bits making the lighthearted Russian slightly richer.

Through the years, Joe the Russian fostered quite a reputation as a huckster as well as accruing a tidy sum of money. He rationalized the stunt as a gratuity, a mere trifling, rather than perceived as a second-rate offense. Profits dramatically increased when social events like a parade or fair came to town.

The trick to the disappearing half dollar was simple. With the sleight of hand Joe substituted the coin with a piece of glass that he had fashioned into the size and shape of a silver half dollar. With a few light taps to ensure the bogus coin settled on the bottom of the glass, the replica became transparent making "it disappear." The palmed coin went unnoticed into the Russian's pocket.

One day the enterprise was seriously challenged. Suspecting a con, a very large and muscular drunk insisted that his half dollar be returned. Joe informed him that was impossible because the half dollar had "disappeared."

In a slow and measured tone, ripe with peril, the Russian was instructed to, "MAKE . . . IT . . . REAPPEAR!"

Joe saw the wisdom in the request and presently the coin reappeared. That evening he carefully avoided the meaty man as much as possible.

Joe the Russian's well choreographed routine was in jeopardy of dissolving were it not been for Beaver. During these years, Beaver had been privy to the disappearing half dollar and the sleight of hand. What the Russian needed was a diversionary tactic and Beaver had an idea.

In the passing of time, Beaver had become a fixture around town. Residents had accepted and overlooked the fact that he had lost a leg during the late war. Except for special occasions like Veteran's Day and Memorial Day, the memory of his service and sacrifice gradually faded with the passing of time. Memory is a peculiar thing; it is a commodity of convenience. Beaver used this to his advantage. If necessity is the mother of invention, Beaver devised a plan that would allow the Russian to continue his fruitful undertaking and lessen the risk.

Should an uncooperative customer create an ugly scene, Beaver would feign a leg cramp. He would ask Joe for the ice pick and then jab it into his artificial leg. He might stab it a couple of times for maximum effect. Placing the pick on the bar, Beaver would give the leg a shake or two and after thanking the Russian, he would smile making his way the restroom. Joe would say something like, "Sometimes he gets these awful leg cramps." Or "It's an eastern European treatment, still used in Kiev." Upon his return Beaver would find a cold frothy beer waiting for him compliments of the house.

All went well for a time. At any hint of trouble Beaver would wince all the while contorting his face. Sucking in air through his teeth, he demanded that the Russian furnish him with an ice pick. Then promptly giving his leg a vicious jab or two, he would leave it lodged upright for supreme effect. Draining his mug of beer, he reclaimed the pick from its plant and handed it back to Joe. He then retreated as planned to the restroom releasing a long and thunderous belch for good measure.

Some of the locals never grew tired of Joe's performance. They hung around in anticipation while business blossomed. The Russian's profits did as well.

Sometimes Beaver would improve on his performance. He might stand up, shake his leg vigorously and howled like a lunatic before he drove the metal pick into his artificial leg.

Yes, it was quite a sight to behold. Beaver even practiced grimaces in the mirror, each one more horrific than the last. Truly, Beaver was becoming a celebrity. A real Humphrey Bogart of barroom antics.

However, one evening as the Russian was making coins disappear into a water glass, a burly stranger became irate and slammed his meaty fist to the bar insisting that he had been swindled. Snatching Joe by his shirt, he drew him close to where the Russian could smell his foal whiskey-tainted breath.

"GIMMIE MY MONEY YOU LOUSE BEFORE I REARRANGE THE BAR WITH YOUR CARCASS. He then threw him hard into the back bar rattling the bottles of whiskey.

Before the brute could complete the intended task, Beaver immediately went into his routine. There was a liveliness heretofore not seen in his performances. Spirited with lager, his grimaces were exceptionally brilliant and the contortions on his face were unworldly. He danced and whooped about like a Plains Indian at the sight of pioneers. He was into his act with such gusto and delight that he not only completely captivated the attention of the entire bar, but he had sidetracked himself.

And when it became time for the peak of his performance, the thrusting ice pick was so swift and sudden that no one noticed that Beaver had stabbed himself in the wrong leg.

Amid the cheers of adulation no one recognized that the grimace and screams coming from Beaver were genuine and unfeigned. And instead of retiring to the restroom as practiced numerous times, Beaver rapidly hobbled to the nearest exit and was absorbed into the night.

It would be many weeks before Beaver returned to his natural perch at the local landmark. Joe the Russian was obliged to purchase a new ice pick for the former one never found its way back. And nobody witnessed any more half dollars dissolving into water, at least that is not while Beaver was on the premises.

MARK A. CLARKE

Conway's Golden Harvest

With the morning milking complete, the dairy herd lumbered to the back pasture. It was late summer and the growing season for once had cooperated with the farmer. Fields were green and lush. This year's crops were abundant and held the promise for a generous harvest.

The trees benefited from the accommodating weather, too. At the base of the oak trees were a wealth of acorns scattered about making the deer population happy and shag bark hickory trees revealed a similar promise of good fortune for the squirrel population. It had been a good year all around.

The sun was especially warm on that afternoon and the dairy herd sought refuge under the shade of some wild crabapple trees. They were attracted partly by the cool shade they provided as well as the abundant sweet grass and tasty wild crab apples that lay scattered about. With ease and contentment, they nibbled the juicy apples along with the tender grass. Together the two make a flavorsome pair. One by one the Holsteins located a comfortable spot to lounge and rest while they peacefully passed the time chewing their cud.

Come early afternoon, Conway, the herdsman, walked to the edge of the pasture and summoned to the "girls," as he called them. It was time for their afternoon milking.

"Here boss, here boss," his familiar voice beckoned them. But they failed to respond promptly to their summoning as they normally would.

Unlike the usual rising, soft lowing, and gradual lumbering to the barn, the herd's reaction was delayed. Perhaps it was a sluggishness brought on by the last warmth in the waning days of summer, Conway thought. He called to them again, this time a bit louder.

"Here boss. Here boss."

This resulted in some stirring. Still, it took a curious amount of time for them to begin moving. The cows found it difficult getting to their feet. Wide-eyed with tongue lulling, one and then another tried rising and standing on all fours. They looked like newborn calves attempting to stand upright for the first time. Those that finally made it upright swayed or tottered about unsteadily. They lurched and rocked somewhat about. Some gently reeled, while some floundered about. Others stumbled as they tried to gain their balance. Once upright on all fours, they walked unsteadily in an uncertain formation with a cow or two seemingly moving lateral for a step or two. One would have thought they were seaman trying to get their land legs beneath them.

The girls gradually appeared up over the rise along the cow path next to the fence row. There came one and then another, but something was rather odd about their gait. Conway, like all dairy farmers, knew his herd. Each were identified by a given name, by their distinct markings and their unique disposition.

Lizzy, one of the older cows, was tacitly accepted as their leader. She led them to and from the barn. Usually, a phalanx formed behind Lizzy and the herd would then amble along behind her in an ad hoc formation making their way either to or from the barn. She was laboring somewhere third or fourth in the line.

"Oh, my God," Conway said aloud. "They're drunk. The whole damn lot of 'em."

It seemed that the herd had consumed the apples that had fallen to the ground. While lounging, the apples fermented in the warmth of their moist stomachs. Chewing their cud further ground the mixture, churning and invigorating the material into a mild form of mash which gradually fermented and formed traces of alcohol. The effect was instant on the teetotaling herd and rendered them mildly inebriated. The extent of the outcome depended on each individual tolerance.

Conway knew they were drunk, "right off" for he was not only acquired the taste for spirits but was renowned throughout the area for his hard cider and apple jack. In fact, it was universally accepted that he made the "best dern cider and jack" in the county. You could say his legacy would have extended beyond were it possible for him to duplicate his joyful concoction in bulk.

Obtaining a glass of Conway's delicious cider wasn't difficult. Just stop by his house during the holiday season with as warm smile and a hardy "Merry Christmas." It was a simple and clear-cut price for a guaranteed invitation to sample Conway's coveted cider. Conway's cider was so good, atheists, agnostics, and twice a year Christians were among those hardy well-wishers who stopped by to pay him a visit around that jolly season.

Conway offered sweet cider for the ladies and teetotalers. The harder stuff was available for those so inclined. However, should you find yourself in the real holiday spirit, there was always the big boy stuff, Apple Jack. Reverend Shufelt preferred the cider because it had "more brace to fend off the ague." Father Flanagan wished neither. He was partial to Conway's Apple Jack because, well . . . it was Father Flanagan.

Conway's holiday hooch was served warm or cold, spiced with cinnamon or plain, straight or with a dram of good Caribbean Rum. The Reverend elected to have the warm, spiced, hard cider "straight if you please." It had just the appropriate boost for his reverence. On the other hand, Father Flanagan was a special order. He opted for the Conway "surprise me special" which required some "big boy stuff" and he never came away disappointed. The "big boy stuff" that Conway served produced somewhere between watery eye to mild numbness to loss of short-term memory. It depended on the year, the batch and the consumer. Father Flanagan took it all in good stride. He was very receptive to Conway's liberal pour around Christmas and Conway's generosity never appeared to have any noticeable effect on Father Flanagan . . . until the following morning.

Yes. Come Christmas, bright lights burned long into many evenings at the Conway homestead. You might say it was very Christian of him to host all those well-wishers during this important holiday season. One participant even labeled it, an Adirondack Christmas Revival.

Getting a glass of Conway's joy juice was not difficult but trying to duplicate it was altogether another thing. Conway was covetous of the recipe and the process. He was intentionally vague about the ingredients and spoke in generalities. All attempts to secure Conway secrets ended in frustration and failure but they continued to try.

"That's a mighty hardy cider you have here," quipped one prober.

"What's in it anyway?"

"Apples."

"Apples you say. What kind?

"Whatever's available."

Trying another tactic, the spy took a sip and then asked, "What make it so juicy?

"I squeeze 'em."

With an appropriate pause the mole takes another sip. "What makes it so sweet?"

"Sugar."

He shot back, "What kind, white or brown?"

"Both."

"How much do you put in it?

"Depends."

"Depends on what?"

"The size of your hand."

"Oh. Is that all?"

"Raisins."

"How much?

"Depends."

"Depends on what?"

"Your hand size." There is another pause and sip.

"It's nice and smooth. No bite to it. I suppose it's the yeast you use. You do use yeast don't you?"

"Nope."

Now, he thought, we are getting somewhere.

"You don't use wine or champaign or brewer's yeast?

"Nope."

"What do you use?"

"You're drinking it. I use some of last year's cider to start a new batch."

Now that's real progress he thought. The subversive holds up his glass to the light.

"It's got a nice clear color to it. Why's that."

"Cracked corn."

"Why cracked corn?

"Filters out the impurities."

"How much do you use?"

As Conway responded, they both said "Depends" at the same time.

Becoming frustrated the snoop asked, "What do you do then?"

"Place the juice in a cider keg and place a corn cob into the bung hole and wait."

"And then what?"

"Wait."

"And then what?"

"You wait some more."

"Annnnnnnnnnnnnd?'

Conway paused for a lasting effect.

"Friend, you have just created paradise in a wooden keg!"

And then Conway laughed until his eyes watered. And then he caught his breath and laughed some more.

The inquiring fellow became so "happy" with Conway's joy juice that he forgot what Conway said and couldn't recall his notations. Conway never repeated them to himself a second time.

Conway's Apple Jack required one additional step. When the temperature drops below freezing, Conway placed a barrel of hard cider on the porch and waited until it frozen solid. Apple Jack is pure alcohol and won't freeze. Using a bit and brace, Conway augered into the center of the frozen cider where the Apple Jack is found. He siphoned the liquid using rubber tubbing into a stoneware jug.

"What we've done here my friend," Conway chuckled, "is capture a genie in a bottle. Uncork it as you wish and then watch the magic begin."

Conway's Apple jack was smooth and made for sipping. Three fingers in a glass was enough to tax the brain. Any more might cause bruising. Although taken regularly, and in moderation, it was "good for the health," Conway claimed. All the ingredients are natural and a dram or two from time to time stimulated the appetite, he declared, "and was essential in maintaining one's wellbeing." Conway issued a general warning. "Apple Jack is flammable," and he mildly cautioned that anyone caught consuming Jack off the premises on a regular basis, might be "viewed as a committed drunkard" and falsely accused of being a worthless ne'er-do-well.

So presently Conway found himself on the horns of a dilemma. Logic indicated that his herd was drunk on a primitive form of crab apple cider. Common sense told him his Holsteins needed to be milked. But what was he to do with the milk when he finished milking his herd? Conway was raised with the simple principal of "waste not, want not." It was instilled in him at an early age that waste was a sin. Therefore, he had only one path. Milk the cows and send it to market. Besides, his milk might stimulate appetites and maintain wellbeing.

It took a long time to get his cows in their stanchions and grained. It took much longer to milk them that evening. Much longer. Conway thought some soothing classical music would help the process but the cows bellowing drowned out the music. And then there was the gaseous vapors and the foul invasive smell. It was reminiscent of a Sunday afternoon football game at O'Reilly's tavern.

Come Monday the milk inspector came and tested samples of Conway's milk from the milkhouse stainless-steel tank. Dipping in a ladle he took a sample for the butter fat content, and other important aspect of the milk. Then he tasted it. He sampled it not once, but twice and then a third time. He seemed quite pleased and left.

Word got around quickly that Conway's herd was rated superior not only in categories like butter fat, but it was ranked "exceptional" and "unmatched" in the most important category of all, flavor.

As one expert taster with years of experience put it, "It is unbeatable in its smooth bold flavor. It is soothing and refreshing. It is balanced to perfection like the taste of fine scotch whiskey."

Conway was delighted with his cider, but he took extra satisfaction over his first-rate milk and his herd of Holsteins known as "the girls." His new-found notoriety spread fast, and his phone wouldn't stop ringing. Buyers wanted to place orders for his superb milk. This became a problem. Conway was kept up at night and he was losing sleep.

Then it came to him in a dream: Conway Cheese. Conway butter. Conway Buttermilk. The possibilities were endless. Fine scotch whiskey indeed. It was more like a fine white cider. Conway spoke confidentially with the president of dairy consortium. Quietly they agreed in private to process Conway's milk into dairy products to be sold only in the fall. They would sell cheese, butter and buttermilk under the brand with Conway's name on it. The product would be marketed by a New York City advertising firm as Conway's Golden Harvest. They created a logo of a Holstein cow with the name Lizzy and sang a jingle that went, "A smooooooth bold flavor" It was advertised as:

"Conway's Golden Harvest. Try our fresh cheeses, butter and buttermilk with the upstate taste of autumn. Balanced to perfection, our cheese and butter have a smooth bold flavor and the buttermilk is soothing and refreshing. Available only in the autumn. You'll fall for it."

Conway's business flourished. His secret would remain and when he died so, too, would his product. He took great pride in his "girls" and in their milk but try as he might he never could quite duplicate the grade of milk he received that late summer when the fields were green and lush. It was the year that the crops were abundant and held the promise for a generous harvest and it was a period when his milk was as smooth and refreshing as a bottle of Glenfiddich scotch whiskey.

GOOGER

When Grover Alexander Cooper was born a scream came from the birthing room. It was naturally assumed that it came from the child, but it hadn't. It came from the mother.

Although physically spent from her several hours of labor, Grover's mother managed a smile when she was informed that she had given birth to a seven-pound two-ounce healthy baby boy. It was short lived for when she inspected the new arrival, she noticed that he had an additional thumb on his right hand. There came a momentary pause and then the screech.

It wasn't really two thumbs. It was more like a cleft right thumb that made it appear the boy had two thumbs. From that day forward his mother avoided mentioning it for fear it would draw undue attention to the issue. Grover's cleft thumb was treated as if it was something uniquely normal like heterochromia iridium - someone born with one blue eye and the other brown.

"God never makes mistakes. He created you special," she told her son when he got older. "You are a limited edition, irreplaceable." And with that, she loved him ever the more.

His immediate family knew him as Googer because as a toddler he couldn't pronounce the name Grover. It came out more like Googer. So, the name Googer stuck and henceforth Grover became known as Googer. It naturally filtered into the neighborhood and beyond until no one remember him otherwise.

Googer grew up in a small town in upstate New York with his parents who were affectionate and devoted to wholesome upbringing. Omar and Gertrude encouraged him to experience everything (within reason). If he didn't care for it, he was encouraged to seek out something that would interest him. However, they insisted that whatever he did, he was to do it to the best of his ability. This was the guiding principle, and it shepherded his way.

Googer was of average height, weight and intelligence. He regularly encountered many things that he found to be challenging. He experienced his share of successes and some failures, but they were no more or no less than the other kids his own age.

Nevertheless, the Lord works in mysterious ways. What may first appear to be a flaw, would sometimes become an asset. Googer's thumb was that way. As he grew, his cleft thumb became more of a blessing than a curse.

Some things came to him easily and he excelled at them. In thumb wrestling he was unbeatable. Another area of interest was the game of marbles of which he became very adept at it. You might even say he was an exceptional participant. His cleft thumb allowed him to aim a marble at the group of marbles placed in a circle with uncanny accuracy. His thumb gave him added stability for the marble fit nicely into the cleft of his thumb. This gave him an advantage in knocking them out of the circle with consistency. In so doing, Googer gained them as his prize and within no time became a school yard celebrity.

Over time, Googer amassed quite a collection of marbles. Many fell victim to his ability, but his friendly disposition won them over in spite of their misfortune. All that is, except a six grader by the name of Michael Harper.

Every neighborhood has a bully and Michael Harper was it. Googer was two grades Mike's junior (actually three because Mike was retained one year), so he, like his classmates, were expected to be subservient to the sixth-graders. Naturally, the grade school pecking order made them all victims of Mike's constant and creative tormenting.

Googer's cleft thumb made him an easy target. Michael Harper, aka as Big Mike to his face or Mad Dog Mike behind his back, was lord and master of oppressors. Always on the prowl for a victim, Mad Dog was mean just for the sake of being mean. The younger ones were told that they could find a picture of Mad Dog Mike in Webster's Dictionary under the word "mad." One studious kid did just that and reported his picture wasn't there. They told him that he had to look in an unabridged version of Webster's Dictionary because pictures required extra space.

While most kids were studying their lessons in class, Michael was constantly plotting. One of his ideas was for everyone to call him by his new name. Mike felt superior to others and wanted to be treated as such, so everyone was required to call him Big Spah. Spah was grade school lingo meaning special, which he shortened it to Spah making it easier to pronounce and quicker to say.

If Big Spah caught you referring to him otherwise, he would make you pay. He might opt to twist your arm behind your back until you said Big Spah instead of the traditional "Uncle." Or place both hands on the victim's wrist and twist it back and forth to produce a burning sensation. The procedure was called an Indian Burn so named after the hot, spicy food enjoyed in India. Mad Dog dubbed it the Spah Burn. His favorite was to place his victim in a headlock and issue a generous helping of noogies. He said it was an "honor" that the victim had earned. To avoid this honor, just refer to him as Big Spah. The younger masses agreed to it mostly because it sounded similar to the sound made when spiting something distasteful out of your mouth like lima beans or liver. So Mad Dog Mike became Big Spah, that brute of a bully worse than a second helping of Brussel sprouts.

Mad Dog's specialty was wedgies. In this line of work, he was unrivaled. Mad Dog would stalk his quarry and then unexpectedly pounce. He would latch onto a kid's fruit of the loom tighty-whities and wrench them upward until they were firmly embedded in their crotch. Then he secured his prey in a firm headlock and while his prey was trying to unjam his skivvies, Big Spah inflicted a series of noogies on the squirming lad. He later modified the technique by provide a series of kudo knocks, or a sudden rapping of a knuckle on the quarry's skull instead. Once seized, no help was in the offering for all his friends had fled for fear of becoming the next victim.

Mad Dog made it a habit of tormenting Googer. He was forever making fun of him by calling him Two Thumbs Googer and trying to make him cry or flee in a panic. But Googer had learned to ignore Mad Dog Mike Harper and move calmly on his way.

On one occasion Mad Dog decided to join the local game of marbles. Not aware of Googer's reputation, Mad Dog promptly lost everything to the fourth grader with a cleft thumb. He would have inflicted one of his extra cruel specialties on Googer had it not been for Mr. Boone on playground duty and a group of sixth-graders spouting humiliating jabs at him.

"Mike you're a moron. You let some fourth grader rob you of your marbles," they derided, which was followed by individual taunts and group laughter.

Mad Dog remained silent and seethed. He would get his just and proper revenge when the time presented itself.

Googer developed another unique skill. It was his ability to pitch a baseball. Googer played on a Little League team called the Holland Patent Hay Hens. As a newly acquired player he started by "riding the pine" or sat on the bench and played second string like all the rookies. That was until his coach, who was always looking to develop team pitching, asked the new prospect to pitch a few balls.

Googer threw the baseball with moderate speed and good accuracy, but the coach noticed it had a funny way of moving. He asked his assistant coach to come and watch.

"Would you throw a couple more for us Googer?" his coach asked.

Googer was delighted to oblige. As he threw the ball the two coaches watched attentively. Googer gripped the ball using his cleft thumb, index and middle finger and threw it with a slight twist of the wrist and in doing so the ball moved in an unusual fashion. Sometimes it moved a little to the left and sometimes a little to the right, but it always traveled in a downward motion. The two coaches looked at each other and smiled. Googer was a natural.

It was early in the season and Googer was encouraged to increase his arm strength. That was easy. Googer loved swimming and he was good at it because his cleft thumb gave him added thrust in every stroke. So, every afternoon (in good weather), Googer would ride his bike to the municipal pool and swim for an hour. Gradually, his arm strength increased to where he could pitch a ball one after another without tiring.

Googer's comings and goings did not go unnoticed by Mad Dog. Once he hid behind a tree in an attempt to bushwack him. But Googer saw him and rushed into the pool. Mad Dog followed, however, in his haste, he forgot that he couldn't swim. In all the years of plotting, he had failed to take the time to learn. So, there he was floundering in the pool, thrashing about, gagging and choking. Googer, seeing Mad Dog was in trouble, swam to him and latched onto the collar of his shirt with his cleft hand and towed him to the shoreline. He was instantly met by a lifeguard who delivered immediate assistance. Googer calmly walked away but it hadn't gone unnoticed. Several sixth-graders saw it and when Mad Dog appeared good enough to walk home, he ran a gauntlet of jeers from his classmates.

"Mike you're a moron. You let some fourth-grader pull your sorry half-drown butt out of the pool," to be followed by individual taunts and group laughter.

Mad Dog was embarrassed, humiliated and howling inside like an angry dog. "Two Thumbs, you just wait. You are going to get yours," Mad Dog thought as he walked home wet and drained from his grueling struggle.

When Googer pitched his first game for the Hay Hens, he was an un-known commodity. The opposing team was the Kayuta Lake Loons, Mad Dog's team. He played right field and batted third. The movement of Googer's pitches were hard to predict but more importantly, the Lake Loons found that it was practically unhittable. Some of the older players would watch Googer throw the ball and try to anticipate its movement and take a good swing,

"Strike one." The more experienced ones would make an adjustment and watch for the second pitch.

"Strike two." Just when they thought they had it down, they waited for Googer to throw a third time. It was then that Googer would slip in a fast ball.

"Strike Three, you're out." And so went the game. Oh yes, there was a dribble infield hit here or a weak arching fly ball just over the infielder's head, but they never amounted to anything of substance. They did manage a run on an error. But that was the extent of it.

Every time Mad Dog came to bat, Googer struck him out which caused Mad Dog to become emotionally dismembered. He huffed and he puffed. He stormed back to the dugout, and he tossed his bat and slammed his hel-met each time. And for his effort Mad Dog was rewarded with taunting re-minders of past failures.

"Hey Mike, isn't that the kid that took your marbles?"

"Oh Mike, isn't that kid who pulled your sorry butt out of the pool?"

"Isn't that a fourth-grader that just struck you out?"

Mad Dog was limited in ammunition but came back with, "Struck you out didn't he?"

"Yeah, but he struck you out THREE TIMES." This was followed by another round of individual taunts and group laughter.

It was the last the inning, and the Lake Loons were ahead by a run. When Googer came to bat there were two outs and someone on first. Mad Dog hoped he might salvage something of his pride by doing something heroic like make a diving catch for the last out or throwing out the tying run at home plate.

"Yeah, that would fix the little snot," he thought.

On a three and two count, Googer managed to hit a high lazy fly to right field. It was a regular can of corn. Mad Dog positioned himself underneath the ball in plenty of time. When it came down something happened unexpectedly. The ball missed Mad Dog's glove and struck him on the bridge of the nose knocking him out cold. By the time the center fielder got the ball and threw it in, Googer was crossing home plate. That proved to be the winning run to the misery of the Kayuta Lake Loons. The final score was two to one – the Holland Patent Hay Hens won.

When Mad Dog came to, he blamed it on the sun getting in his eyes which was ridiculous because it was an overcast day. Now, Mad Dog was going to do REAL damage on that Two Thumbed little wretch.

The following day Mad Dog lay in wait, hidden in a dark alley in Googer's neighborhood. When Googer walked by on his way home, Mad Dog made his move. He pounced, grabbing Googer's skivvies and yanked them upward. Mad Dog then quickly slipped his arm around Googer's head getting him into a solid head lock and commenced inflicting kudo knocks unmercifully. . All the while Mad Dog was chanting in a singsong fashion, "Two Thumbs Goooooger. Two Thumbs Goooooger. Two Thumbs Goooooger."

It was somewhere at the beginning of the fourth rendition of the song that Googer (unintentionally) reached up with his right hand and latched onto Mad Dogs package. It was like when his family doctor struck his knee it involuntarily flexed. Latching onto something was just natural but in this case it happened to be Mad Dog's family jewels. Because of Googer's congenital anomaly of birth, his cleft thumb pinned BOTH of Mad Dog's testicles to the palm of his pitching hand, which had increased in strength since the beginning of baseball season.

A paroxysm of pain instantly shot from Mad Dog's crotch directly to that little bit of gray matter that he called a brain. It instantly dispatched a communication to his vocal cords stating PAINNNNNNN! Upon receiving the message, Mad Dog's voice was elevated several octaves higher than normal. So, when Mad Dog started to say Goooooger, he sounded more like a mad dog baying at the moon, OOOOOOOOOOOOOOOOOOOOOO.

Mad Dog continued to howl even when Googer unlatched his gripe and sprinted down the street, up his front steps and into his house. The elderly neighbor across the street kept looking at his watch in confusion. He thought the noon siren at the fire department was in error now because it was three fifteen.

I am reminded of an old North Country adage that maintains "Once you have them by the b---s, their hearts and minds will soon follow." There must be an element of truth to it because from that day on Mad Dog avoided games of marbles, baseball and Two Thumbs Googer. Mad Dog Mike clearly had a change of heart and mind.

As we get older and look back into the past, we are reminded of the Googers of the world. They are those who overcame adversity and left their mark on those who pass. In our small town, Googer was a shaft of light softly filtering through the forest canopy shedding light along the path. Unheralded, he directed us along the way.

DRAGONFLY

Some say there are two seasons in the Adirondacks; July and winter. Somewhere in between you will find Halloween.

Cold weather sets in early in the small Adirondack town of B'ville where I grew up. It is a small hamlet nestled in the foothills of the Adirondacks. A quaint, quiet little place that everyone should visit once in their lifetime – or so the sales pitch goes. There is nothing extraordinary about it except perhaps its bitterly-cold winters, which accumulates an abundance of snow annually that is measured in feet not inches.

B'ville has a main street like most small towns in upstate New York, which doglegs into a not-so-thriving two-stored downtown business section. There is a postage stamp park in the center of town which hosts a bandbox once used for weekend entertainment and a lofty granite Civil War monument topped with period cannon noting the community's sacrifice to a very un-civil war. Both bandbox and cannon are mute relics of the past. Today, its cannon serves for an occasional pony ride for youngsters or a slam dunk soda can receptacle for the yougotnochance NBA-aspiring teenagers. However, it mostly serves as a point of reference for some wayward traveler seeking directions.

Main Street hosts a couple of dozen stores with large thick-plated display windows. The second story is prominently crowned with ornate façades which celebrates a prosperity lost to the memory of all except the most distant generation. An occasional store entrance, stairway or alleyway disrupts the otherwise trim ground-leveled frontage. All in all, its parking meter-lined cement sidewalks could be found anywhere in small town USA.

Halloween is the beginning of the holiday season and understandably, youthful excitement. It is a time when the days shorten and the air becomes crisp while the leaves begin to change into a marvelous array of almost mystical pastels. It is a time to don the heavier coats and mittens as well as hats (wool is best). It is a momentary reprieve of the impending, unavoidable winter misery looming beyond a low Confederate gray sky.

Leaves are raked, piled and burned. Its aroma is a harbinger of festivity. Youths are invigorated with joyful thoughts of colorful costumes and plentiful candy. Even the poorest children are not denied. What with an old pair of pants and shirt, handkerchief stuffed with newspaper and tied to a tree branch, face blackened with a burnt wine cork; these ready-made hobos share in a cornucopia of candied delight and thus rightfully given their proper do.

This autumnal ritual has evolved very little. Inspired by creativity and novelty; homes, stores and classrooms are ghoulishly decorated accordingly. The energy level increases with excitement, culminating in "The Day" when school children bring their costumes to school. Little learning takes place, not because of diminished effort by teachers, but rather unbridled youthful restlessness.

Having paraded around the village block in costumes by assembled classrooms, dismissal explodes with the scattering of spirited youngsters. Many will stop at the Main Street bakery for a free cup of cider and a donut before scurrying home. As night nears the street lights begin to illuminate, officially heralding the beginning of this eagerly anticipated hallowed night.

Devilry takes many forms depending on the level of delinquency. Socially sanctioned forms of mischief manifest itself with strewn toilet paper and soaped windows. Acceptable folly is aerial water balloons or lofted rotten tomatoes. Lavishly applied shaving cream may be added to this witch's-brew of mischief. The more demonized youth will substitute paraffin for soap, eggs for water balloons and molasses for shaving cream.

A successful evening might come in the form of bulging bags of assorted treats for the benign ghostlings or goblinettes. And those older specters, cold and wet teenagers more recently smeared with a mosaic of eggs, molasses and shaving cream - cheerfully shiver in the cold night smelling like yesterday's compost. They, too, share in the rapture of the evening's activities.

However, it was toward the end of the 1960s that another game was afoot – black plot, more diabolical in nature, slowly brewed. Sinister in design, it had been metastasizing for an entire year.

Women and cars were a hot topic growing up in the 1960s. The poet once said that "in the springtime a young man's fancy lightly turn to thoughts of love," and I might add there is no stronger love like the first.

In B'ville, first love came in the form of muscle cars: Camaros, Mustangs, Chevelles, GTOs and Vettes. The vibrant colors: emerald greens, candy apple reds, night watch blues; captured the eye and enchant a young girl's fancy much like the flashing array of spring flowers would a honey bee. And the roar of a 409 or a 389 horse power engine had the same luring effect as that of a Rocky Mountain herd to the bugle call from a rutting bull elk. High octane in your late teens was an aphrodisiac.

However, should one have to choose between a coke and fries for a sweet young beauty or a dram of high octane for "the beast," then engines must roar and tires shall squeal. When it came to love, sacrifices had and must be made. Youthful love, especially first love, is enigmatic.

At seventeen, Tom Dragon was the hard-working son of a local dairy farmer. Around B'ville, husbandry was a cherished way of life; cultivated with devotion and care from generation to generation both in practice as well as study in clubs like the FFA or "Future Farmers of America." Yet, Tom's primary affection wasn't farming; it was his 1967 Aleutian blue, 4 speed, 400 cubic V8 Pontiac GTO.

It was commonly referred to by car enthusiasts as a "GOAT." It was hardly your typical meandering, grass-eating kind of goat. It came with chrome valve covers (brightly burnished), gloss black air cleaner (ne'er a speck of rust), and a brilliant white interior which sported bucket seats, full center console, a deluxe steering wheel and a four speed chrome shifter crowned with a black eight-ball.

Its exterior sparkled with the frequently washing, waxing and buffing from Tom's callused and battered, yet, gentle and loving hands. This gorgeous GTO was not any GOAT; it was the prized possession of Tom Dragon, the son of a humble dairy farmer and a sparkling marvel to everyone's envy.

When Tom fired up the engine it barked and snarled, then settled into a deep rumbling idle. A mere tap of the gas pedal unleashed a paroxysm of caged fury, roaring to alarming heights matched only perhaps by the now defunct Civil War Cannon perched idly on a block of granite in the town square. What the senses beheld was wonderment, a marvel, an extraordinary testimony to some supreme celestial power or the manifestation of a Dr. Franken/Hyde-like MIT graduate; yes, a wild, unsettled man.

Tom would drive his 1967 GTO to school and like an immerging storm on the horizon; you could hear the distant rumble of its high performance engine long before he appeared. He would proudly parade it around the block before class to admiring eyes. Moments after the final bell for dismissal sounded, Tom could be seen bursting through the braker-bar double doors, run down to his sleek Aleutian Blue GTO, fire up the engine, and then racing through the gears, catapulted out of town – squawking the tires as he disappeared, errt . . . .errrrt . . . errrrrrt . . . errrrrrrrrrrt !!!!

It was one day in late October that Tom blundered. While the civil and not-so-civil urchins were making merriment dressed like ghoulies and ghosties and long leggety beasties this Halloween night, he decided to parade the Aleutian blue, 4 speed, 400 cubic V8 Pontiac GTO around town.

Its distinct deep rumbling engine and Tom's trademark errtity-errrrt-errttttt tire squawks had forewarned the juveniles, delinquently skulking within the dark shadows of the store entrances, stairways or alleyways of the village main store frontage. Each possessed a cache of eggs, water balloons and rotten garden vegetables. As one dressed in Paul Revere garb recalled wittingly, "No one needed to wave no lantern in my face. Tom's was commin', and he'd be commin' by land, 'cuz Tom can't swim."

What happened next was swift and impromptu; not a crime of conspiracy but one of chance. From the time that his GTO chrome grill and headlights appeared protruding around the corner at the red light of Post and Main, until he fully negotiated the doglegged stretch of the downtown, the sparkling marvel of everyone's envy now looked more like a sad soiled sow than a gorgeous GOAT.

Flanked on both sides of Main Street an explosive barrage of decayed produce found its mark. Having finally negotiated the end of the gauntlet, Tom in a burst of smoke, screeching tires and fit of anger spun a one-eighty, to the awe and wonderment of all. Was Tom fool enough to risk another run?

The offending hands slowly reached into soiled bags or pockets for another putrid projectile. But it was not to be. No, discretion overruled valor. Tom slowly turned into a side street and made his way out of town.

For several weeks, Tom was not to be seen. Some thought he sold his GTO while others stated that he had just put it up on blocks in a shed for the winter. He started to drive an old blue and white pickup truck back and forth to school.

Tom just wasn't Tom. The experience had changed him. He lacked the bounce in his step and stayed to his own. When he wasn't in school, he was working on the farm. Winter slowly came to a close and a wet, brown spring followed. Still there was no sign of Tom and his GTO.

As spring made its way into early summer, Tom appeared one day in his GTO. Yet, something about it was different. Some say it appeared bigger, better, faster. Not only had he polished the chrome to a brilliant sheen, rebuilt the engine to purring perfection and tinted the windows a smoky gray; he had repainted the car with several coats of lacquer which gave the Aleutian blue a deep, three dimensional appearance. It was like looking into a small dark mountain pool.

But the biggest change was Tom. He seemed happier, livelier and more gregarious. If there were hard feelings, it wasn't evident. He appeared to have forgotten the whole ugly affair and got on with life.

Another summer quickly came to a close and school started with renewed excitement and energy. By mid-October teacher's scowls gradually shifted to occasional smiles as the autumn leaves took on their annual array of vibrant clusters of color.

The crisp autumn air initiated the onset of two things: the rut of the white tailed buck and youthful unrest. Lunch period became extra lively with talk of costumes and candy. The upper classmen quietly and discreetly renewed their stock of villainy. Parents fretted about costumes and decorations, striving to accomplish two things: exceed last year's efforts and outdo this year's competition. In all of this self-centeredness no one took notice that Tom began to drive the old blue and white pickup truck once again.

Then came "The Day." Children were cheerful, colorful and effervescent. When dismissal came they donned their costumes, paraded around the block and quickly scurried home. Porch lights appeared as the street lights gradually came to life. And as if by decree children burst forth from their homes like startled quail before a springer spaniel. For the next few hours one could hear the swishing of costumes, rustling of leaves, and the sing-song chant of "Trick or Treat."

On the other hand, tricks were played regardless of treats. As the evening progressed windows were soaped, pumpkins were fragmented and trees were draped with tattered remnants of toilet tissue. Those with devilry to spare quietly slunk to darkened store entrances, stairways or alleyway of the business district with a cache of water balloons, eggs and rotten tomatoes in tow as they waited in ambush. Patience would reap reward.

And it did.

Suddenly there appeared protruding from around the corner at Post and Main Street, a small, dark, motorized mountain pool. A 1967 Aleutian blue, 4 speed, 400 cubic V8 Pontiac GTO with tinted windows to be exact; chromed, lacquered, and polished to a high sheen. In a deep low rumble it idled at the stop light.

Just as suddenly, its engine barked to life, sending the GTO screeching sideways 90 degrees, settling in a cloud of smoke. To those skulking in the shadows good fortune had arrived with royal grandeur. Here for the second year was the opportunity to show their disdain for the gods of fortune; to defile and deface this grail of adoration.

The Pontiac GTO gently rocked to and fro to the idle of its powerful engine.

And let these water balloons, eggs and rotten tomatoes be a clear message to the gods; that we – those less fortunate, those by our fate deemed to be unworthy, those who must trod the highways and byways on foot – will not passively accept this injustice.

The chromed grill of the GTO sneered with distain.

One by one the tormented stepped out onto the sidewalk. There were demons and goblins, rogues and fiends, ghouls and ghosts, scalawags and scamps each clutching in their fetid fist some reeking, rancid, slimy object of their discontent.

The taunting began. Jeering, shaking their fists, they challenged him to venture forth if he dare. The engine revved louder. They doubled their threats. Sparks flashed from the exhaust pipes. The crowd increased as the sneers grew louder and louder.

Finally, when the cauldron of chaos seemed ready to boil over, all 400 horse power of the GTO erupted. Swinging the rear bumper 180 degrees, the Pontiac reversed it course and in a cloud of smoke scooted around the corner and out of sight.

And then just as quickly there emerged from out of the smoke a large Ford tractor. It must have been waiting just around the corner out of sight.

Racing through the gears the tractor rapidly increased its speed and behind it was a manure spreader filled to capacity. At the wheel was Tom Dragon, eyes fixed ahead with a wild grin spanning his face. The heap of manure that he had been saving from his dairy herd overflowed the sides of the spreader. To ensure that it had the right consistency Tom added water just for good measure until it reached the texture of a rich milkshake.

By the time Tom reached the stunned crowd, he was flying in high gear (later some would recall it as rapid ... speedy ... fleeting... almost airborne). Reaching down he engaged a lever (PTO) causing a Vesuvius-like eruption of animal pooh. His exact timing and agile movement (no doubt practiced numerous times in some secluded section of the farm with an accomplice) left the hooligans paralyzed with utter bewilderment. In the next few moments, he had emptied the entire contents of the manure spreader the length of Main Street, covering any and all in a shroud of slop.

For as far as the eye could see there was a coagulated corridor of cow crud – on the whole generous and ubiquitous. It was a wet, glistening glaze of earthy excrement, a veritable mound of manure, a plush pile of poop, a defective drenching of do-do – in short, it was a steaming, smelling, soaking shower of shit. And smiling back at this defiled group of miscreants was Tom Dragon beaming with contentment.

Spring seemed to come early the next year. As the robins returned downtown shop owners found sprigs of clover emerged from the sidewalk crevices and timothy and alfalfa dominated the grassy areas. Oddly, shoots of oats appeared in flower boxes, while flowers bloomed early and with the most vibrant colors.

In the years that followed after a long hard winter it was said around B'ville that should one see a dragonfly on Halloween, it was a sure sign of an early robin spring.

SECTION 4

~~~

Otter Creek

~~~

DOING MY PART

The room was cold with a bright florescent light humming overhead. A stainless steel table with small black wheels was off to one side. Under a white sheet there was a visible mass that appeared to be the shape of a human body.

When you are young, death is a like some distant relative who rarely comes calling. One day unexpectedly, great-uncle so-and-so appears at your door from out of the blue. He lives in some remote, outlying region not easy to pronounce. You don't recognize him, yet once you are introduced, he is permanently etched in your memory, impossible to forget. Death was like that to Phyllis in 1943.

It was pinnacle period. America was at war and nearing the end of its second year. In 1943 there were many great-uncles who appeared on door steps all across America. Gradually war was taking a terrible toll and few managed to avoid the clutches of its sinister and indifferent hand.

At seventeen Phyllis was full of hope and promise; as were many her age throughout America. She wished to do her part in the war effort but she was too young for military service. Some of her classmates lied about their age and enlisted in the armed forces. They wanted to do their part but sadly their names appeared in the local paper as a casualty and became a statistic.

An opportunity, however, presented itself. Phyllis heard about a program where she could volunteer to help out after school at the local hospital. Much like the USO, her duties at the local hospital consisted of assisting the medical staff. She quickly found herself usefully doing her part by getting a glass of water here, a pillow or extra blanket there. She was needed to fluff up the pillow of patient #5 in ward B, or empty the contents of the bed pan at bed #7 in ward A.

Her duties were benign. She might be asked to serve a treat from the snack tray or read to those visually impaired. Angelically, she would dispensed words of kindness and was universally viewed as a younger sister from back home. Nonetheless, the war pressed on and there just weren't enough hands to provide ample assistance.

Phyllis, who was not trained in the formal arts of medicine, lacked the skill to care for the tender needs of the patients like taking temperatures, registering vitals or administering medication. Out of necessity Phyllis was approached by the head nurse to help with a special assignment. Determined to do her part, Phyllis consented to assist as needed.

"I want to do my part," she was overheard saying.

Before the head nurse's gratitude withered away, Phyllis was told that she would be needed to wash a recently deceased patient for transportation to the funeral home. While this came as an unpleasant shock, Phyllis was determined to be as gracious and genial as if one's great-uncle so-and-so had suddenly come to pay a visit.

The deceased were located in the morgue in the basement of the hospital. She followed a staff nurse down four flights of stairs and was shown a small room where there was a stainless steel table and a body covered with a white sheet. Next to it was a basin with soapy water and a sponge. She was instructed to wash the body by an attending nurse and when she was finished to report to her, who would be in the room next door preparing another for transportation.

"Any questions?" she asked.

With nothing more said, she passed by her and left the room.

One feels weak and unimportant in the company of death. Darkness exists even in the most luminous surroundings. Phyllis paused for a considerable time, thinking about what to do next. A couple of times she attempted to draw the sheet back and examine her task, but she was weak with apprehension. Uneasiness disarmed her, she went limp with indecision.

She kept repeating to herself, "I will do my part . . . I will do my part . . . I will . . . And before she knew it her hand had drawn back the sheet exposing the upper half of the cadaver.

The first thing she noticed was that there were no notable injuries. In war the dead don't always come ravaged with severed limbs and gaping wounds. Death can appear subtly as with a bout of pneumonia or the flu or some other peculiar affliction.

Now revealed, the young man appeared to be resting. Death's confederation had come to him with the kind of serenity that one might experience at sundown with the close of day. Calmly, death's tender hand caressed. Oddly, Phyllis recalled some lines of poetry from Miss Dubois' English class.

"But now go the bells, and we are ready,
In one house we are sternly stopped
To say we are vexed at her brown study,
Lying so primly propped."

Why she had thought of these lines, she will never know. But the momentary distraction permitted her to grasp the sponge unconsciously in the basin and begin to cleanse the body.

Just how does one wash a dead body? She imagined it was just like washing herself, first one arm, then the other. Yes, and then next the chest and so on. It seemed like a good plan and with that she began the task.

The young man must have recently died for his limbs were still supple. Lifting the arm she went up one side and then down the other. She paused to rinse the sponge and repeated the procedure, careful to remove any telltale soap or excess moisture. She proceeded to wash the other arm in the same manner.

Little by little she became absorbed in the task. Instinctively, she moved to the chest. Much like when she was young and her mother would comb out the snarls in her hair; Phyllis' motion became rote and unconscious. The task became automatic and unyielding - scrub, wash and rinse and then scrub some more.

It was somewhere in the process that the man let out a painful groaning.

"AHHHHHHHHHH!"

Phyllis became paralyzed with fear. A voice screamed in her head, "HE"S ALIVE!"

But like the finger when first cut and it doesn't immediately bleed; so too was Phyllis' voice. She couldn't – didn't express her fear. However, it was momentary and like the rich red fluid which gushes forth from a wound, so too was Phyllis' cry.

"AHHHHHHHHHHHH! HE IS ALL-EYE-EYE-EYE-EVE-VA!"

Understandably, Dr. Frankenstein would have been envious.

Fortunately, the morgue is located in the bowels of the building, for was it not, chaos and confusion would have ensued. With the alarm levied, Phyllis bolted for the safety through the door before anyone could react. In the process she collided with the nurse in the other room and was gibbering to herself in a high pitched voice.

"He's alive . . . he's alive . . . he's alive . . ."

"Who?"

"IT! IT, HIM, IT! . . . HE'S . . . HE'S . . . HE'S . . ." wide-eyed Phyllis paused and then catching her breath, very low tone whispered her inner most fear . . . "alive."

"Who? That man in the room? Don't be silly. Trust me, he is not alive. I examined him myself. Now follow me."

The nurse gently grasped the young woman's arm and escorted her into the room's florescent interior. The nurse placed two fingers on the prone man's neck, checking for a pulse. Nothing. She next placed a stethoscope on his chest, listening for several moments. She repeated the procedure in different spots. Still nothing.

Presenting the stethoscope to Phyllis, she suggested, "Here listen for yourself."

Halfheartedly Phyllis placed one end of the stethoscope to her ears and the other on the prone man's chest. She listened long and hard, but try as she might she could not locate a heartbeat. There apparently was none to be discovered.

"See? No heart beat. He is very much not with us - living I mean. Clinically, he is deceased. It is nursing 101. No heart beat means he's dead . . . and dead he shall remain. Now, finish up here for, I have another task that will need some attention."

With that she left Phyllis standing alone with the cadaver and the stethoscope dangling from her hand.

Bewildered, Phyllis slowly backed away from the gurney and looked long and hard with suspicion. In due course she slowly took a step forward. As she neared the prostrate man, she again placed the stethoscope on the man's chest. Concerned, she listened for a long time with care. Only then was she certain that there was nothing, like the Munchkin Coroner decree, she concluded that he was not "only merely dead" but "really most sincerely dead."

She must have imagined him breathing. Perhaps it was like the story she read in Miss Dubois' English class "The Tell Tale Heart". It was about a man who imagines hearing the beating heart of a dead man who he dismembered and placed under the floor boards of his room. Like the man in the short story, Phyllis was allowing her imagination to play tricks on her.

Whatever happened earlier - imagined or real - this man on the cold stainless steel gurney was, without a doubt and with a certainty, very much dead.

Reassured, Phyllis continued with her task emancipated from her ridiculous adolescent imaginings.

The wisdom of her father came to mind. "A job worth doing is worth doing well."

Renewed with inspiration, she set to the task once more with the best measure of her ability. She thoroughly washed the toes and the ankles and then the legs.

Next she applied the sponge to the thighs, the hips and then the private area - careful to avert her eyes to save the deceased man a bit of human dignity.

She then washed the stomach and chose to complete the chest area that she had previously started earlier.

Dipping the sponge into the basin, Phyllis worked the sponge about his chest lost in thought. She became fixed on the man's face with steady intent. He didn't appear much older than herself and it suddenly reminded her of her own mortality. Oh, how she wished she could speak with him or anyone who could impart something reassuring about the afterlife.

Death was the ultimate mystery. Phyllis believed in an afterlife, but "what must it be like?"

Pausing she thought, "Does the sun shine day and night? Don't be silly. If the sun shown at night, there would be no night. However . . . if God was All Powerful . . . he could make the sun shine at night and still make it night."

That was a difficult bit of theology, but then again it worked and she took pride in the results.

Phyllis slowly worked the sponge in a circle around the sternum.

"I wonder if there is ice cream in heaven. I do hope they have black raspberry ice cream. Oh, I would miss black raspberry ice cream."

Yes, Phyllis concluded that if God could make the sun shine at night, he would certainly provide black raspberry ice cream.

Now her thoughts began to wander to the subject of animals and heaven.

"Take my Stamper; he's such a beautiful dog, a brindle boxer. If anyone deserved to go to heaven it would be our Stamper.

"Mary Jean Wittbeck, that prissy little wretch, said that dogs don't go to heaven. It is reserved for humans. She said that there wasn't even a dog heaven. 'Dogs just die.'

Mary Jean's father was Dr. Wittbeck, our family doctor who everyone likes and respects.

Mary Jean Wittbeck was a miserable little snot. Everyone calls her 'Crisco Kid' because she is fat in the can. What does she know about dogs and heaven, anyway?

"Dear God I do hope you allow dogs in heaven, for I just couldn't bear living without Stamper."

It was at this time, when Phyllis was consulting with the Lord on the pressing issue of whether dogs were allowed in heaven, that she leaned forward on the dead man's chest deep in thought. In her agitated state she leaned a bit too hard and the air in the corpse's lungs rushed out in the form of a groan.

The issue of pets and heaven remained unresolved, for the scream that followed, rivaled that of the wailing howl of the specters and spirits, the ghosts and ghouls, the devils and demons all combined into one very mournful cry.

"AHHHHHHHHHHHHHHHHHHHHHHHH!"

IT LIVES! And that agonizing wail trailed Phyllis out the door, down the hall, into the staircase and out of the building and off the hospital grounds.

When Phyllis' mother came home from work, she found Phyllis sitting on the couch with her legs comfortably tucked under her, reading a book.

"Hi, honey."

"Hello mom."

"Home a bit early. And how was your day?"

"Oh, the usual," she responded without taking her eyes from her reading. "Just doing my part."

Snakes

Northerners, as a rule, do not care for snakes. The first time I saw a REAL snake was in Louisiana going through infantry training.

We were cutting vegetation with machetes at the clogged opening of a culvert where water drained from one side of the road to the other. Someone yelled, "SNAKE" and without even a glance everyone leapt out of the ditch; everyone, that is, except the guy from Texas. He positioned himself about three feet in front of the culvert entrance and waited.

A rebel stood like the Colossus of Rhodes as an adult water moccasin exited the culvert. He made one quick swipe with his machete and decapitated the cotton mouth in a flash. Still squirming with life, the Texan proudly displayed the snake as we all gazed in utter revulsion and pure adulation.

As a part of our training, we were required to navigate a compass course. Divided into small groups, we were required to plot our way through a marshy terrain. The drill sergeant gave strict instructions,

"Thars all kinds of snakes in them there woods. Y'all not to bring any back. Ya hear?"

A hardy, "YES SERGEANT!" was given and away we went. The first thing the northern boys did was find a sturdy stick the length of a rake to mash any legless reptile, should we encounter one. It wouldn't take long.

Using my army issued compass, I shot an azimuth in the direction into the southern swamp. I instructed a fellow trainee from Detroit to head in that direction. He gave me a flat, "NO!"

"What do you mean, no? We work as a team like we were told. I'm supposed to shoot an azimuth using a compass and you are to walk in that direction counting steps. That's how it supposed to go." He vigorously shook his head from side to side.

"Why's that, I asked?"

"Cause Jake the Snake is out there and I'm from Detroit and we ain't that stupid."

It appears no one in our group (all northerner), weren't that stupid either; especially this one from upstate New York. We settled on finding a safe place and waited a reasonable amount of time before we returned. After a couple of hours, we thought that it was ok to retrace our steps back to the assembly area. Walking single file down a shady trail the person in front of me stepped over what he thought was a good-sized stick. That is what he THOUGHT it was. Extending across the trail was a sizable snake lurking in the shadows.

I yelled, "SNAKE."

The guy in front of me leaped into the air and before he could land the rest of us beat the B'Jesus out of that snake. As it turned out, it not only was a snake native to Louisiana, but it was a large cotton mouth just shy of three feet. Forgetting what the instructor told us, someone had wrapped the snake around a stick and paraded around with it like Jack in William Golding's "Lord of the Flies."

"You stupid *bone-headed' IDIOTS," the drill sergeant yelled! "I told you not to bring any * snakes back with you. Get rid of that *blitherin' snake NOW!"

My brother-in-law was in a rifle company in Vietnam. While on patrol his platoon stopped for a brief rest. As they were catching a breather a FNG (Frigger New Guy) turned to him and said, "Hey Sarge, look at this cute little snake I found. The new guy had a little lime green snake woven in fingers of his hand. "Does this little fellow have a name?"

"Yeah, we call it a two stepper."

"A two stepper? Why do you call it that?

"Because if that little snake bites you, you will take just two steps and drop dead." He had just enough time to throw the snake before he passed out from shock.

Northern boys just do not like snakes. Take Tavis for example, he might have been the most base human being you were liable to meet, but he was likeable and came from up north.

Tavis was the size of a prairie buffalo, and he drank and swore like a platoon of drunken Marines on a weekend pass. Tavis was known for his hard work and his hard drinking. Tavis was able to consume a case of beer at a sitting. He was a man who remained firm and attached to his beliefs. Once he had made up his mind; he never deviated. Reverently, his friends called him *The Beast and his profanity was legendary.

Tavis was afraid of nothing and no one unless snakes were involved. When he said he hated snakes, you took him at his word. He hated all kinds of snakes and would spit at the mere mention of the word. It would be followed by chugging a beer just to purify his throat. If you happen to mention the word snake, you could expect Tavis would latch hold of you and give you a lecture on the subject.

"I tol' you not to use that * pea-pickin' word around me. I DON'T want to hear that *mud-mucker again" There ain't a *goldarn" snake on this planet that I care for. You know that Irish guy named Pat had the right idea. Kill every last one of those *somsabritches."

Tavis dreaded the legless, wiggly creatures for as long as he could remember. He was once overheard to have said, "Snakes, I hate the nasty little *buggers. My momma raised only one fool an' that was my younger brother. And I thowed him in the swamp up to his neck one day when he brung home a *feather-plucking snake."

Sometimes it was difficult to tell when he was only joking.

During Army basic training someone tossed a harmless rubber snake over a metal wall locker, and it landed on Tavis's bed. Seeing the rubber reptile, Tavis bolted for the door in a panic and in the process knocked over an entire row of metal lockers in the effort to get as far away from the snake as possible.

The impromptu entertainment resulted in laughter. When Tavis stormed back in the barracks, he was shown the harmless rubber snake. Suddenly, like the hood of a King Cobra, Tavis's neck enlarged noticeably and his body became perilously rigid. Tavis's facial expression was alarming. The main arteries along his neckline became visibly crimson and pulsated which suggested imminent peril.

Starting at the first cubical he hissed at the tenant in a low perilous voice,

"Did you throw that *clam-shuckin' snake?"

Without saying a word, the accused jerked his thumb over his shoulder. Tavis went to the next cubicle with the same results. One by one he went down the row of cubicles from one squad member to another, asked the same question and getting the same results. Finally, Tavis ended up at the very last cubical and demanded coldly,

"Did you throw that *feather-pluckin' snake?"

"Yeah, what of it," the jokester replied and then smirked?

"The *shirt-tucker didn't get out another word," Tavis recalled. "I like to beat that poor * lip-pucker to death. The Company Commander called me in to his office," he continued, "And told me I shouldn't have hit him that hard. I told him, "Sir, that * dice-chucker ought not t' have thrown that * cotton-pickin' snake on my goldarn bed."

Tavis's first duty stationed was Panama and he was ordered to deliver a truck load of supplies to a company in the field. While driving a loaded two-and-a-half-ton truck down a jungle road, Tavis came around a sharp turn. There, extended full length across the road, laid an enormous snake.

"I first thought it were a tree trunk. Its head was hidden in the bushes on one side of the road and his tail was somewhere buried on the other. It liked to be the size of a fire hose," Tavis recalled. "I stepped on the gas and the *mud-mucker made the *goldarn truck leap in the air when we hit it. When I came back to that same spot in the road, do you know what? That *thumb-suckin' snake was gone? Can you imagine that! I ran over that *friggin' snake with a two-and-a-half-ton truck and the * bull-bucker was GONE!" HE UPPED AND CRAWLED HIS *BAD-LUCKIN' *BUTT AWAY!"

Another time Tavis recalled, "I was fixing a fence one day and I looked down and there was this * corn-shuckin' snake on the ground. I took a fence post and pounded that *huckster halfway to China. I kept driving the post deeper and deeper into the ground. My partner told me that the snake was dead. I tol' him the *whisker-plucker wasn't dead 'til I SAY its dead. I like to break the *goshdern post in two driving that * toe-pickin' SNAKE into the * thumb-suckin' GROUND."

He then spit and chugged a beer.

After his enlistment, Tavis worked for a fuel company. He made a service stop to clean a woman's furnace. While at the home he politely informed the lady that he would be back when she got rid of her snake problem.

"I don't have a snake problem," she said trying to reassure him. Tavis led her down into the cellar. He pointed with his sausage-like index finger to a shadow that looked like an unfurled condom extending from behind the furnace.

"That," Tavis declared politely, "is a snakeskin. He then gave a mini lesson on the subject. "Ma'am that is a snakeskin and snakeskins come from a snake. If this is your house and that is your furnace, you got snakes and that is a problem. She tried everything to convince him that he was mistaken; but Tavis would not have any of it. "Ma'am," he finally said. "I'll be back when you get rid of those sorry *spear-chuckin' snakes."

Tavis left. He spat several times as he went to his truck, and drank as many beers when he came to the nearest tavern. Tavis wasn't sure if or when that woman got her furnace cleaned. But one thing was certain, if her cellar had a hint of a snake, it was not going to be cleaned by him.

Tavis was the most vulgar person I knew especially when it came to snakes. Raised in the north, I shared in his contempt. As a rule, most northern boys did not care for snakes, and it was obvious that Tavis had a deep-seated hatred for the *gol-darn little *beasts himself.

*__Warning__: *Mothers for a Better America have censored vulgar language that the reader may find offensive.*

DID YOU KNOW?

At any given moment over the course of the past four decades, my wife will inevitably mention something that I haven't a clue and then wait for my response. It goes something like this . . . .

Wife asks, "Do you think so-and-so should or not?"

I respond, "Should or shouldn't what?"

"You know . . . .?

"Know what?

"That so-and-so is . . ." It is then she fills me in on the rest of the riddle.

In a quandary I state, "I didn't know that."

"Well, I didn't know you didn't know that."

"But how was I supposed to know?"

"I don't know," she reasons. "Everybody knows that."

"Well, I don't. To start with you should have asked me if I knew that or not."

"How was I to know that you didn't know that in the first place?"

"You would think after 40 years, you would know if I knew something or not."

"Well, for your information, I don't know."

"Ok, I'm letting you know now that when I don't know something, I don't know it. I'd even go as far to say that when I don't know something, you can be certain that I definitely don't know it. Capeesh?

"Capeesh? What is that suppose to means?"

"It means . . . never mind. What I am trying to say, without mincing words is, my unknowing is a state of which I don't know. And there are times that I am inflicted, even crippled by unknowing. You must realize that when I don't know, I just plain don't know. It can be very disturbing."

"I can imagine that it may be disturbing, but crippling? Come on."

"Yes crippling. I'm like that blind ex-soldier in the movie, Scent of a Woman. When I am expected to know that which I don't know, it becomes ...yeah, crippling."

"Don't be silly. It is only a movie. I'm trying to be reasonable. Can't you see?

"Nope. 'I'M IN THE DARK HERE!'"

"Once again, how is it that you do not know that you did not know?" she asks.

Pausing to collect myself, "I don't know."

"And when is it that you knew that you didn't know?"

"When ...you ...ask ...something ...and ...I ...don't ...know...it."

"So how am I expected to know that you didn't know until I ask you and you tell me you didn't know it."

Sigh, "I don't know."

"There you have it. Seems to be a lot of not knowing around here and clearly it isn't me."

Out of frustration, "I CAN STATE WITH A HIGH DEGREE OF CERTAINTY THAT WHEN I SAY I DON'T KNOW SOMETHING ...I DON'T KNOW IT.

"Well ...THAT'S very good to know! Sooooooo."

"So what?

"Should they or shouldn't they?"

"Should they or shouldn't ...ummmmmmm. What do you think?"

"I say they should."

"Me too."

"Why didn't you say that I the first place?"

"I don't know."

ANGELS OF OUR BETTER NATURE

When my wife entered the backdoor to the kitchen, I could sense something was amiss. She had a look of both anger and disgust, which immediately told me to tread lightly for the hounds of hell were about to be unleashed.

It is said 'God hath no fury like a woman scorned.' These are soundly pragmatic words derived from difficult lessons of our forbearers. These also are prudent words of advice for divorce proceedings.

My wife Susan, is well-known for her pleasantness and gentle disposition. So I was taken aback when she came lunging into the kitchen glaring menacingly.

"IT IS WAR!" she bellowed, "WAR!"

War?

My beloved was so flustered that she had not specified to whom and why she was at war. Being a woman true to her word, a state of war undoubtedly now existed. Hostilities had been openly declared. Yet, she being the slighted warrior, I was left clueless as to who was the offending warree and what could have possibly caused my wife to morph into Mrs. Hyde.

Just a few weeks ago this gentle, kind-hearted bride of mine strolled light-footed into the kitchen through the front entrance. She whispered that I should not (which meant could not) use the front entrance into the kitchen because there was a nesting mourning dove in her flower pot hanging on the front porch. I was to use another entrance so as not to frighten her being that she was resting and in such a delicate condition.

In a melodious voice she informed me ever so sweetly, "I think she has little ones. She mustn't be disturbed."

The homestead law having now been announced, it may as well have been etched in stone. Consider it as firmly and as rigidly enforced as a sturdy switch on the butt of a wayward youth. In short, if you MUST enter this house – use another entrance.

My general merriment and future joviality depended on by bride's happiness. Not to mention those added pleasantries that I have grown accustomed to and relied on for lo these past forty years – blueberry pie, fresh clean sheets, back scratching in that hard to reach area and . . . you get the idea.

A "Yes dear" was in order. With an agreeable smile, I promptly went to work taping muslin cloth over the glass on the kitchen door and drawing the shades to the window above the kitchen sink that overlooked the nesting nursery.

Days passed and after a few weeks the nestlings hatched and had flown their geranium sanctuary. As the saying goes, "Happy wife, happy life." My wife's happiness now became my happiness. The nestlings' liberation now became my liberation. I was free to come and go as I pleased. Peace and tranquility ruled – that was until in the words of Franklin D., "A state of war now exists . . ." Susan's declaration was less diplomatic.

"YOU MUST KILL THEM!" KILL THEM ALL!"

"ALL of them?"

"YESSSSSSSS," she hissed. "ALL OF THEM! NOT ONE IS TO BE LEFT ALIVE!"

"Not one?" I inquired.

"NOT ONE!" she confirmed.

Well, well this was serious business.

Next, after having painfully discerned that THEM was in reference to the rabbits that had free run of the farm and that ALL specifically meant every filthy, furry little hopping beast and the YOU was in reference to me.

Furthermore, if I SHOULD take on this mission (and I WOULD – see afore mentioned pleasantries) she meant by KILL to: destroy, dispatch, slay, annihilate, abolish, extirpate, wipe out, eradicate, exterminate or murder those grubby little creature in a method of my choosing. Their end would justify the means.

However, it must be performed immediately if not a minute sooner.

I instantly surmised that if regular meals were to continue, the bunnies must go bye-bye. In her state had the Easter Bunny been fool enough to wander near our homestead, a scattering of chocolate, jelly beans and Peeps would be strewn about its dead carcass like the poppies at Verdun.

With a little bit of diplomatic inquiry I was to ascertain that she had lost her patience when she noticed THEY (the furry little buggers) had consumed her lovely impatiens flowers that she meticulously and with care had planted in a bed around the bird feeder out back. In short, she lost her patience when she lost her impatiens.

"How many flowers were eaten?"

"All but one," she pleaded. "And it would have eaten THAT if Jordan (our beagle) hadn't spooked it and it ran off into the woods. You must get them. They ate all of them."

Then she started to access the meaning of the calamity. "There are four plants per box; I had four boxes at three dollars and fifty cents per box. Now there is only one puny one left.

As I quickly added up the price it became apparent that the going price for a "whack" in Ghent was fourteen dollars. Life was cheap when it came to Susan's flower garden.

"YOU must get him. He was a big one TOO."

Somehow the size of the critter seemed to justify its forthcoming departure.

In a low, child-like voice she continued, "When I looked they were gone. Once there were impatiens and then nothing. They were gone. Nothing. Not even a stalk. I kept looking there to see if there were any left. There was just that one puny ..." her voice trailed off. Pausing momentarily to gather herself, she added, "Had Jordan not scared it away, I'm afraid it, too, would have been eaten."

Now fully fortified, she blurted out, "YOU MUST GET THAT RABBIT!"

The sentence for willful destruction of flowers beds around here was death by firing squad. With the Elmer Fudd mantra "Kill the wabbit, Kill the wabbit" quietly playing in my head, I got my trusty bolt action 22. Removing the screening in the back bedroom window, which overlooked the crime scene, I scanned acres upon acres of farmland and waited and waited and waited.

I knew that the furry little buggers frequently came out at dusk and dawn. Dusk is difficult time for me because the Yankee game was usually on and it was a sacrifice I just couldn't make. However, I am an early riser so seven-ish was a better bet.

Rising between six-thirty and seven I quietly walked to the back bedroom. Slowly raising the shades I peered out over the stretch of land that was our back lawn. Nothing.

I got my sniper weapon with a full clip and set both on the bed. I waited some more. Still nothing. After about fifteen minutes, I snuck into the kitchen to make a quick cup of coffee in the Keurig.

Returning to my perch as the hot coffee was burbling from the Keurig into my cup, in the gray first light, I thought I could just make out a mysterious gray mass low in the grass. Was it a shadow? Perhaps some leaves? I waited and I watched for several moments. It suddenly moved. Or I thought it moved. The morning dimness can play tricks. Slowly opening the window several inches I stuck the rifle out the window and chambered a round. Nothing.

As I centered the sights on the shadowy clump of mystery-mass it moved again. In a scurrying-loping-hop-pity-hop-hop, the shadowy mass looked like, and had the distinct characteristics of a "THEM." And he was a big "THEM" too.

I'll not get into the sanguinary details, but a shot rang out and a live "THEM" resulted in a dead "IT."

In the aftermath of this event as I pause for reflection, I am reminded of the consoling words regarding harmony and discord as expressed by our late president, Mr. Lincoln. We are reminded that when our passions become strained and the bonds of affection are broken; we as flawed human beings can be governed by raw emotions. But we must take a moment to pause and look within, striving to seek out and touch "the better angels of our nature."

This expresses positive words of wisdom to guide our paths as we go forth in life. However, I wouldn't recommend picking any flowers too soon along the Ghent Flats. That is at least until Susan has had time to compose herself.

The future is unpredictable and forthcoming events may rely heavily on mystic cords, better angels and flower beds abloom.

Mark A. Clarke

'What We Have Here is a Failure to Communicate'

A nasty stomach bug was going around, and my wife was weathering it well. She appeared to be on the tail end of its untimely wrath. I stuck my head into the spare bedroom.

"How are you feeling today hon?"

"k vdd> z snl>d >lg >k<d tls gndt k ckc mjxg z xnlfg snk> zbl," came the reply.

Having grown up in the Adirondacks, I had a working knowledge of the native tongue. Majoring in English at college and an advanced study of the vernacular in the Army, I found it at times a challenge to understand a low-lander such as my wife.

Knitting a brow, I politely responded, "Huh?"

She repeated it again, "k vdd> z snl>d >lg >k<d tls, gndt k ckc mjxg z xnlfg snk> zbl."

Earlier I had a bout with the same nasty bug, and my hearing must still be somewhat affected. Politely I inquired a second time, "Huh?"

Thinking that I didn't quite hear her or that I was temporarily rendered feckless, she rephrased it for my benefit. "Z xnlfg snk> zbl, K ckc tlg vdd> mjxg >k<d gnkx."

I thought to myself, "No, you heard her correctly." So, it must be one of those temporary disruptions that occasionally hinders the husband/wife line of communication. As long as we have been married, we have experienced a messaging problem from time to time. We sometimes speak in a different language often in a different dialect. What I needed was a wife-to-husband translator to decode what she was saying to what I was hearing.

Now if I were her what might this mean? Hummm. Let me see? If I replace the vowels with A=Z, E=D, I=K, O=L and U=J. What does that leave us?

"I vee> a sno>e >og >i<e tos, gnet I cic muxg a xhofg sni>e abo."

Needs more work. It is still more of a mess then a message. My wife continued to smile as I worked the problem. Now if I replace a couple of consonants like the R=F, the L=>, the T=G, and the N=T, what would we have?

"I veel a snole lot li<e nos, tnen I cic muxt a xhort snile abo."

There's movement in a promising direction. Be patience. You're getting closer. Let me see what this will do. Make the D=C, the H=N, the B=R, the G=B, and the F=V. That would give me . . . .

"I feel a shole lot li<e nos, then I did muxt a xhort shile ago."

Now, if I could only make the S become a W, the X an S, the < equal a K and now convert the M into a J we arrive at . . . Oh, but of course.

"I feel a whole lot like now, then I did just a short while ago."

"Is that it honey?"

"Is what it?"

"You feel a whole lot like now, then you did just a short while ago?"

"Yes! Yes! That's it. That's how I feel right now," she beamed back with her lovely, genial smile.

"But of course, you silly goose," I thought to myself. "Oh, how foolish of me."

I returned a friendly smile and came away scratching my head dazed and deeply puzzled or so I thought. . . for that is how I felt right then, which was different from what I had just a short while ago.

Hummmm.

*Cool Hand Luke

Mark A. Clarke

A Day with Dad

Death is the finality for everything except baseball. Baseball has a life of its own. It transcends time and space. It is said that what makes man standout in all the animal kingdom is the flexible thumb and the ability to bestow on future generations the knowledge of the past.

The thumb allowed mankind to grasp and manipulate tools – from the club to the computer and a simple system of communication granted the following generations the benefits from their forefather's successes and failures. That in a word is baseball.

We tend to view baseball in terms of success or accomplishment. However, baseball is essentially a game of failure. If a person consistently hits a ball three out of ten times, he qualifies as an all-star. Should he hit a ball four out of ten times he is a candidate for the Baseball Hall of Fame. Yet, that same Hall of Famer or All-star has failed six and seven times of ten at bats.

Despite this, we erect citadels or baseball stadiums designed to test man's ability to exceed the given limitations of mere mortal and then meticulously record every minutia affiliated with its noted accomplishment. Nothing escapes the measuring eye of the statistician.

For a lifelong lover of the game, this was Charles. But there was more.

Charles had a passion for baseball. Retired, he would visit the "Club" and nightly explored a brandy (with ice-water back) fixed intently on the evening baseball game on TV. It was more than the familiar; it was intimate, close to sanctimonious.

One evening as the Yankees were about to lose their third straight game, one patron declared that "the bums will pass Reggie Jackson. He's got the team record for the most strikeouts with the Yankees."

"That's a bunch of malarkey. Everyone knows Babe Ruth's got the record. It's hit a homer or strikeout. Feast or famine. Ain't that so Charles?

"Nope, you're both wrong. It's Mickey Mantle. Reggie Jackson has the most strikeouts in the major league, but Mickey Mantle has the Yankee team record."

Everyone at the "Club" knew that Charlie had a great knowledge of the game of baseball. However, from time to time a challenged would issue forth.

"Not so. I got fifty dollars that says that you are wrong. It's Reggie Jackson."

"Save your money. Look it up if you don't believe me," Charlie added mater-of-factly as he relit his pipe.

"Not until I lighten your wallet of a farthing or two," the challenger quickly added.

"If you wish. It's your money."

They shook on it. Two days later payment was made and Charlie's reputation was secure.

Although I was never the Doubting Thomas, I was intrigued with Charlie's zeal for baseball. Not too long afterward I found out.

I found Charlie in his usual spot at the bar watching a baseball game. When there was a break in the action I asked him why he had such a deep interest in the game of baseball.

"Baseball is not just a game. It's about people," Charlie told me one night at the "Club" while he and I sat alone.

"You mean players and the fans?"

"Something like that. When I think about baseball, I think about my father," he began. "When we are young, life seems simple. It is a game of good and bad. Good is determined by the shade of their socks not the color of their hat. Baseball is uncomplicated. It is a game of balls or strikes, safe or out, win or lose. Yet it's a game of magic that comes to life before our very eyes. Some will speak of the game in terms of talent, hard work or luck. Whatever it is, it has captured the imagination of every boy from nine to ninety-nine.

I thought about my youth and listened. Charlie took me back to a simpler period in time, the age of innocence.

"Players will shuffle, leap or glide in one spontaneous motion to gather in a hit baseball and in the process they seem to defy even the forces of gravity itself. It is an athletic ballet; part skill, part art. Their craft is developed and honed through years of pain, failure (lots of failure) and disappointment which place the chosen few and placed in a pantheon for the immortals and gods.

"Quickly won, young boys lift these heroes above earthly existence nearer to the realms reserved for honored saints. When placed in an arena of peanuts, popcorn and soda pop, a boy is transported into the land of promise and possibilities, an adolescent Garden of Eden. This is how I felt when my father took me from Brooklyn to Ebbets Field."

I waited as Charlie took a sip of his brandy and then continued.

"My dad was a hard working man from Brooklyn. We didn't have a lot of money but what we had was honestly earned. Squeezing a quarter here and a quarter there he saved up enough to take me to Ebbets Field."

He paused and smiled. It was as if he were speaking to someone other than myself.

"Ebbets Field. Magical or it seemed so to me at the time. It was the home of the Brooklyn Dodgers and there we stood at the entrance to the stadium. Not any stadium but The Stadium. I can still remember the day. It was a bright summer day. The sky was a robin's egg blue. Not a cloud in the sky. A light breeze stirred the air and with it came all the smells pleasing to a young boy. Sweet mouthwatering smells that seduces the senses. Like the sirens to the ancient mariner. Hot dogs, sodas, popcorn, peanuts, they lured me deeper into its dark interior."

Charlie looked at me for several moments, allowing me to sift through his words to find a shared understanding.

"Once inside there were thousands of people: tall, short, thin, stout, young, old and the not so old. Some glanced at the sports section seeking out each minute detail of today's game; like precious nuggets at the race track to the serious gambler. There were the wavers, the hand-shakers and the occasional crying child in tow. There was an array of colors as bodies swished by, a multitude of mankind in motion. There was the momentary aroma of a gentleman's pipe tobacco or the pungent scent of a lady's perfume. In this tribe of waifs and workmen and masses of a common humanity, I stood with my dad in awe."

Oddly, I felt as if I, too, were invited to watch the game with his dad.

"A short walk drew us into a shaded passageway that led to the playing field. Entering the stadium, the place was aglow. Blue sky above and bright green field below. And then there they were my heroes – all of them. There was Robinson, Reese, Hodges in the infield. Snider and Furillo in the out-field. Campanella was behind the plate while the Great Don Newcombe went into his ritualistic warm ups. They were all here with me and my dad. It was perfect."

Several moments passed as I watched Charlie spend that time again with his dad. I remained silent as Charlie took a sip of his brandy and then continued.

"That was the beginning of my lifelong love affair with baseball. But you see, baseball isn't just about hits and runs, winning and losing. It is about shared time with special people like my dad. When I think about baseball I think about Ebbets Field that one special day that I spent with my dad. When I think about baseball," Charlie concluded while relighting his pipe, "I think about my dad."

That conversation with Charlie was one of those rare moments when we are allowed to peer into the lives of another. I likened it to Hank Aaron when he hugged his dad at home plate after breaking the major league home run record. Hank was just a kid again, sharing a moment with his dad and the game of baseball.

SECTION 5

~~~

WHITE LAKE

~~~

LOG JAM'S MUTT

He was the most obnoxious animal alive or so thought the men in Lumberback Camp #13, above Thendara in the Adirondacks.

Lumbering was a cold weather occupation of seclusion. Isolated men find them sequestered in the high timber region of the Adirondacks with limited companionship. As the weather grew colder, the days became a long gray monotony. The only entertainment was what imagination can manufacture in the form of tales and long lost loves. However, the narratives quickly became stale and repetitive.

Working in the Thendara camp in '88 there was the monumental figure of a lumberjack by the name of Log Jam McLaughlin. He was so named because given his massive stature, his talent of navigating logs with cork shoes and unraveling blockages on the river was viewed with amazement.

Good natured and poised, he was universally liked by all. Log Jam had one distinct flaw and that was his flea ridden, ill-tempered crossbred mutt was a misery to the entire camp. Roughly the size of a fox, the mongrel's bristly gray hair shot out in all directions. It looked as if it had been involved in a mine explosion. Temperament and looks placed aside, the critter was Log Jam's comfort and companion on those long desolate nights of continual cheerlessness.

When the creature wasn't chewing or stealing something, the under-handed beast would mark anything and everything with a warm steady stream of dog piss. Log Jam tried tying the dog to his bunk while he was away laboring in the woods, limiting his area of operation. Later, however, when Log Jam returned, he discovered that the dog had chewed through the rope and made a shambles of the bunk house.

Moreover, he anointed the wood box, potbelly stove and several pairs of boots with the foul fragrance of dog urine. It took some time for Log Jam to mollify the men; what with two hours of scrubbing and straighten-up and the promise that come payday there would be a jug of Dust Donnelly's best "Oh Be Joyful" home brew for his bunkmates.

Still there was the undertone of constant uneasiness loitering close by. Although Log Jam utilized a metal chain to tether his mutt to a tree, there was no stopping the yipping and the yapping and just general turmoil the diabolical cur created. It seemed the only solace that his bunkmates had was when Log Jam was allowed to pet the beast while it lay on the floor next to his bunk. Even then it would shed copious quantities of hair which would naturally stick to woolen socks like burdock to winter mittens. The dog could instantly destroy any semblance of bunkhouse harmony. The days began to grow colder and the nights considerably longer; misery was stirring.

One evening Frenchie Dubois, a reserved woodsman, had just finished supper when Log Jam entered the mess tent followed by that yipping-yapping mutt, spryly leaping to and fro. The critter was especially rambunctious during mealtimes. This performance persisted for about twenty minutes, all the while Frenchie stared unresponsively at the performance to the canine clamor. Several of his messmates were taken by his unwavering interest. Finally, one spoke up. "Say Frenchie what's on your mind?"

He responded in his slow and measured manner, "Just thinking."

"'bout what?"

"Thinking . . . that I'd like to own that dog."

"What? That dog?!" a bunkmate added in astonishment.

"Yep."

All eyes looked to Frenchie in disbelief. One whispered, "He must be afflicted with cabin fever."

"This cannot be," a third logger gasped. "Why would Frenchie wish to own such a dog as this?"

Still eyeing the canine, Frenchie slid his chair away from the table and quietly affirmed, "I'd kill that dog."

It was sometime in late January when the west wind whistled through the woods and cut like a double-bitted axe. Provisions were getting lean and wild game became a steady subsidy for general consumption. There would be venison, rabbit, turkey or lake trout. Occasionally there would be a partridge or perhaps two.

Stumpy, the camp cook, took pride in his "bill of fare." Short and stout, Stumpy was built like a Roman warrior. Agile too, if it weren't for the double-bitted axe that glanced off a pig-headed red oak tree and buried the blade into Stumpy's right calf. Had it not been for this ill-fated incident, he would still be logging alongside the rest of the boys. After an extensive recovery and a slight limp, Stumpy came to the painful decision that lumberjacking as he knew it had come to end.

But his love of the singular life and the wonderment of nature guided him to a culinary pursuit in the camps. Quickly he honed new-found skills to his delight and equally to that of his former lumberman mates. Soon he was back working in the camps in the Adirondacks.

He wielded the spatula as adeptly as he did an ox head or hand sappie. He not only prepared hot, freshly ground coffee, but scratch flap-jacks and sizzling heaps of smoked bacon and honey ham before dawn. The bread was homemade along with his splendid soups and stews. The menu varied to the delight of his fellow lumberjacks. Whatever Stumpy could flip, ladle or spread was second only to what dear old mother created at home. They became dietary disciples of Stumpy's delicious concoctions and regarded him as the anointed one.

It was getting on toward the end of February when the wild game was scarce and Stumpy happened to come into the possession of several respectable partridges. Using a hunting trick taught to him by an old Oneida Indian, he fashioned a snare out of some birch bark and boot laces. With a small section of white birch bark, he carved some circular openings into it, slightly larger than a partridge's head. Then scattering cracked corn about the trap and a generous portion in each hole, he looped boot laces around each hole and secured them to a tree. His snare was complete. All he needed was some dim-witted birds to investigate and when their protruding neck feathers became ensnared in the loops, something novel would appear on the menu. The entre would be baked partridge floating in a thick pool of gravy with the added assortment of Stumpy's resourcefulness.

It took several days before Stumpy had enough to make an ample meal for the boys. Leaving the wild birds hanging in the kitchen to cure, he momentarily turned his attention to other duties.

It was sometime later that menace of a mutt got loose and skulked into the kitchen while Stumpy was away splitting some firewood for the evening meal. When Stumpy returned he found feathers scattered throughout the kitchen and that demon of a dog greedily gnawing on the evening's meal. If it hadn't been for that old logging injury, Stumpy and his meat clever would have sought justified compensation for such wickedness.

That evening's dinner was especially somber. Instead of the intended delectable dinner Stumpy pledged, there was plucked porridge ala whatever, with a slight wisp of a feather or two.

The meals for the next week or so were both uninspired and uninspiring. It had a deep and lasting effect on Stumpy. In the days to come, his meals nourished the body but were characterless, unimaginative and bland to the lumberman's palate. It was a blessing, except to Log Jam perhaps; that that mountain mongrel slipped its leash unnoticed and vanished into the wilderness, destination unknown.

It was after this timely occurence that Stumpy became revitalized and began cooking his celebrated specialties. There was homemade cornbread slathered with butter, fresh steaming coffee and a huge pot of aromatic stew. It was teeming with numerous vegetables: corn, carrots, beans, fresh cubes of potatoes and hardy chunks of meat all in a thick rich gravy generously united with an assortment of agreeable spices. For dessert there was a mouthwatering cherry (canned) cobbler. It was truly a culinary extravagance, a gastronomic garland, a crowning diadem of all of Stumpy's handiworks. In fact, it was so well received that seconds were offered and one and all eagerly accepted.

Log Jam restlessly waited his turn with great anticipation. He was eager for another helping and perhaps more if he could finagle it. Stretched to his full six-foot-four-inches and balancing on his tip-toes, Log Jam craned to see if there might be enough for another helping. There was.

When Log Jam reached the front of the line, Stumpy ladled out a generous helping onto his plate. Log Jam was so free with his compliments that it prompted Stumpy to dip his scoop back into the pot.

"Stumpy, this stew is first rate. What is it?"

"Oh, it's a recipe I got from an old Indian who was part Huron and part German."

"What is it called? He asked.

"I call it Hund Stew."

"What's in it that makes it so tasty?"

"Have you ever heard of succotash?"

"Yeah."

"Well it's like that. In the dead of winter when food is scarce around the camp they take whatever's available and make it into a concoction. It is sort of like Mulligan Stew but Huron style. You know, whatever you got around camp. Spice it up a little here and there. And what you have is Hund Stew . . . Indian style. Here have some more."

He placed a steaming ladle into Log Jam's bowl. He was quite proud to be honored with an extra ladle of Stumpy's specially prepared Indian stew.

"Hey, guys this is some kind of Huron stew. He got it from an old Indian. He was part Huron and part Hun and it's called Hoot Stew."

Klaus Gunter, a beefy German born in Mainz asked, "Are you sure it was 'hoot' and not 'hund'?"

"That's it, hund . . . hund! Huron style Hund Stew. It's got vegetables like succotash and things like that. Whatever is around camp. Hey, Klaus I know that Hurons are Indians from Canada where do Hunds come from?"

"Most everywhere," he said as he kept eating. "It is German for mutt."

"Mutton huh. That's must be what those chunks of meat be."

"Nah." Klaus continued with his stew. "I said mutt. Hund is German for dog."

The men did not think that one man could vomit so much and for so long. Well, why not? Log Jam was a very large man and he was well into his second helping of Hund Stew.

In fact, he threw up long enough for Stumpy to hastily gather up his cutlery and hobble out of camp. No one ever saw Stumpy again. Some say he was in the Yukon panning gold. Others argue he was living on a reservation somewhere or other in Alberta raising sled dogs for the Royal Mounted Police. Some folks heard he was herding sheep in the outback in Australia. No one was quite certain of the particulars.

However, Log Jam did work in the Adirondacks lumbering trade the following season though he was noticeably thinner. He had taken up eating mostly fruits and vegetable. Log Jam was reported to prefer spring water and nibble on bits of goat cheese now and again. But he mainly subsisted on canned sardines with a cracker or two.

DEAD EYE

He was born Poindexter Louis Duchamp, but those who grew up with him called him Dead Eye Duchamp or just plain Dead Eye.

Poindexter Louis Ducharme stole the suspenders off Mr. Yeoman's back porch. Old Man Yeoman always washed his suspenders every Saturday and then hung them on the back porch to dry. One day his suspenders were found in the bushes with one of the elastic straps missing. The following week Poindexter was seen sporting a new slingshot made of a forked hickory limb and something that looked like Old Man Yeoman's missing suspender strap.

When he was confronted with the issue, Poindexter said he found the sling shot in a vacant lot. Shortly an unusual amount of mischief occurred in town. Poindexter had been seen on more than one occasion shooting pebbles with his new found sling shot at salamanders on the rocks along the Black River. Thereafter, when a window was broken without accounting or a beloved bird's sudden departure couldn't be pinned on a badly-behaved village cat, Poindexter became suspect.

Poindexter was not a popular boy in the neighborhood. There is was a troubled history behind Poindexter. His checkered past included smearing peanut butter on door handles, spitting dry peas at unsuspecting classmates through a straw, placing gooey chewing gum on class chairs and tying stubborn knots into the laces of unattended sneakers. When he visited the doctor's office for his yearly checkup, he would sneak an extra lollipop from the nurse's station "for later."

The fact of the matter was that Poindexter was not much liked by most because there was an air of sneakiness about him. When some damaging gossip came his way, it appeared on the bathroom wall as truth, in indelible ink. School lunch bags were often rifled through and sweets like cookies went missing. When cold weather arrived, mittens and scarves were found floating in one of the school toilets, or worse, clogging it.

The shadowy offender was dubbed "the mad flusher." Poindexter became the prime suspect.

It wasn't that Poindexter was born with the mean gene because he had three older sisters who were genial and universally well-liked. His mother was generally regarded as a saint. Even when Poindexter was caught red-handed in some misdeed and confronted by his mother, Poindexter would stare back blankly with doe eyes and innocently deny it.

This noble woman was filled with unconditional love. After mildly admonishing him she would forgive him, giving him some sweet treat and sending him on his way. "He is such a good boy," she would state in his defense.

Some children just need extra attention. Perhaps Poindexter felt that he was neglected. His father, returning home from work, ruffled Poindexter's hair with a pleasant, "What's up, sport?" and then retired to his pipe and paper. One would hardly mistake that for quality time.

His older sisters were more than willing to spend time with him pointing out his numerous defects. "Don't slouch. Close your mouth when you eat. Stop picking at yourself. No running in the house. Stop fidgeting. Pay attention to the minister's sermon." Adding in resignation, "Lord knows it might do you some good," and then they rolled their eyes.

On and on they would persist correcting every flaw and misdeed of his that would materialize. Annoyed, Poindexter would curse under his breath, "damn 'em." If he were real angry he would add, "Damn, Damn . . . double damn 'em." Occasionally when he become livid, his face would turn a crimson red and he would follow the degrading oath with a wad of congealed spit.

He turned to his mother declaring that his sisters were a wicked group of nasty witches." His mom would listen, smile and then replied with the usual, "But they are such good girls."

Still, when Poindexter was alone and certain no one was listening he referred aloud to his siblings not as "witches" but in an invective sounding similar to it.

Getting away from the house was somewhat of a blessing for him but not for the neighborhood. He would pinch the younger children until they cried and teased the girls with the same results. He cheated at games whenever possible.

Animals didn't seem to care for him either. Mr. Dubois' graylag gander honked at him and violently flapped its wings as he chased Poindexter down the road – all the while pecking at his leg.

Mrs. Merle's submissive dachshund named General Grant generally spent most of its time either sleeping on the porch or licking itself. When Poindexter came into view the dachshund would bolt after him. Down the street the two would sprint with the General nipping at Poindexter's heels.

The kids called it the dachshund dash and placed odds on the event. General Grant wouldn't be deterred until he could latch onto something solid, usually the seat of Poindexter's pants. He once tore Poindexter's back pocket getting at his sling shot. General Grant promptly chewed it to splinters with a vengeance. What made the General act in that manner was puzzling.

One might expect empathy for poor Poindexter if it weren't for the way he treated Stanley Dawson. Stanley was a quiet kid, small in stature with no particular talents. He wasn't muscular or fleet of foot. When he was the last player selected for a pickup game of baseball he stood grinning with delighted just to be a part of The Team.

Stanley was the first to pat a teammate on the back when they struck out with a reassuring word. Yet, when failure came his way he graciously smiled saying, "I'll get 'em na-na-next time."

Stanley had one noticeable flaw, he stuttered. Everyone overlooked his minor imperfection – all except Poindexter.

Poindexter was good at one thing and that was marbles; even when he didn't cheat. Marbles were made of glass and came in many colors and designs. The more common ones were single colored and named Ade (lemon-ade, lime-ade, and orange-ade). A cat's eye was made with swirls of various colors. The more exotic marbles like aggie, bumblebee, sunburst or dragon fly were as well as all the metal marbles that were commonly called steelies. The more unusual the marble's design or color, the greater it was admired and coveted.

Every boy growing up in the village had a sack of marbles they would collect and trade. Most would play the game of marbles. The participants would place 5 to 10 marbles in the center of a circular ring scratched in the dirt. While kneeling outside the circle, a player used his thumb to shoot a marble held in his fist at the group of marbles. Any marble knocked out of the ring was the shooter's property and he got another turn.

Poindexter held his own, coming out even or winning in these regular matches. However, Poindexter didn't like to play fair. He was always looking for an advantage. On this one particular day Poindexter found Stanley alone and lured him into a game of marbles. When it became Stanley's turn to shoot, Poindexter would mimic Stanley saying, "Stanley's Tatatatatatata-turn. Stanley's Tatatatatatata-turn."

Stanley, who was not usually self conscience of his stuttering, was thrown off his game. He missed hitting his mark time and time again. This delighted Poindexter and he roared ever the louder when he scored a marble, "HA-HA-HA another one."

This threw Stanley off his game ever the more. At the conclusion of this one-sided event, Poindexter had Stanley's entire assortment of beautiful marbles. As Poindexter was counting and admiring his undeserved plunder, Stanley slugged his way home in tears – an emotional wreck.

The moniker "Dead Eye" did not come from Poindexter's aim with a sling shot or with his talent with marbles. His baptismal debut would come sometime later.

Stanley was a quiet youth and stayed on the outer edge of general conversation. He mostly liked to tag along, lost in the shadows of group activities. But like Black River that ran through the village, Stanley's waters ran still and deep.

This quiet youth developed a keen sense of observation and he had a quick, intelligent mind. These attributes lent themselves to a kind of mature craftiness, matchless in scale and scope for his age. Time would provide Stanley with the opportunity for reckoning and like an autumn harvest; Poindexter would be ripe for the picking.

In the weeks that followed, Stanley groomed his skills and replenished his sack of marbles taken by Poindexter. When playing marbles, Stanley was focused on the more colorful, unusual and rare marbles in the circle. He would take the more difficult shot angle at a prized marble. Quality over quantity played an important part in his plan.   All the kids knew that Stanley was compiling quite a notable collection of marbles.

One day during recess, while Poindexter was in a crabby mood alone in the corner of the playground, Stanley pulled out his bag of marbles. Making sure he was close enough for Poindexter to survey the action, he began to admire them one by one by holding them up to the light. When Stanley was sure that Poindexter was sufficiently captivated by his doings, Stanley reached into the bag and extracted a rather large and very unusual marble.

Holding it up to the light it had become evident that Poindexter had never seen a marble like that before, ever. He was certain that no one had either. He rushed over to Stanley and insisted that he show him the unusual marble that he had in his hand.

 "Na-na-not here," Stanley stuttered. After school. I'll sha-sha-show it to you then." He slipped the rare novelty back into his sack with the rest of his marbles."

Poindexter was fidgety all afternoon in school. When he was called on by his teacher, Poindexter couldn't answer even one of the simplest questions posed to him.   He appeared distant, as if he was someone just visiting from another planet.

When the bell rang Poindexter was out the door like a shot and impatiently waited in the shadows along the route Stanley would take home. As he was passing by, Poindexter got his attention.

"Psst, Stanley over here."

But Stanley continued to walk. He wanted to increase the possibilities. Poindexter scurried alongside him.

"Lemme see it. Lemme see it."

"I'll let you see, but you can't ta-ta-touch."

Stanley retrieved it from his sack of marbles and displayed the rare oddity in the palm of his hand. There it was in all of its splendor. It appeared to be made of glass the size and shape of a human eye.

Poindexter was bedazzled with amazement. Stanley carefully held the glass eye in such a way that it appeared to be looking at him. When the light hit the marble eye just right, it seemed to wink at him. Poindexter decided then and there that he must have it.

He tried to lure Stanley into a game of marbles, but Stanley would have nothing of it. If Poindexter couldn't win it from Stanley, he thought, maybe he could buy one. He kept pestering Stanley to divulge where he got the eye-like marble.

"Where, where did you get it?" Poindexter pleaded.

"I can't tell you. It's a sa-sa-secret."

"Come on. I'll let you choose any ten marbles from my sack for just that one."

"Nope. It's a sa-sa-secret." Stanley was toying with him. He reached into his bag and displayed the iconic marble a second time.

"Wow! That's some marble. Please-Please-Please. Tell me where I can get buy one just like it."

Stanley had played this fish long enough. "Tell you what. I'll sa-sa-show you where you can get one but it will ca-ca-cost you."

"What? What? What? Anything, Anything. Just name it. Anything."

Stanley didn't stutter this time. He had practiced it in the mirror for weeks.

"It will cost you all of the marbles you have in your bag."

Thunder struck. That's how Poindexter appeared. There was no way he was going to give up his bag of marbles. He was willing to give back perhaps some or all the marbles that he had won from Stanley but his collection of marbles? No way. Poindexter tried bartering but Stanley wouldn't budge. All or nothing. That was the deal. Stunned and speechless was how he left Poindexter.

The following day Poindexter made it a point to meet Stanley before he entered the school. He would agree to Stanley's terms but he must get more than one glass eye. They settled on three: one blue, one green and one brown. Stanley had figured that negotiation would end up that way.

At lunch Stanley made an inventory of Poindexter's marbles. They appeared to be a few less than what there should have been. He took them just the same. He planned that that would happen, too.

"Meet me in the sa-sa-same place as yesterday.

Poindexter came early and was waiting when Stanley appeared.

"Where's the marbles?"

Stanley explained that it would take a fifteen or twenty minute walk. They ended up in front of Barkley's Funeral Home.

"They're in th-th-there. Follow me."

"In there? Not me. That's where dead people live."

"No they don't. They la-la-live in cemeteries. This is where they spa-spa-spend a night or two."

"I don't know. I don't care for no dead guys."

"Suit yourself. But there's a whole ba-ba-bunch of dead eye marbles in there." Reds, blues, greens. A whole ba-ba-bunch."

"How do you know?"

"My dad helps Mr. Ba-Ba-Barkley when there's a wa-wa-wake. I help clean up. I seen 'em. Mr. Ba-ba-Barkley gave me this one."

Stanley displayed the dead eye marble again. It glittered. It sparkled. It seemed to almost speak to Poindexter. Like the Sirens melodious voices in Greek mythology it had a mesmerizing effect on him. He paused long in thought.

Finally he said, "But you go first." And with that Stanley opened the side door and walked down a set of steps that led to the basement and work rooms.

Stanley entered a door on his left that had a large pane of glass with gold lettering that read, "Supply Room." Trailing behind, Poindexter stopped and peered through the glass window as Stanley opened a cabinet door and pulled out a tray. He turned to Poindexter and motioned him in. Tentatively, Poindexter entered slowly all the while he kept glancing from side to side and occasionally behind him. Poindexter's nervousness diminished when he set eyes on the tray. Shimmering and glistening, the tray of colorful glass orbs seemly came to life.

"These are for folks who la-la-lost an eye and need one," he gestured to the tray.

Poindexter could not have been more euphoric if he was a gold prospector hitting the mother lode. His hands trembled with excitement. He was overjoyed. He was ecstatic. He was thrilled beyond measure.

He grabbed a handful and rolled them in his hands with momentary delight. Their smoothness had the sensation of spring water flowing though his cupped fingers of a man dying of thirst. He savored the moment like a connoisseur sipping a fine Louis XIII brandy.

"Wait, there's ma-ma-more."

"More?!" Did he just say more?

Stanley opened the cupboard where there were several more trays. One by one he slid them forward displaying glass eyes of assorted sizes and various color. Poindexter could hardly believe his own fate. Picking each glass eye up individually with thumb and forefinger, he delicately examined them as if they were the diamonds in King Salmon's mine.

One tray was an autumn forest of browns. Oh what joy. Another tray held an Irish field of Emerald greens. This was seamless rapture. And a third tray held a heavenly array of blues: robin's egg, azure, denim, aquamarine … Bliss came to him quietly undiluted. It came unblemished. Bliss flourished within, simple and pure. Poindexter wanted them all. But then he remembered that the deal was for three.

He finally settled on an autumn brown, an Irish green and a blissful blue. When they departed, the two did not take the same path used when entering. Stanley made a left, up a flight of stairs, a right and another left where the two ended up in a spacious room, dimly lit. Poindexter was too preoccupied with his treasure that it passed unnoticed.

When they stopped Poindexter looked up and saw several sizable caskets stored in the room.

"What's this?" he asked.

"This is the salesman's room. People come here to ba-ba-buy a casket."

"No kidding. Can I look inside one? I never saw the inside of a casket before."

"Sure, but you probably don't want to la-la-look in this one," he said standing in front of a smaller wooden casket.

"How come?"

"Did you hear about the ba-ba-boy who drowned over in West Lyden?

"No I didn't hear that."

"Well, his family is ca-ca-coming for him tomorrow to bury him."

"The dead boy's in there?" he said pointing at the casket in disbelief.

"Yep. Did you ever see a dead person before? I ma-ma-mean up close."

"Nope. What do they look like?"

"Oh, like most dead folks I ga-ga-guess. Like they're sleeping. I'd show you but you'd ta-ta-tell."

Normally Poindexter would pass on an offer like this. But this was an extraordinary day. He got not one but three dead eye marbles all in different colors and now he had a chance to see dead person, up close.

"Does he have a glass eye like ours?"

"Naw, he drowned. People don't usually la-la-lose eyes when they drown."

"Let's take a little peek. I won't tell."

"You promise not to ta-ta-tell?"

"My lips are sealed," Poindexter said making a zipping motion over his lips.

"Ok. Just a peek." With that Stanley lifted up the half lid of the casket. There was just enough light to see a heavenly interior of white linen surrounding the young figure of a fair boy about their age. He was dressed in a dark suit with a pallid face that matched the interior of the casket and he appeared to be asleep.

Poindexter stared at the dead boy for a moment and then asked, "What does a dead person feel like?"

"I don't know. Go ahead and fa-fa-feel 'em"

"You first."

Stanley touched the pale hands folded on the dead boy's chest. "It feels like cold rubber. Go ahead, your ta-ta-turn. Unless you're chicken."

Poindexter moved closer to the casket. What he really wanted to do was touch the dead boy's eye to see if it felt similar to the three glass ones he just acquired. Reaching into the casket he bent over the ashen boy to touch his eye lid. At that moment the dead boy's eyes opened wide and at the same time he smartly grasped onto Poindexter's outreached arm with a powerful grip. Poindexter froze. Rising upright in the casket, the dead boy made a motioned with his other hand for Poindexter to join him in the casket. Without uttering a word the dead boy kept pulling Poindexter toward him closer with a white hand and motioning him with the other.

It was about this time that Poindexter's movement was restored and he let out a scream that could have been heard all the way to Alder Creek. He tore himself from the grip of the dead fiend, leaving behind the cuff of one sleeve, three dead eye marbles and a line of yellow liquid marking his flight of terror.

One thing about childhood nicknames, they remain with you for a lifetime. Some wanted to call him "yellow sneakers." Others were partial to the title "rusty zipper." To combine the two was awkward and too long. So they branded him with the nickname "Dead Eye." It was accurate, concise and worthy of reflection. Dead Eye had a brilliant range in meaning: sling shot, marbles, cadavers. Dead Eye it would be.

Dead Eye wasn't seen around much after that nor was Stanley's cousin living two towns away who had agreed to play the dead boy when the opportunity presented itself. The glass eyes were returned to their rightful place, no one the wiser. Stanley's mother noted that she had somehow misplaced her container of talcum powder and please let her know if anyone should find it. They never did.

Old Man Yeoman got a new set of suspenders and the only time you could see them were when they were holding up his trousers. General Grant lived a long life and passed away one summer afternoon while sleeping on Mrs. Merle's porch. Such a saintly woman she was that upon Mrs. Duchamp's death the villagers donated a stained glass window to the local church in her honor. Her three daughters remained "good girls," married quite well and moved to the big city.

God has a sense of humor. Dead Eye (Poindexter Louis) Duchamp ended up in the Midwest working as a successful optician with a wife and three lovely, however, annoying daughters. He could never shed the handle "Dead Eye" by those who knew him.

As for Stanley, well I overcame my speech impediment right after that episode with the glass eye and the dead kid with the talcum powdered face. It simply faded away. I became a university professor and today you can find me giving spirited lectures on the subject of adolescent psychology.

P. S. My father once gave me a bit of practical advice. He said, "Stanley, you know you can't get even with all those who have done you wrong in this life. But when you find that one …

Oh, how sweet it is!"

Patsy Two Pie

Beagles have two passions, eating and chasing rabbits. Patsy Two Pie enjoyed both. Patsy was a beagle.

Patsy Two Pie got his name on a warm summer afternoon when Grandma Eunice placed two blueberry pies on the kitchen windowsill to cool. Patsy naturally noticed.

Was it the amber butter glazed pie crust that captured his attention or the sweet saliva inducing aroma of freshly baked wild blueberries? Humm? Difficult to tell. In either case, Patsy must rely on the "I'm a beagle" for his defense.

Adirondacks beagles are the Huck Finns in the animal world. They were not required to attend school, church, or account for their whereabouts, generally speaking. Reciting lessons or memorizing passages from the "Good Book" was not required of them, which gave them ample time for creative idleness, that took up most of their time. In short, they were accountable to no one, no way, no how. Creative idleness meant laying around licking, scratching, and sniffing in some sunny spot to their liking (pardon the redundancy). Mealtimes were festive occasions and a beagle's whereabouts was never in doubt.

One can be assured that a beagle's is somewhere in the vicinity at mealtime, theirs or yours. By beagle standards humans are considered food sources and register in all the categories on the beagle food pyramid. Wide-eyed, panting and under foot, they eagerly loiter about in the kitchen. Food is more of a want rather of a need. My grandfather said that beagles don't eat to live but lived to eat.

Therefore, it was quite natural that Patsy became attracted to the two pies like a bee to honey. People who are acquainted with beagles should expect that.

Note, I don't use the term owner in reference to these people. At the absolute best, humans are patrons, benefactors or perhaps sponsors but they are never owners. Ownership requires servitude, a degree of fidelity. Beagles serve primarily their own needs and wants. Fidelity on the other hand is a two-way street. The range and depth of meals can be directly correlated to beagle devotion.

Food filching in the beagle world is a minor offense and should warrant a mere reprimand like "bad dog." Were a stronger measure required, then a simple "bad, bad, dog" would be in order. But this offense was not your typical case of "bad dog" or even "bad, bad, dog." Patsy ate not one but two of Eunice's' blueberry pies.

Early on a drowsy summer day, Patsy had just finished his morning meal and was lounging about in the warmth of the mid-morning sun. Between the licking and the scratching, Patsy hadn't noticed that Eunice had gone missing. When she reappeared sometime later, Eunice set two freshly baked blueberry pies on the kitchen windowsill to cool.

Eunice, like most folks in the Adirondacks took great pride in her baking skills. It was a testament to her natural ability and culinary heritage. A slight to her cooking was taken as a direct assault on her pedigree.

Cooking was viewed as much an art as it was a science. It required generations of carefully kept secrets, the tedium of gathering ingredients (in this case fresh blueberries), time measuring, mixing, assembling. If scratch blueberry pie was to be carefully crafted, the process should begin with a novena and then followed by a whole host of activities.

Consider for a moment that not all scratch pies are the same. Take your average homemade blueberry pie. Pies that are prepared on different days, in different months, in different seasons may use the same ingredients but end up with different results. Legendary pie making requires unique talent, the kind that comes with aptitude, proficiency and breeding.

Eunice's award winning, number one, blue-ribbon, Grand Champion, best in the County Fair blueberry pie required reflection, for no two pies can be replicated. She had to consider the slightest differences and adjust accordingly. Not only the day, the month, and the season shaped the outcome but the time of day, room temperature and humidity as well.

Then there was a passel of other hush-hush necessities like a cup of raw good fortune, a vital ingredient in baking. Many award-winning bakers view "good fortune" like the finest yeast. It must be carefully cultivated. Those relying on chance are thwarted and own the ignominious labeled of "also-ran." They must endure a dismal case of the blues until the next bake off. As the saying goes "second place is the first loser."

But Patsy Two Pie was ignorant of all this fuss, the pies were simply tempting. Still, Eunice was partially to blame because she overlooked one especially important detail. Eunice failed to secure Patsy by a rope to the base of a sturdy oak tree.

When Eunice went to check on the pies, she found them GONE or more accurately, gone except the pie tins. A wrenching scream hastened Dade to the scene with his shotgun. He thought a bothersome black bear had wandered into the area and Dade quickly surveyed the scene. He came to the same conclusion as did Eunice. The modius operandi was familiar, "Round up the usual beagle suspects."

Dade, the lead investigator, quickly followed a trail leading from the crime scene (gooey specks of pie fillering) to Patsy who was resting in the afternoon sun with the telltale tinge of blueberry about his muzzle. In his frenzy Patsy's pelt was dappled with cobalt blue spatters that mottled the white of his coat. He looked like a canine version of a Jackson Pollack painting, and it gave the appearance of him having a smattering of blue-tick hound somewhere in this blood line.

Patsy was found preening himself of the remnants of the culinary delight. Upon completing the pleasant task, Patsy sat upright with wagging tail. He cheerfully slavered as Eunice appeared with clenched teeth seething. Her looming presence wore the mantle of judge, jury and the executioner. Hell, hath no fury like that of a woman whose pie has been pinched.

Humility is a proven method of deflecting moodiness. Patsy donned a mask of guilt and wore a mantle of shame. Careful not to make direct eye contact, Patsy slumped dog-hung, baby-browns peering downward in a posture of submission and remorse – one in pursuit of reconciliation. But none was being offered this afternoon. Understandably so, for one of those prized blueberry beauties was destined to grace her dinner table. The other was intended to surprise and underscore Eunice's unmatched talent as the number one, Blue Ribbon, Grand Champion, best in the County Fair blueberry pie baker for the ladies bridge club that afternoon. But the surprise was all Eunice's.

Had Patsy the Pie Poacher been able, he might have suggested something in the line of assorted dog treats from his hound-hutch. These choice morsels, neatly stacked and artfully arranged on bone China would do nicely. Eunice's heirloom platter would serve the cause well. And why not? Was he not fond of those delicious treats himself? Did Patsy not find those doggie delectables pleasing both day and night?

Eunice's afternoon luncheon would be a fitting time when the ladies had freshened up a bit after the card game. Patsy always felt that way when refreshed and renewed after a brief visit to the backyard. With a lick here and a lick there, Patsy eagerly looked forward to one of his prized biscuits. But would his biscuits measure up to Eunice's blueberry pie? That's difficult to say. Sometimes humans can be unpredictable. Sometimes they're funny that way.

Take for instance that last bridge club party when Patsy and Ms. Wildermuth had a slight misunderstanding over proper protocol when welcoming guests. Mix-ups will happen when two cultures encounter one another - human and canine cultures that is.

Patsy, as host, eagerly greeted the guests as they arrived. He properly performed his duties, wiggling back and forth and wagging his tail. The traditional beagle baying was in order as each guest entered the home. Charm naturally came to a beagle.

Then there were his winning eyes, his cute lolling tongue. He was careful not to slobber too much or as little as was canine possible. When a friendly hand was extended, Patsy licked it appropriately, cordially. All was going well until the two cultures clashed.

Customarily, when dogs greet there is the expected sniffing. It is quite common. It is just as common when meeting, to exchange a quick examination of the other's posterior. In canine culture, it is expected, proper and much appreciated. It is a compliment, a tacit sign of approval.

Unlike those cheeky Frenchmen, who practice the in-your-face, doublecheeked kiss; dogs prefer a more subtle approach. Face to face greetings often lead to misunderstandings and result in dog fights. Even the French Poodle, known for their grace and civility, favored the routine canine salutation over their human counterparts.

So being a gracious host, Patsy naturally greeted Ms. Wildermuth in beagle fashion. Patsy could immediately sense that something was not quite right; that Ms. Wildermuth rejected the customary canine salutation. The sure indication was her sudden and unexpected shriek. This unpredictable response left Patsy bewildered.

The incident resulted in quite a fuss. Embarrassed, Eunice secured Patsy by the collar and hastened him from the room - all the while apologizing with, "I'm so sorry" and "He's still in training" and "He's young and hasn't acquired proper manners yet."

But Patsy had in the dog domain. But Americans are peculiar in some things as their British cousins will attest. Americans do not appreciate things that are cold and wet except maybe their beer. This became strike one for Patsy and the two blueberry pies were strike two and three.

For the next two weeks Patsy was restricted to quarters, bound by a rope to an old oak tree. He was henceforth branded ignominiously with the nickname, Patsy Two Pie. The misery of it all was that Patsy was not allowed the freedom to follow his second passion in life, chasing rabbits.

Speed was in Patsy's blood. He would chase practically anything but when it involved a rabbit, all the better because rabbits were his favorite. Patsy was a natural rabbit dog, and his devotion to chasing rabbits was in his DNA. The challenge of pursuing rabbits wasn't just an inherent ability but more of a native calling. In the Adirondacks, beagles were meant to run rabbits and that is what they did best.

Patsy loved to sprint about, dodging left and right through woods in pursuit of the elusive hare. Should Patsy Two Pie encounter two rabbits, he elected to sprint after the younger and leaner of the two.

A beagle's prowess is measured by the talents of its adversary. The greater the challenge, the more noble the reward. Chasing rabbits was competition, a test of Patsy's ability. It invigorated his spirit; it kindled his soul.

But Patsy was now a prisoner of his own undoing. A wayfaring spirit is a princely virtue in both dog and man. It contributes substance to life, a rudimentary pathway forward to a meaningful existence. The spirit seeks validation, fulfillment, and self-worth. When an adventurous spirit is imprisoned, it becomes hobbled, wounded, subdued. A stifled soul is a lonely soul. It questions life's meaning, its purpose and intent.

So it was with Patsy, tethered to a tree unable to dash about in search of meaning and purpose, the fulfillment of life. Then fate took an unexpected turn. His friend Dade entered into the scene.

Friendship is a warm and wonderful thing. It tends to the lonely. True friendships are guided by love, a healing balm that mends all wounds. It was this sort of friendship that restored the trust that Patsy Two Pie had lost and sought to regain.

After a week in exile, Dade's own wayfaring spirit revisited the demanding sentence for his hunting companion and accepted friend. After one week, Patsy Two Pie was permitted to run free. His listless spirit was instantly revived. Patsy wiggled, Patsy danced, Patsy spun about in eager anticipation. Adventure was afoot and Patsy knew that he would be a part of it.

It is said that friendship beget friendship and love begets love. This new adventure wedded man to dog and dog to man in a kind of friendship that is bound by a mutual love of sport. Strange as it may seem, Patsy and Dade's common love of hunting led to Patsy's strange encounter with a new love. Unlike those other passions that came before, food or rabbit quest, Patsy Two Pie fell deeply in love with a train. Yes, a train.

Love came knocking the day after Patsy's sentence was commuted. As he and Dade made their way to their favorite rabbit run, Dade stopped briefly in town to get a few supplies for the afternoon. While driving out of town Patsy was drawn to a new sound in the distance. Dade took no notice because he had heard it a thousand times, but Patsy was immediately alerted by it - no he became entranced by it. A short way off as a train approached a road crossing, it blew its horn announcing its passing.

"HONNNNNNNNNNNNNNNNNNK, HONK! HONK!"

Startled, Patsy bolted upright in the back seat of the car. His head swiveling to the left and then to the right, trying to get a better fix on the foreign sound.

Drawn by its odd bellowing, Patsy listened intently, caught in its spell. There it was again, further off.

"HONNNNNNNNNNNNNNNNNNNK, HONK! HONK!"

Patsy was captivated by the extraordinary sound. It appealed to his innermost self. His excitement was electric, barely containable. Never had Patsy heard such a deep and rich sound. It barked like the calling of Canada geese, but it wasn't geese. This sound was captivating. It was exciting. It was enchanting. Tilting his head, Patsy waited, carefully listening. It blared forth a third time farther off.

"HONNNNNNNNNNNNNNNNNNNNK, HONK! HONK!"

Patsy vented a howl, long and loud.

"OWoooooooooooooooooooooooo."

It nearly caused Dade to have an accident. Thrusting his head back, Patsy exploded again with another howl. This time Dade was ready.

"OWoooooooooooooooooooooooo."

Patsy's baying continued intermittently the entire trip to their destination. Patsy Two Pie was distracted with delight. Rabbits no longer held his attention. The thought of rabbits had been replaced by the thought of that strangely wonderful and thunderous sound. It stole his concentration and Patsy was unable to focus on anything else.

Along a narrow trail a spooked rabbit unexpectedly rushed out of the brush. Confused, the rabbit bolted directly towards Patsy, leaping in flight and vaulted over him before the beagle could focus and react. Just as suddenly the rabbit disappeared into the dense undergrowth that boarded the woods.

The hunt was over even before it began. Whatever made that uniquely wonderful, bizarre and beautiful sound had captured Patsy but good. His new passion eclipsed his desire for hunting and unlike the rabbit, Patsy couldn't let the thought of it pass.

Patsy's new passion wasn't the kind of romance in a traditional sense. Although his obsession conveyed a heartfelt infatuation of a sort, there was no doubt Patsy was smitten as if a fair-haired beagle had smugly sauntered into his yard.

In the days that followed, Patsy remained subdued as all young lovers appear when first struck by the tenderness of a newfound love. He lay about in idleness. Oddly, there was none of the usual licking and scratching and sniffing.

Dade and Eunice took note. Every so often Patsy Two Pie would perk up, raise his head and give out a long, deep full-chested howl. Yes, Patsy had all the signs of being love-struck but good.

Some may argue that dogs can't fall in love. "Certainly not with a train. Never!" But how strange was it really?

Man has long had love affairs with their machines. Why not a dog? In the not-so-distant past, what young man hasn't had fond thoughts at the passing of a sleek maroon Chevelle with chrome wheels, white interior with matching convertible?

In a similar manner, Patsy's fixation on a train was not unlike our foolish fondness for automobiles.

In the days to come, Dade elected to visit a new rabbit run near Thendara, a small hamlet less than an hour away. Patsy was her old self again. She dashed and darted, rushed and ran, sprinted and scampered amid the green ferns and underbrush of the unfamiliar woods.

In fact, Patsy Two Pie lost all sense of time as he entered deeper into the alien surroundings in hot pursuit of the elusive rabbit. Patsy Two Pie's baying became smothered in a dense mantle of wood. Dade waited patiently with concern.

By then Patsy was hot on the trail of a feisty rabbit. The challenge prompted Patsy to dash about in close pursuit. His nose followed the scent of an invisible trail that coursed through the woods. Patsy stopped, sniffed this way and then that.

After picking up a fresh scent, off he scurried bounding up and onto a railroad bed. His nose led him on a trail that followed the railroad tracks. Just then Patsy heard a familiar sound. He stopped, raised his head to listened. There came that strange goose calling off into the distance again.

"HONNNNNNNNNNNNNNNNNNK, HONK! HONK!"

If it had wings it was no ordinary Canada goose. This goose calling blared forth in a long, deep honking followed by two short honks. It sounded again but closer.

"HONNNNNNNNNNNNNNNNNNNK, HONK! HONK!"

This last honking was louder, and the ground began to tremble. From around the bend came something that Patsy had not seen before. It was big and black. It may have sounded like a Canada goose, but it wasn't.

This goose was HUGE, completely black and without feathers. The featherless goose was bigger and faster than anything he had ever seen before. It loomed large and was barreling towards Patsy with a big bright light that led its way.

The featherless goose blared forth another loud and long honking followed the two shorter ones. It was so loud that the ground rumbled even more, and the sound boomed throughout the forest as it rushed forward.

"HONNNNNNNNNNNNNNNNNNNK, HONK! HONK!"

It reverberated with resounding force. The featherless goose raced onward in the direction of Patsy all the while it bellowed even deeper and louder. It thundered. It echoed. It shook the very ground Patsy stood on. It became for that moment the lord and master of the entire domain. Patsy looked on in amazement, in wonder.

"HONNNNNNNNNNNNNNNNNNNK, HONK! HONK!"

At the last moment Patsy leaped aside and howled. He tried to match the featherless goose in volume and might. But all he could manage was a meager beagle yowl.

"OWOOOOOOOOOOOOOOOOOOOOOO!"

As the train passed a man with a blue and white striped hat from an open window smiled and waved at Patsy. The big, black featherless goose bellowed louder,

"HONNNNNNNNNNNNNNNNNNNK, HONK! HONK!"

And again.

"HONNNNNNNNNNNNNNNNNNNK, HONK! HONK!"

Patsy was still howling as the train made its way down the tracks. Patsy had never seen anything that big or that fast before. He followed it howling down the tracks in a dead run.

"OWOOOOOOOOOOOOOOOOOOOOOOOOOOOOOO!"

He continued until the train disappeared.

It took Patsy Two Pie the rest of that day searching for the Big Black Canada Goose. It grew very late, and Dade sadly made his way home. He left his jacket where Patsy would easily find it. Attracted by the scent, he hoped to return in the morning to retrieve both it and Patsy Two Pie.

The following morning when Dade returned, he found Patsy Two Pie laying on his coat like he thought he might. Patsy was muddy and his fur was matted with burdocks.

Dade stroked Patsy's head and took him home. After a good brushing and a thorough washing, Patsy found a sunny spot close to the house and laid down. It troubled Eunice that Patsy passed by his dog dish without a sniff or a glance.

She first thought that he was just exhausted from his adventure but after a while Eunice grew more concerned. She tempted him with tender morsels that he liked. Nothing. She even baked a fresh blueberry pie and placed it near him. Patsy just lay about and was not interested.

The vet gave Patsy a thorough examination and reported that he could not find anything wrong with him. The vet had seen similar cases, but they were all associated with dogs being placed in a kennel while the owner was away.

"I would call it separation syndrome. You know it better by the more common term, lovesickness," the vet said.

In truth, what Patsy Two Pie suffered from was unrequited love. That is the unanswered love of one to another.

Trains are the lifeless creation of man. This particular one became Patsy Two Pie's mysterious sweetheart without a face or name, just an alluring golden voice.

Gradually, like all quick summer romances, eventually this too ran its course. Patsy's appetite improved. Keep in mind he's a beagle.

Time passed and Patsy aged. He went on to new adventures and found new loves. He sired several litters of beagle puppies that grew up and discovered adventures of their own.

In the years that followed, on warm summer days you could find Patsy Two Pies as in the old days lounging in a sunny spot licking, scratching, and sniffing. As he got older, he got grayer about the muzzle. His naps were longer and more frequent. Occasionally he would lick his lips, give a yip and suddenly out of nowhere bolt upright, wide eyed and give a deep and rich howl.

"OWOOOOOOOOOOOOOOOOOOOOOOOOOOOOO!"

Dade came to recognize something others seldom do; that love is a winged creature which leaves no footprints, save those that mark its passing on the heart.

As Patsy Two Pie slept away his senior years, he recalled his halcyon days when he ate blueberry pies, chased rabbits and a fleeting locomotive. To Patsy Two Pie it was a featherless Canada goose that captured his young imagination and with it his heart. And every so often, Patsy would articulate a princely howl.

Dade, his life-long friend would smile and think, "It's just an old beagle allowed to howl once more."

Passions come and go, some friendships lasting, but first loves are never forgotten. They will always prevail.

THE MAGIC OF CHRISTMAS

The holiday came on swiftly yet not unexpectedly. The mood was cheerful because it was Christmas, a time to pause for reflection and remembrance.

It was late one evening and shoppers were busy culling through the stores looking for that one special thing, for that one special person that would convey that one special message. You need not ask why because it was Christmas, a festive time.

You wouldn't have notice Mildred when she entered the store. Why would you? What with colorful Christmas lights flashing, Santa ringing a bell and soliciting donations, the loud, ever-present music, heralding the holiday appeal of Frosty, Rudolf, and Santa with their eyes of coal, red noses, and bellies that shook like bowls of jelly.

The older, white-haired woman in an ordinary hat, generic scarf and a run-of-the-mill overcoat simply went unnoticed.

But had one paused for a moment, they may have commented that something was oddly remarkable about her. It wasn't her tinted glasses or her elegant walking stick with her initials embossed in sterling or the quiet formality that attended her. No. What made her notable was her ordinary appeal and authentic charm that embodied the true spirit of Christmas. Mildred was genuine. She was commonplace. And that made her special in the veneer world of holiday glitz, glitter and rank commercialism. She simply walked quietly amid the holiday crowd and went unnoticed.

As Mildred shopped, she recalled her beloved childhood days of sledding, warm cinnamon cider, gingerbread cookies, the sweet smoky scent of applewood burning in the fireplace and most notably were those fragrant tangerines imported all the way from Morocco. Christmas produced a symphony of sights, sounds and smells that awakened and renewed the spirit.

For Mildred it was a time of recollection and reflection. Like a child tossing a pebble into a pool of neglected memories, her long-ago, sought-after days came rippling back from her past. Yes, for Mildred it was Christmas and Christmas was special.

Mildred stopped at the produce section which held a large stack of tangerines. Gently she selected one and squeezed it tenderly while raising it to her nose. It had the scent of the faded past.

"Ahhhh, stocking stuffer," she thought.

Carefully she selected several of the treasured orbs, one for each of her three grandchildren, her daughter, son-in-law and that someone special. Of course, the last one was for herself. She carefully placed them in her macramé shopping bag and continued on her way.

Next, Mildred located a large container of sweet cider and some cinnamon sticks to spice up the holiday elixir. Then she selected some fresh eggnog intended for the adults that would be braced with a spiced rum imported from a Caribbean isle. Finally, she made her way to the aisle where she found the section marked "Holiday Cards."

There was a vast array of colorful cards from which to select. Hundreds were neatly on displayed so she took her time. An instrumental version of "Come All Ye Faithful" was playing throughout the store as Mildred eyed one card of a manger scene with three men bearing gifts and bowing. The bold gilt lettering caught her eye and held her interest. It had "Christmas a renewal of Faith" gilded in bold lettering that caught her interest. Mildred picked up the card, opened it and started reading, "Goodness may not always be visible but very real." Mildred closed her eyes as the words quietly resonated. She felt a deep warm from within.

Opening her eyes, she continued reading. "Faith is like gold. Treasure it" and the words strangely illuminated and became encircled by a warm, radiant light. The Christmas card shifted gently in her hands and suddenly WHOOSH, a gust of frosty air blew strands of her fine white hair all about. Looking up, Mildred was momentarily surprised. There on a stool sat a portly man, gazing out a window as a red neon sign hummed above his head proclaiming, "The Stumble Inn." Clayton North was the proud proprietor and a public official. Locally, they said he was the perfect politician, a man for all seasons for he was for he was "frank and made a great deal of sense."

"Why," Mildred exclaimed, "It's the mayor."

~ ~ ~ ~ ~

It was a chilly December evening when an older man entered the Village Tavern. Stooped shouldered, he deceptively wore a worn brown overcoat like the humble frock of a monk. His hard eyes made contact with the bartender. With a slight jerk of his head, he indicated that he wished to have a private word in the other room. Sensing that he might be away from his station for an extended period, Clayton grabbed a clean glass and drew a fresh frothy beer from one of the taps. Renowned for tightfistedness, Clayton uncharacteristically slid the foaming glass to the lone customer, tapped the bar with a finger, smiled and said, "Merry Christmas, Jake."

"Well, what do we have here? A cold free one. Well, well, it must be Christmas."

Frowning at Jake, Clayton turned toward the kitchen without saying a word and followed the visitor into the kitchen and gently closed the door.

It was an unusual evening. Clayton, the proprietor and barkeep, rarely served a drink "on the house" unless some service was rendered like changing a keg of beer or running a personal errand. When he wasn't tending bar, Clayton would sit on his stool located at the entrance, observing the ebb and flow of his town through his window.

Clayton was mayor and outside his tavern window was his settlement. He viewed the small world as his private domain, fiefdom if you wish, and each person who passed by were one of his subjects, fittingly bequeathed to him by the good citizens who thrice elected him mayor to manage the town. It was an office that Clayton took seriously, and he managed with a small-town attentiveness. Just spit once and see if it went unnoticed by His Honor's keen and perceptive eye.

Being mayor of his small town, Clayton was tacitly granted the uncommon ascendancy to peer into the lives of its inhabitants. He was an engaged social voyeur. While mothers were telling their children to "mind your own business" it was he and Agnes, the postmistress, who conducted this dubious business without reproach.

He was Lord Mayor, and they were his vassals. Perched high on his barstool throne next to a large picture window, he minded over the comings and goings of the town outside his place of business. It was an obligation he took seriously. If his eyes (or ears) detected anything improper or amiss, Clayton would have a private word or two with the transgressor to rectify the wrong to see that there was not a recurrence.

When the world outside his window wobbled, Clayton made sure it returned to its symmetry. Clayton dispensed his duties as Lord Mayor with faithfulness and resolve. Perched upon his barstool with a keen nomadic eye, the village was properly served. All was well in both his and their world, both were one and the same.

The door to the tavern eased open and a second rather portly visitor entered without fanfare. Glancing around the near deserted taproom, he nodded to Jake, smiled and then sat in an empty seat at the end of the bar. A couple of minutes passed. Smiling, he asked Jake if someone was on duty.

"Yep. Clayton. He's conducting personal business in the backroom. This may take some time. What is it that you are having?"

"Whatever you're drinking will be just fine."

Going behind the bar, Jake poured a tall cold beer and slid it to the stranger. "What did you say your name was?"

"I didn't, but it's Chris. And you are . . . Jake, I take it."

"How did you know that?" The stranger pointed to the name on his work shirt. Jake glanced at his shirt pocket where his name "JAKE" was blazoned in red letters.

"Yes of course. Duh! For a minute I thought you were some sort of a mind reader.""

The stranger gave Jake a friendly smile.

"I've been told that before."

Jake returned to his chair and drank what was left of his beer. Taking a sip from the Christmas beer he turned to Chris.

"Play your cards right and Clayton - that's the owner - might give you a free one. But I doubt it. He's tight fisted. But who knows? Christmas is coming and you never can tell."

Chris nodded pleasantly in assent.

Jake paused rolling his eyes and added, "Whatever that means."

"You know it's one of those feel-good things. It strokes the heart strings."

"Feel good things? What do you mean?"

"Christmas is about buying and selling. People are eager to sell anything to those sold on that tale about wisemen, camels and shepherds. You know what I mean. Someone's always hawking something that you don't need but somehow you can't live without. Just name it and they'll be selling it."

"I take it you're not . . . excuse me for saying . . . sold on the story about the child and Bethlehem?"

"Myth. Like Santa Claus."

Chris smiled. "It's a pretty nice myth wouldn't you say?"

"Yeah, sure. But let me tell you something, er . . . Chris, the head is located over the heart. Not the other way around. I let the head do my thinking for me, not my heart. And my head's telling me that the little town of Bethlehem stuff is a catchy tune but a big nope."

"You seem certain about things."

"Not everything, just some things. Take the God thing. There's no proof that He even exists. Show me something tangible. Show me some proof. Something I can see and touch." He pauses long enough to take a swig of beer. "You can't. And do you want to know why? Because it doesn't exist."

"What is it that you believe in, Jake?"

"Science. Now there something you can see and touch. Science is like a watch; it is predictable, and you can depend on it."

"Like a watch, huh?"

"Take this watch here." Jake pointed to his wristwatch. "It was my dad's. It's a Swiss watch that he picked up in Europe after the war. It is accurate down to the second and it is something you can see and touch. Now that is something you can rely on. I couldn't live without it."

Chris extended his hand, "May I take a closer look at it?"

"Sure." Jake took off his watch and handed it to the rather rotund man. *If he bolts with my watch,* Jake thought, *he'd be easy to catch what with him being old and carrying all that weight.*

Chris looked at the watch and then at the clock over the cash register. Pointing to the bar clock he asked, "Is that time right?"

"No, that's bar time. Clayton always sets it ahead ten minutes to get everyone to drink up and get out by closing.

"That's a nice watch. Made in Switzerland, you say?" Jake nodded while he took another swig of his beer.

"They are the best watchmakers in the world," Jake said proudly. "People come from all over to buy their watches. It not only accurately tells the hour, the minute and the second, but it strikes on the hour and the half as well. Look here. It gives the date and the phases of the moon. Waterproof, too." Jake added with satisfaction, "Some of their watches have a lot more features. I couldn't live without it."

Chris looked the watch over carefully. "Pretty complicated stuff?"

Then Chris hit him with something unexpectedly.

"Jake, would it be reasonable for me to say that this watch has a specific purpose, yes?"

Jake glanced at the stranger thinking that perhaps Chris wasn't as sharp as Jake first thought.

"Like I say, it's really complicated and accurate, too, down to the second."

"What would you say if I told you that your eye is far more complicated than your watch?"

"I'd say where are you going with this?"

"Science. It's the science of logic. Don't take my word for it. Ask any doctor. They'll tell you it's true. The human eye has two million working parts. There is the cornea; pupil, lens, retina, and optic nerve that send visual messages upside down to the brain that then recreates the image so we can understand it. It can pick up 10 million colors. Now, that is complicated stuff."

Chris now had Jake's full attention. He continued.

"Now, using the science of logic, would you say that if someone looked at that watch, they would conclude that some skilled watchmaker created your watch?"

"He'd be a damn fool if he didn't."

"Follow with me for just a moment. Just suppose you and I were to take a trip on a rocket ship across the galaxy and we found a planet like ours with a vast ocean and coastline," Chris began.

"You want me to suppose that we take a trip to another galaxy and find a planet like Earth?"

"You got it. Now suppose as we were walking along the shoreline you happen to come upon something shiny in the surf. Reaching down you picked up an object just like your watch. After examining it, you would conclude that this was a complicated object, and it has a specific purpose. It could not have just washed up on the shore in and of itself. You would logically come to the conclusion that if there was a watch, there must have been a watchmaker. Yes?"

"Yes." Jake began to think that perhaps Chris might be a bit sharper and slightly odder than he first thought.

"Let us say we continue down the beach and we notice something rolling around in the surf. Bending down you pick up an eyeball."

Chris, Jake thought, had just advanced beyond the mere oddball into a full-fledged screwball.

"How about you pick up the eyeball?"

"Ok, I pick up the eyeball." Chris continued, "After careful examination and reflection you, me . . . we would logically conclude that if there is this watch there must be a watchmaker and if there is this eyeball, there must be an eyeball-maker. What I am suggesting," Chris paused, "You may call this eyeball-maker anything you wish. But whatever name you settle on, I'm suggesting that the name is God.

Jake placed the watch back on his wrist. Jake heard one of the voices in the back room become elevated. "No, I will not!"

Jake turned his attention to Chris saying, "Well that doesn't prove that there is a God, now does it?"

"No, but it does causes one to pause and think. How about a little bit more of science? You got iron in your blood, right? That is the same iron you will find scattered throughout the universe. That goes for oxygen, carbon, hydrogen, nitrogen calcium, and phosphorus, too. The science of physics tells us that you can't create matter, nor can you destroy it. Matter just changes. Scientists tell us that all the matter that exists in the universe was at one time in a large mass. Then something happened. And that something was a gigantic explosion. They call it The Big Bang Theory. So, if they are true, we are made of the same stuff that stars are made of, now, aren't we? But more importantly, who made it go Bang?"

Jake stared blankly at Chris then added, "My theory is . . . spontaneous combustion, I guess. It's my theory against your theory."

"What time is it? Chris asked.

"10:37."

"Sorry, I've got to go." Chris stood up and finished his beer and looked at Jake. "You know Jake, when I look around in the spring and I see the first flower or I smell the freshness that comes after a summer rain or hear the lone call of the whippoorwill at dusk, I cannot help but see the fingerprint of God. All the proof in the world will not make a believer of those who doubt and for those who believe, none is necessary."

Chris neatly stacked several coins next to his empty glass. "This is for the beer. Thanks for the company and the chat. I hope I didn't trouble you."

Walking to the door he turned. "God's hand is in everything, watches, worlds and whippoorwills. Somewhere in between there is an eyeball or two. Enjoy the rest of your evening. Merry Christmas." He then added, "Oh, what time did you say it was?"

Jake looked at his watch again. "It's now 10:38."

"You know Jake, it would be really difficult reading your watch if you didn't have an eye." Chris winked and then walked out the door and into the night.

Clayton and his mysterious visitor entered the taproom from the other room.

"I said NO!" Clayton barked. "I will not be a part of it. For Christ sake it is almost Christmas. Now get the hell out of here before I lose my temper."

The stranger with the worn overcoat glanced in Jake's direction without making eye contact. Pulling its collar about his neck, he departed in haste.

Clayton was still fuming as he paced behind the bar. He used the bar rag to re-clean the same section of the bar.

"Why that miserable son of . . .," he mumbled.

Whatever they were discussing sure got Clayton steamed. He poured another draft beer and placed it with in front of Jake and begrudgingly growled, "Merry Christmas."

That was two free beers in one night. Jake was tempted to remove the page from the leaf calendar and keep it for posterity, but he thought better of it. Who knows there might even be a third beer in the offering before the night was over?

"Do you know what that son of a . . . gun . . . wanted? He wanted me to evict a family who hasn't paid their rent in a couple of months. He said it was my duty to evict them. Duty like hell. I told him to get out or I wouldn't be responsible for what came next. Imagine that. And it is almost Christmas. It will be a cold day in hell before I become part of that sort of thing. Imagine . . . Christmas."

There was a long pause and then Clayton asked, "Whose glass is that?"

"Oh, some old guy named Chris. He just left."

"What did he want?"

"A drink, some company, I guess. Lonely fellow. Funny that you should mention it, but he rambled on about God being some kind of a scientist. Had his hand in everything.

"Who, God? Had his hand in everything you say?

"Yep, flowers, birds, the air. He even found time to make watches."

"God makes watches? I never heard such a thing. Did he look like he had too much to drink when he came in?

"Not any more than your usual customers."

"Strange fellow. Well, I hope he gets home safely. It's Christmas."

"He told me to have a Merry Christmas and left some change. I guess that means if there's anything left over you were to pour me another one. It's on Chris." Jake looked at Clayton and smiled. Clayton took the empty glass, washed it in the sudsy water under the bar, rinsed it and then set it on the stainless-steel tray to dry. He scooped up the change and counted it.

"Nope, he shortchanged me. See here's a bus token." Clayton slid the token to Jake.

Jake looked closely at the token. "Put your glasses on Clayton. That's no bus token. It's a five-dollar gold piece."

With that, Clayton snatched his glasses off the backbar to have a closer look.

"Well, I'll be darned. Jake, I think you're right."

Clayton squirted some seltzer water into a shot glass and dropped in the coin. They waited and after a sufficient amount of time the coin began to dazzle a bright yellow as gold will do.

"Well, I'll be. Merry Christmas, Jake."

Clayton slid another frothy cold one in front of Jake as he stared back in disbelief. That made three free drinks from the tight-fisted Lord Mayor-barkeep.

"Yeah, and a Merry Christmas to you, too, Clayton." He paused. "You know Clayton, if this continues, you might make a believer out of me yet."

Clayton didn't appreciate the humor and glared back at Jake, who was the only one smiling.

~ ~ ~ ~ ~

The store was playing a Christmas favorite, "Oh Holy Night," in the background as Mildred smiled and placed the card in her satchel. She scanned the Christmas Card selections until another card caught her eye. Drawing it from the display, a second card hidden behind it gently floated to the floor at her feet. Bending down, she picked it up as the choir sang . . .

"the stars are brightly shining ...". The card had a pleasant picture of a night scene where a bright star was shining down on shepherds in a field with their flock. Its message was "Christmas is a Time of Hope." Opening the card, Mildred continued reading, "Light shines brightest when it is the darkest." Thoughtfully she closed her eyes in contemplation.

Over the store speaker a woman's voice announced, "Attention shoppers. For the next twenty minute this evening there will be reduced pricing on hand tools in the hardware department and in gardening there will be half off the listed price on freshly dug fox holes.

Mildred felt an icy wind slap her face like a handful of stinging nettles. Startled, she opened her eyes and found herself standing in a fresh deposit of fallen snow. An army jeep zipped past her with four scruffy looking soldiers who were in need of a shave and a good hot bath. Mildred wasn't sure but one of them looked like her brother.

It was December 20, 1944, and the Germans broke through the American lines along a 75-mile front of the Ardennes with 200,000 troops and nearly 1,000 heavy tanks. The German thrust was like wading through fields of grain, trampling all before them. The Nazi juggernaut sent the untested green troops, fresh from the States, into full retreat. The lack of experience, not personal courage, resulted in the collapse.

This midwinter offensive became known as the Battle of the Bulge.

Smitty had a mere eight months in the army with less than eight hours of combat experience when he found himself sharing a fox hole with a tall Texan. Infantry units shattered by the initial Nazi thrust were hastily formed. Those not killed, wounded or captured were assigned to defensive positions in and about the Belgian countryside.

The surrounding foxholes were loosely organized; and like Smitty came from outfits that had been overrun and piecemealed into a nascent perimeter. Though ad hoc and ripe with uncertainty, these units were instructed to defend at all costs. Several roads converged at a small town named Bastogne and were crucial to American resistance.

"Hey Smitty," drawled the tall Texan. "No winter gear?"

"They said we would get some when we got to the front. That was two weeks ago."

"Temperature's droppin.' Gonna be mighty cold t'night. Yessiree. A mighty cold one."

Smithy's wet leather boots and field jack were inadequate for winter warfare. What he needed were the rubber boots and a woolen overcoat like Tex had.

"Where'd you get the wool coat and rubber boots?"

"The same place you'll get yours. Off a one who don't need it no more ... if you know what I mean. Better hope he's your size. This fella was as big as a phone booth. It could fit me, and the missus and I'd still have room."

Smitty shivered in the cold.

"I'll be right back. Need to move around a bit to get some of the blood moving."

"Get shot and there'll be plenty of blood a moving'."

Smitty came back about twenty minutes later dragging a mound of spruce branches.

"Psst ... Tex. Here. Find a place in the fox hole where it will do us some good. I'll be back in a jiffy," and then Smitty slipped away into the soft grayness of the approaching dusk. He returned with a second load of spruce boughs and began to fashion a primitive canopy over their fighting position.

"It wouldn't stop a bullet or an artillery shell, but it may help with the snow." Smitty stood back admiring his work and then crawled into the foxhole lined with evergreen.

"Ain't much but call it home," Tex added with admiration. Time passed as night neared. "Hey Smitty, is it the 24th?"

"Yup. Tomorrow's Christmas."

Another period of silence passed. They then noticed a series of flashes to the east followed by a series of low distant rumblings.

"Someone's catching hell over there."

"But who? Them or us." Smitty reached into his field jacket and took out his last piece of Wrigley's peppermint gum his mom had mailed in her last package from Upstate New York.

Breaking the stick of gum in two, he offered half to Tex. "Here, Merry Christmas."

Tex unwrapped his half piece and placed it into his mouth, savored the taste and began to chew.

A minute passed and he added, "You Yanks aren't all that bad."

There was a rustle just outside their fighting position. Tex grabbed his M1 and leaned forward, alert. Smitty slowly grabbed a hand grenade and slipped his finger through the circular ring.

"Psst . . . Smitty . . . Psst . . . Tex. It's me, Polanski."

Raising a challenge, Tex cried out "Halt." He paused then growled the password, "Tigers." Clicking the safety off from his M1, he nervously waited. "Damn it I said Tigers." Raising his rifle into the firing position a response immediately came.

"Detroit."

"Who won the MVP in the American League?"

"Newhouser . . . the southpaw from Detroit."

"Advance."

"I thought it was Spud Chandler," Smitty whispered to Tex, "from the Yankees."

"That was last year. This year was Hal Newhouser. He won 29 games with an ERA of 2.22. You Yanks only remember Yankee stuff like Babe Ruth."

"A lefty too and a pretty good one at that," Smitty boasted.

"Pipe down and listen up you guys," Sergeant Polanski began. "G2 says Jerry might hit us again tonight. Be alert. Oh, Doc asked me to see if you guys had any medical supplies?"

Tex handed over his bandage.

"And you Smitty?"

"I gave Doc mine this morning. Here's a sulfur packet. It's the only one I got."

"Well, I suggest then, that you don't get shot," Sergeant Polanski grinned.

"You're a real comedian Sarg. A regular Bud Abbot and Lou Costello?"

"Cozy little place you've got here." Sarg said admiringly. "A real Waldorf Astoria. Got room for another?"

Before either of them could say no, Sgt. Polanski announced, "Here's a replacement. His name is Bradway from Cleveland. Be sure one of you guys stay awake. Oh, here's a chocolate bar. Split it among yourselves."

He handed Tex a 4 oz. D ration bar that was a mixture of Hershey chocolate, sugar, cocoa butter, skim milk powder and oat flour.

Tossing an opened pack of Camels to Smitty he added, "Merry Christmas and be sure you don't let Jerry catch you napping or taking a cigarette break."

Then he quietly crawled away.

"And a jolly Noel to you, too, Sarg. What is needed here, Tex, is a wise man and what do they send us? A wise guy."

Turning to his new companion, Smitty immediately noticed that Bradway was dressed in a warm woolen overcoat.

"D rats are like chewing on boot leather," he groused. "But you'll get used to it." Taking out his trench knife he carved off three pieces of the rigid chocolate and handed one to Tex and the other to Bradway from Cleveland.

"I'd rather snack on a boiled potato. At least I'd be warmer. DAMN. IT IS COLD!"

The chocolate was bitter and bland, but it served the immediate need.

Tex took a bent Camel from the crinkled pack of cigarettes. He straightened it with his soiled thumb and index finger, ducked below the lip of the fox hole and lit it. Taking a deep, long drag into his lungs; he tipped his head back with delight. He took two more quick drags, nudged Smithy's leg and passed it to him.

"Here, this might warm you up."

Smitty sat amid the sweet, scented boughs and took a long drag. It was followed by another and another and then again another. He would have remained content where he sat had it not been for Bradway snapping his fingers. Like two sprinters exchanging a baton, Smitty carefully handed him the glowing nub as he rose to resume his vigil into the dark overcast night.

Just then they heard the sound of a mortar going off from behind their lines. It was followed by the incandescent glow from a flare to their immediate front. Instantly, the night became like day with shadows scampering about in their field of fire. Eerily, the flare created phantom animation of elusive shadows as it oscillated beneath its small parachute.

All three looked up at the glowing orb. Smitty whispered in awe, "People that walked in darkness have seen a great light.'"

"What's that supposed to mean," muttered Bradway?

"It comes from the Bible, Isaiah chapter 9, verse 2. The prophet foretold the coming of the Messiah, the anointed one. You know Jesus." He finished the passage with, "'And they that dwelt in the land of the shadow of death, upon them hath the light shines.'"

"Now that you mention it, it looks a little like the Star of Bethlehem," drawled the Texan.

"Very fitting I'd say," ribbed Bradway.

"How so," asked Tex.

"What we have here is Christmas Eve, there's the Star and someone in this foxhole smells like a Camel." Both Tex and Smitty sniffed their armpit.

"Tex, when would you say you last took a shower," complained Smitty.

"What day is it?"

"Saturday, I think."

"Last Monday. Why?"

"It's got to be you then, because I took a shower just last Tuesday."

Tex took another sniff under his arm. "Nope, it's you Smitty. I smell more like a herd of sheep."

That launched the three into a round of snorts and giggles. The unexpected lightheartedness added momentary warmth to a cold unforgiving night.

As the night progressed it got more wintery. It began to lightly snow. Smitty stomped his feet and complained he couldn't feel them anymore.

"Your problem is that your feet are wet. Here put these on."

Bradway reached into his shirt and handed Smitty a dry set of second-hand socks.

"Take your wet ones off and put them under your shirt – next to your body. It'll keep 'em warm and dry. Change them every hour or so."

"I can't take your last pair of socks," Smitty argued.

"Worry not. I've got another pair. The fellow that was wearing these ..."

". . . I know," Smitty interjected, "he didn't need them anymore. Whew wee. That guy must have been part goat?"

Taking off his boots and wet socks, Smitty rubbed his raw toes and then put on the dry soiled socks.

'Dry aren't they?"

"Warm too. Thanks."

"The guy sends you season's greetings."

A little after twelve the snow picked up. There was still the flashing and rumbling off in the distance. Hell was assembling a deadly gathering. From time to time a lone flare would ignite overhead and the sinister sky would light up with a radiant glow. Unlike Tex and Bradway, who wore wool overcoats, Smitty suffered terribly in his pitiful clothing. Both had the warm woolen collars drawn close to their faces.

"Hey Tex, be a sport. Why don't you let me wear your overcoat for a while?"

"Cause fools don't run in my family."

Smitty stomped his feet and shivered, wearing a mask of misery and utter despair. Several minutes passed when Tex spoke.

"Tell you what Yank. This here coat is big 'nough for two." He opened his jacket as an invitation. "You just latch right onto ole Tex's waist and share in some of this here Waco warmth."

Friendship has a way of separating men from their manliness. The heartfelt offer was accepted. And on this bleak winter night, while exposed to the dangers of combat; these two soldiers shared in a rare camaraderie of note. It was the lasting solidarity of true friendship, bound together by a simple woolen overcoat.

In the days ahead there would be more brutal fighting but for that one night on December 24th at Bastogne, Belgium there was a coregency of the heart and mind between friends.

The night would be notable for there were three wise guys, sharing stale chewing gum, bitter chocolate and a crumpled cigarette. Huddled in a fetid fox hole, reminiscent of the earthy scent of camels and sheep and goats; they exchanged gifts of dirty socks, an oversized woolen coat and an abiding friendship. All three were quietly praying for the same thing; that come morning there would be for them a tomorrow.

"Hey Smitty…Tex. Would you like me to call room service in the morning and order the two of you love birds breakfast in bed?"

"Shut up Bradway. You're an idiot," his companions instantly shot back in rapid succession.

"And a very merry Christmas to the both of you, too."

~ ~ ~ ~ ~

Throughout the store Bing Crosby was crooning, "White Christmas," as Mildred stood in the aisle humming along. Centering her attention back to the Christmas card, she finished reading the passage, "Peace on Earth, Good will towards man." That, she thought, would do nicely, and she then placed it with the other card in her shopping bag.

With some hesitation Mildred browsed through the vast selection looking for a third card. Pausing at one she muttered, "I think I'll … no, no not that one."

She was in the strange habit of talking to herself when confronted with indecision. Mildred had reached the age where others overlooked the practice. It was a weakness of children and seniors but drew neither alarm nor mockery.

Johnny Mathis started singing the lyrics to the "Sleigh Ride," a Christmas standout as fellow shoppers hummed along while stepping gayly to its lively beat.

"Just hear those sleigh bells jingling Ring-ting-tingling too…"

Dithering over a card, Mildred muttered to herself, "How about this one?" But no, it was too late, for her resolve had weakened. "That won't do either," she mumbled. The song continued with the pleasant sound of sleigh bells in the background.

"Come on its lovely weather for a sleigh ride together with you."

And as if someone were reading her mind, a stranger walked up to Mildred and said, "Here's one. It has a pleasant ring to it."

When Mildred turned to say thank you, no one was there except the spirited voice of Johnny Mathis singing,

"There's a happy feeling nothing in the world can buy . . ."

The card she held was a timeless scene of a sleigh gliding over snow towards a well-lit country manor. It read, "Merry Christmas. Peace, love, and goodwill." Mildred opened the card and the inscription inside read, "No one has ever become poor because of charity." Mildred closed her eyes deep in thought. "Peace . . . love . . . goodwill . . . It has a pleasant ring to it," she thought. Sleigh bells jingled lively in the background as Johnny Mathis sang,

"As we pass around the coffee and the pumpkin pie . . ."

Mildred musing came to an abrupt end with the sharp ringing of a cash register and the sweet scent of freshly brewed coffee. Before her stood a man and woman. They had just finish paying for breakfast at the Blue Stone Café. Next to the cash register was a sign that said, "Christmas Breakfast Free. Call for reservations" and then listed the business number. Tomorrow was Christmas. It was the same sign that had been posted prior to Christmas for the past four years.

"How was everything," asked the hostess?

"Very good, especially your coffee. Do you put something special in it," the man asked.

"Columbia grows the beans. We add the love." They laughed.

Paying his bill, the man pointed to the sign next to the cash register, "That's very nice. It's got to take a lot of work and take you away from your family on Christmas."

"Not really. This is a family run business. We all help out on Christmas and spend the rest of the day and all of the next together as a family."

Curiosity prompted him to ask the hostess why?

"Some people ask the same question, Why? It's a reasonable question and it requires a straightforward reply. My nine-year-old daughter thinks that people probably wouldn't' understand, but I tell them anyway. I tell them, we do it because we want to. It is as simple as that. When I get a blank stare I add, 'It's a feel-good thing.' That seems more understandable to them."

Just then the phone rang. The hostess excused herself, picked up the phone and in a cheerfully voice asked, "Blue Stone Café. How may I help you?"

The man remained close to the hostess station counting his change. He could overhear a young man on the line ask, "Are you serving breakfast Christmas morning? And is it free?"

"Yes, we are serving a free breakfast on Christmas morning. How many will be in your party?"

There was a pause, and the man could hear the man on the line ask in a raised voice someone with him, "How many? The lady wants to know how many."

In the background an older man voice was overheard, "Are you SURE it is free?" The young man politely asked the hostess again.

"If we come, will we have to pay for anything? I mean, we don't want to appear ungrateful but is there some kind of a gimmick or something?"

Still doubtful, the older man pressed the younger man in the background, "Free you say. Are you sure?"

The hostess replied, "There are no gimmicks. You simply make the reservations and come Christmas morning, breakfast will be waiting for you and your party. There is no charge. Breakfast is free."

She eventually convinced the young man despite the continued inquiring from the older man in the background, "Are you sure? Are you sure?"

The younger man reserved a table for Christmas breakfast for a party of seven under the name Otis Starks.

On Christmas morning the party of Starks arrived early and patiently waited in the cold. They were greeted with a smile and escorted to their assigned table. The older man walked with a cane. He tilted his head with his free hand cupped around his ear whenever someone said something of interest. It was apparent he was hard of hearing. He was likely the younger man's or perhps the woman's father.

The younger man, Otis, brought his family. The woman, Lille was about his age while the four children (three girls and a boy in descending order) looked to be separated by two years of age starting with Sissy who was eight, Emily who was six, Maggie who was four and finally Buster, the toddler who appeared to be two. They followed their mother closely in a group like a brood of chicks. Their clothes were loosely fitting, slightly threadbare, neat and clean.

The two men were clean shaven with hair slicked back and noticeably in need of a trim. The girls were outfitted in colorful dresses that were outdated. Their hair was neatly assembled into ponytails, braids and pig tails. A bright red ribbon, the kind found at the Five and Dime, was gathered into a curlicue bouquet and meticulously fastened to each of the girls' hair by a loving, maternal hand. It was the crowning touch before public exhibition. It was the kind of suitable presentation fitting for the common man.

Lille wore a common non-descript coat that seemed designed more for warmth than fashion. On the lapel she had arranged the same hallmark red bouquet except hers was adorned with a costume jeweled bauble that glittered when she moved. Its impact would have gone generally unnoticed were it not for the seven assembled and this special occasion.

The Starks were seated at a table tucked in the corner of the room. The young girls gazed about in awe as if it were their first visit to a fair as their mother seated them one by one. Buster sat in a child's seat next to his mother who was watchful and close at hand. When he grabbed the tablecloth and began to tug, Lille gently removed his hand and placed a spoon in his reach. It wasn't long before he began drumming away with no discernible cadence.

The menu had a fixed fare for the occasion. It consisted of eggs with pancakes, home fries, toast, slice of melon with bacon, ham or sausage, orange or apple juice, coffee, tea or milk.

It took some extra time to order because of indecision but Lille, who had the final say, sorted things out. The girls became antsy. They squirmed. They giggled. They beamed at one another with joy because it was all new, different, and felt special … because it was Christmas.

Lille looked at Otis with soft eyes and smiled. The older man, a born spectator, looked around and made comments about nothing of importance to no one in particular. It was obvious he was delighted, too.

When their meal arrived, it was as if the heavens opened, and a flight of angels had descended. The girls' wonderment wouldn't be bridled. They wiggled and wiggled and then wiggled some more.

Never was such a feast more suitable for the little ones as a meal such as this. There were eggs with pancakes, home fries, toast, a slice of melon with bacon, ham or sausage, orange or apple juice, coffee, tea or milk.

The waitress placed a container of creamers and sugar for the tea and coffee on the table with an assortment of jellies, syrup and butter. REAL BUTTER. Lille looked closely at the syrup. It was REAL MAPLE SYRUP. The kind fomred from the Sugar Maple sap she and her father gathered in the early spring. Lille's eyes moistened as she reflected.

"Can I get you anything else," asked the waitress?

Lille, containing her joy, shook her head from side to side and whispered, "No. Thank you, ma'am. This is quite enough."

The waitress exchanged a smile and left the family to their meal.

The children were prepared to delve right in were it not for the stern look from their father.

"There'll be grace said at this table."

And then he bowed his head, laced his fingers in prayer and paused for the rest to do likewise. Otis glanced about the table. When he was satisfied all were in compliance, he began, "Bless us, O lord, for this thy gifts …"

Murmuring in unison, his charge and understudies followed his lead with their heads bowed and eyes closed. Lille ended grace with "Amen." It was repeated around the table. Otis smiled his approval and then nodded to those assemble to begin.

And thus, they did, with the proper restrictions. Napkins in the lap. No elbows on the table. No speaking with mouths full. Please and thank you would be generously applied. Spillage would be considered a major offense save Buster, who was still exploring that untamed stage.

In their delight the Starks' clan didn't notice those that followed. Many were older couples or families that wore the mark of the common man. However, there was one couple that pulled into the parking lot in their expensive import. Their dress seemed out of place, especially the gold and diamond jewelry. When shown their table, they requested another more noted yet apart from the others.

Ordering became lengthy and complicated. They inquired if the breakfast was gluten free, with free ranged eggs, smoked Canadian bacon, and Earl Grey Tea. When they were not satisfied with the response, they said that what was offered would have to do.

They did manage to get their eggs poached on toast with a glass of tomato juice with a stalk of celery of which they promptly added salt, pepper, and hot sauce from the tray of condiments. They quickly produced two 1.7 oz mini bottles of Grey Goose vodka to "freshen it up a bit." Before departing they placed the left-over in plastic container for later, "Just in case we get hungry."

As the family departed the older man remained behind saying, "I know this is free but ... I would like for you to have this. He placed a worn dollar bill into her hand, smiled and quietly departed.

The sign next to the cash register read, "Christmas Breakfast Free. Some people may not understand why. However, it was done for the same reasons why most folks are compelled to do the unnecessary things they do.

They do it because they want to. The party of seven paid for Christmas breakfast with a simple gesture and in that gesture rests the answer to the question why.

~ ~ ~ ~ ~

The melody and lyric to "Jingle Bells" played over the store sound system as Mildred made her way to the checkout counter. It filled her with holiday spirit and added strength and spring to her stride and step. Checking her list and checking it twice, Mildred made sure she purchased that what she needed.

As the clerk was ringing up Mildred's purchase, she spied a lovely, organized display of bright red poinsettias. It was labeled "Christmas Star." That was the expression her late husband used when he first brought one home.

Pleasantly addressing the bagboy, Mildred asked, "Young man, would you please select a poinsettia for me?"

The teen, who aimed to please, hastened to the poinsettia display asking, "Which one would you like?"

"You pick one," she said. "I always place trust in the merit of a man's good taste."

After some thought, the fair-haired youth touched one and glanced at Mildred. She smiled and then nodded. Beaming, he placed it with her other purchases on the counter and was rewarded with a silver coin for his trouble.

"Most insist it's a poinsettia," he said, "but some call it a Christmas Star. Look," he said pointing to the accompanying card. "It's all explained right there."

"Thank you for that bit of information. You have all the makings of store manager in you," she said and smiled again as she departed.

Exiting the store, Mildred was greeted by flashing lights, Santa and some robust music with holiday charm. Reaching into her purse she selected a bill and placed it into the slot of Santa's red kettle.

She was greeted with a "Thank you" and a "Merry Christmas to you and yours."

Grinning, Mildred politely returned with, "Likewise, Santa."

Taking a few steps toward the parking lot, Mildred made an attempt to orient herself with her car. A store announcer interrupted the pleasant holiday musical score to inform prospective buyers of a storewide sale.

"Attention shoppers! For the next twenty minutes there will be an additional ten percent off the sticker price of all merchandise purchased in our jewelry department."

Mildred's attention was drawn above to a clear raven sky that was bejeweled with a seemingly limitless display of unending stars. They stretched from horizon to horizon with a display of endless stars.

"The heavens have quite a lovely collection of gems of its own," Mildred thought. "Priceless. And free."

Mildred located her car after her third attempt and safely negotiated the troublesome traffic home.

In the days that were to follow there would be the eleventh-hour tree-trimming, decorations, baking and the rush to wrap presents. Mildred would scour the bathrooms, place clean bed linens in the spare bedrooms and complete her final touches for her expected guests. There would be her daughter and son-in-law in one bedroom with her three grandchildren (ages four, six and eight) in another. They were Mildred's pride and joy and she consigned them pet names: Cookie, Cup Cake and Coco. In return Mildred was christened simply Nana.

There would be freshly made gingerbread cookies and warm cinnamon cider to be consumed on Christmas Eve. It was what Mildred referred to as "core memories."

The stocking would be hung from the fireplace mantel each by name. There would be one for her daughter, Phyllis and her son-in-law, Bill. Next to them would be three stocking with the names of Cookie, Cup Cake and Coco. Each of these would be stuffed with a generous collection of an assorted seasonal trinkets.

Three cryptic Christmas cards would top each grandchild's stocking and inside they would discover a crisp, newly minted five-dollar bill – a king's ransom for those so young.

But at the very top, a fresh tangerine that had come all the way from Morocco would be wedged into the stocking.

"Mmm, the unmistakable scent of Christmas."

Beneath the tree in the morning would be a battery of presents. Why? Because it was Christmas. To avoid a tangle of sibling rivalry, Nana would ensure each child would receive the same number of presents because it was certain not to go unnoticed by those so young.

This would all come to pass, however, in the days to come. For the moment, Mildred decided to relax. Taking a seat in her lounge chair, she picked up the card that came with the poinsettia. On the front it said, "Christmas Star." She opened it and continued reading.

"The Magic of Christmas

"Soon a shadow will move train-fashion across the star lit sky. It will appear from out of the north and move its way south, zigzagging its way east and west. Swiftly it will descend below the horizon and return airborne within the blinking of the eye. It would seem to spirit its way about the black winter night by the power of a wizard's chant. Whatever it is that makes the shadow move, it is not believed by most grown-ups, nor is it fully understood by children. But its reality and splendor can only be explained through the eyes of a child as the – The Magic of Christmas.

"For those who believe in the Magic, would not see a funny old man riding across the sky but would see a messenger. The messenger and his journey are a story that has been told and retold for two thousand years. This is a tale that comes in many forms. For some it might be a story about reindeer, elves and a portly old man who for one evening is transformed into an angel in white. While for others it is about camels and wise men whose faith directs them by a bright distant star. Yet, both journeys will end before a child and gifts would be exchanged, bringing happiness and joy.

"The expensive gifts of the Magi were meager compared to the precious gift that they received in return. For on that day the child gave to them the true meaning of Christmas. It didn't come in a box, nor was it wrapped in fine ribbons. Yet, when they left the gift went with them and they handled it as gently as it had been given. They would share it throughout their land.

"It was years later that an enchanted old man with white hair and beard happened upon this gift. He was so taken by this gift that he decided to share it with the world. In his humble shop to the far north, he made toys with a special addition. Placed within each toy was a message that came from an ancient time. It was the Magic of Christmas. Each year around this time, the crazy old man boards his sled and rides the ebon currents of

the night to bring a message in the form of gifts.

"On Christmas Eve, when you look into the night sky, those with a sharp mind and a keen sense of sight will not see an old man and reindeer but wise men and camels crossing the black sands of time. They bear a message from a time of great darkness, and it speaks of hope.

"For those who don't understand, rise early on Christmas morning. There beneath the green boughs and amid the pine scented room you will find it. For delicately encased in the shinning eyes of a child is the Magic of Christmas. Perceive and protect it, and you will be the wiser man."

~ ~ ~ ~ ~

Before Mildred went to bed that evening, she placed the Christmas Star on the fireplace mantle. Next to it she placed a card addressed to her late husband that simply read, "Leon."

Mildred made a mental note to add another stocking next to the others. In it she would place some seasonal trinket from their past Christmases with a note she would write, the contents of which would be known but to her. And of course, a fresh tangerine that came all the way from Morocco would be stuffed in the very top of the stocking. They would both enjoy it even though he was not there.

As Mildred dimmed the lights before going to bed, she surveyed the room with a final glance. There was the Christmas Star with its red leaves reflected vibrantly in the mirror behind it. Beside it was the card with the name of her late husband printed on the envelope in reverse. It read "noel."

Mildred smiled and whispered, "Likewise, Leon."

For Mildred, Christmas had come swiftly, yet not unexpectedly. She was cheerful because it was Christmas and that was a time to reflect and remember.

Like the little girl from her past, Mildred glanced under the green boughs of her Christmas tree looking for a present that bore her name that held one special thing, from that one special person that conveyed that one special message. She had little doubt that it will be there come Christmas morning.

When Mildred rises early on Christmas morning, she will not find one, but three presents. Each will be delicately encased in the shining eyes of her grandchildren. However, for Nana, that would all have to wait till Christmas morn.

NIGHT VISITOR

The chimes of an antique wall clock from a room downstairs tolled the early morning hour. It was one a.m. Spontaneously, as if given the gift of life by a mystical hand, the pendulum was set in motion. Reinvigorated, the ancient time piece found a youthful tempo and beat with a steady cadence.

Tick-tock, tick-tock, tick-tock …

High above in the evening sky, an autumn moon slowly emerged from a broken bank of thick clouds. A soothing shaft of light entered the upstairs nursery through the window casement. It appeared as if a veiled hand had unexpectedly ignited the wick of a bedside candle. The beam flickered and then blossoming into full incandescence as the room at the top of the stairs became flush with light. Faintly, the voice of a young child began singing.

"Pony boy, pony boy, won't you be my pony boy."

Softly his voice trailed off.

There was a momentary lull in the melody and then the song began anew as the now animated moon suddenly took refuge behind the nearest cloud. In an adjacent bedroom a woman stirred. Her bed springs squeaked as she pitched to secure a more comfortable position. Drawing the covers closer to her chin, she listened passively as the young boy continued to sing.

"Pony boy, pony boy, won't you be my pony boy."

The child's voice trailed off into the cool September night and for a moment the melody departed, and amnesty filled the room. Like the vortex of a gentle whirlpool the child's words journeyed inward and drifted around and around in the woman's listless head. Amusingly, her unbridled imagination took hold as an inner voice asked,

"Do you remember those words? Yes. Of course, you do."

The voice joined in singing, "Pony boy, pony boy, won't you be my pony boy."

The words emerged like the long-forgotten faces of childhood friends. Adrift, the lyrics came full circle reciting those words.

"Pony boy, pony boy, won't you be my pony boy.

Pony boy, pony boy, won't you be my pony boy."

Like a lone hawk slowly gyring in a dark canyon, Barbara felt herself slowly slip into the dreamy abyss. In her wistfulness there appeared a beautiful woman with red hair in a rocking chair. With her was a young child dressed in a pink laced dress positioned on her lap. Soothingly, they rocked back and forth, singing the mellow tune.

Unconscientiously Barbara smiled. The woman's voice was soothing, distant, detached. Puzzlingly, the woman's voice seemed familiar, yet elusive. Rocking to the song's gentle rhythm the two sang, "Don't say no, 'cause here we go, riding down the lane."

The dream-child giggled and then joined in the singing, "Giddy-up, giddy-up, my pony boy."

Laughing, the young girl leaned closer and gave the red-haired woman a caress. The song was about to start anew when Barbara stirred.

"That song was familiar," she thought. Long ago she had sung that very tune as a child. She recalled that it was a time full of warmth and innocence. And because dreams allow for the freedom of untamed flight, Barbara dreamed happily on, soaring away on the warm currents of her childhood memories like her dream-hawk to the sanctuary of a distant and more innocent time.

The clock continued into the night. Tick-tock, tick-tock, tick-tock. Barbara's opened her eyes, and she was again back in her own bed. Jed, her two-year-old son, was still singing.

"Pony boy, pony boy, won't you be my pony boy. Don't say no ... here we go ... riding down the lane ..."

"Isn't that odd," she thought, "that Jed should be singing at this time of night?" Barbara felt young again and enjoying the moment she quietly listened to the voice of her son singing from across the hall.

"Giddy-up, giddy-up . . . my pony boy." Wistfully she thought, "Um, that's funny, I don't recall having taught Jed those lyrics."

The clicking sound of a rocker prompted Barbara to rise from her bed. Folding back the covers, she slid her legs over the side. Blindly she placed her feet into the openings of her slippers. Donning her bathrobe, she walked into the faded hallway.

Across the way was the nursery that for the past two years had become her son's room. She was familiar with it for it had been her room as a child. Except for the printed wallpaper and a fresh coat of paint, the room had remained comparatively unchanged.

From beneath the door the moonlight glimmered, and the room seemed to come to life. She heard the gently click-clicking of wood on wood and a hushed voice. Nudging the door slightly open, Barbara noticed the image of a child reflected in the mirror. The young boy was gently pitching back and forth on a rocking horse. Lightly, he was singing to himself.

"Pony boy, pony boy, . . . be my pony boy."

As if on cue a cool gust of autumn wind playfully whipped the white nursery curtains back and forth against the half-opened window, prompting night shadows to scurry about.

Entering the room, Barbara walked to the rocking horse and began stroking the boy's strawberry hair with affection. Delicately, she raised Jed up from his rocking horse and placed him into the folds of the sheets. Placing the covers over him, she detected the scent of lavender. "Um fresh sheets" she thought and then tucked the loose covers between the mattress and the box springs.

"Good night, Jed. Please go to sleep"

"Go to sleep, pony boy," he insisted.

"Ok. Goodnight and please go to sleep, Pony boy."

Rolling onto his side Jed mumbled, "Night mommy," and then closed his eyes.

Turning to leave, Barbara thought she noticed movement in the distant corner of the nursery. Just then the moon re-emerged from behind a cloud to reveal an antique rocker slightly pitching back and forth in the dark recess of the room. A rogue gust of wind simultaneously tossed the folds of the curtains, prompting phantom shadows to scurry eerily about on the colorful wallpaper.

Dismissively she muttered, "Why you old fool, it is only the wind."

Relieved, she drew the window sash down until it was slightly open and then quietly slipped into the hallway, leaving the nursery door slightly ajar. Returning to her room, she slid between the sheets and drew herself into a comfortable position. Closing her eyes Barbara tried to fall back to sleep, yet that tune haunted her. The song played over and over in her mind.

"I wonder ... where ... Jed ... learned ..." Those were her last conscious thoughts before she fell asleep.

The chimes of the downstairs clock stuck two tolling the early morning hour and it continued with its rhythmic tick-tocking. Barbara abruptly bolted upright. The dining room clock had revived her memory with greater clarity. She had a heightened account of the origins of the song. As a young girl, she and her mother would sit rocking in an old wooden rocker, singing bedtime songs. Pony boy had been one of her mother's favorites.

Glancing across the hall, she saw a pair of shadows dancing about the nursery floor. The performers were a creation of the moonlight and the curtains which lightly twisted and swirled about in the evening air.

"Where could Jed have learned that song," she thought? "I don't recall having sung it to him. Where then, could he have learned it? The only person besides me that knew that tune was ..." A tingling sensation engulfed her, and she shudder. "My Mother . . . No, that couldn't be. She died before Jed was born."

The sound of the rhythmic clicking of the antique rocker returned. Barbara hopped out of bed and proceeded slipperless to Jed's room. Opening the door, she glanced quickly toward where he slept. His bed was empty. Across the room in the far corner of the nursery was the source of the steady click-clicking. Perched high on the old wooden rocker was Jed rocking back and forth. All the while he was grinning.

"Pony boy," he giggled. "Pony boy."

~ ~ ~ ~ ~

The next day Barbara entered the Ye Olde Village Clock Works with a grip on Jed, wriggling beside her. The establishment had a first-rate reputation for clock repair. A white haired, bespeckled gentleman eyed the time-worn Seth Thomas wall clock with care.

"You say this clock has remained in your family for quite some time and it hasn't run in a while?"

"Yes, for the past few years. You see my mother passed away on a Wednesday and I never took the trouble to rewind it. Silly, isn't it," she said nervously. "It may seem strange to you, but it has remained sort of a . . . memorial to her. It hasn't worked since then. That is," she paused, "until just the other night."

"Silly? Not at all," he said while opening the back panel of the old clock. Gazing into the dark, dusty interior he continued. "Seems a fitting tribute I'd say. A nineteenth century concept by nature. It was quite common back then for folks to stop a clock when a loved one passed away. You know, as a memorial so to speak."

Raising his head he added, "Then again, it's not unusual for these old clocks to start up again. Reactivate, I mean. Sometimes a passing truck will rumble past the house, creating a vibration that will set the pendulum in motion. The pendulum oscillates, the mechanisms move and BINGO, you've got yourself a nice working time piece again."

Squinting into the aged interior, the white-haired man became lost in thought. Barbara became preoccupied as well. That was a chance for an unattended child to wander off. f

With all its splendid sounds and endless motions, the universe of clocks was attractive to a child. Some clocks clicked and ticked while others gonged and chimed. The shop was a cosmos of disorder comprised of innumerable chronometers. They were miniature worlds in disconnect. Microcosmic heartbeats independently piloted each ticking gadget.

One timepiece enclosed in a glass dome was particularly pleasing. It displayed a flashy interior with a multitude of exposed brass wheels, which whirled and pivoted in prearranged agreement. Unified by the touch from a seemingly phantom and enigmatic power, these time pieces became members in a symphony of synchronized activity. They pitched. They spun. They twirled. They turned. They were refinement. They were movement in elegance. They were the allied assurance that set order resided somewhere in this chance world of the unpredictable and the unruly.

Impulsively, Jed reached for the fragile dome of the glass timepiece, however, Barbara's maternal instincts made for quick reaction and cradled the squirming child in a firm yet gentle embrace.

"Seems to be in decent shape wouldn't you say," she managed to say while holding firmly onto the squirming tot like a hook fastened to the mouth of a tormented trout.

"Indeed. It is in remarkable shape." Looking at the struggling mother and child, he good-naturedly quipped, "I'd say you were as well."

"Would you care for me to spruce it up for you? A bit of oil wouldn't hurt."

Barbara nodded her approval. "That would be nice. My mother would like that."

"You may pick it up next Tuesday," the clock smith replied and then tearing a numbered ticket in two, he attached one to the Seth Thomas wall clock and handing the other to Barbara.

"I'll see you Tuesday then. Thank you," she responded politely and then made an exit.

A lengthy ringing of the shop's bell announced their departure. The late autumn sunlight painfully stole Barbara's sight, and she raised her left hand to shade her eyes. With Jed in tow, Jed paused, sneezed, and then proceeded with his mom to the car.

Wrestling Jed into his car seat, Barbara fastened the safety harness. Earlier that day Barbara had given thought to last evening. Lately, Jed had displayed curious behavior. There were little games that occupied him. Barbara had taught him games like "So Big" and "I'm a little Tea Pot," but she could not figure out where he learned to play "Itsy-bitsy Spider" and "This little Piggy went to Market."

Perhaps Jed had learned it by watching television or from someone at play in the neighborhood? But then there were the songs. Surely "Farmer in the Dell" is a tune everyone would know. But "Pony Boy"?

Barbara fastened her seatbelt. Engaging the directional, she pulled into traffic. Since the episode with the clock, she had fondly been thinking about her mother. Her mother had always been a caring, loving person, even when her father departed for the west coast. When he moved away, he took a used car, a younger woman, and left the wreckage of a maimed marriage and a broken heart.

Barbara had been too young to remember all the sordid details, but she could remember that her mother appeared hurt and distant. But gradually the void and unpleasantness disappeared. Her mother was moved to tenderness and affection, which comes with the kind of love that binds a mother with her child.

Barbara glanced at the light and waited for it to turn green.

At first times were difficult but somehow, they endured. Her mother worked two jobs to pay the bills and often they went without the little extras. Once while passing a clothing store, Barbara spied a beautiful pink dress with lace prominently display in the store showcase. Barbara often dreamed about wearing it. Every time Barbara passed the display window she would pause and imagine putting on the pink laced dress. She fancied herself dancing about like a whirling dervish. She would spin and twirl around an elegant ballroom like Cinderella, the girl in the storybook that her mother read about at night before bedtime.

But this was just her imagination. It was make-believe for they never had enough money to pay for all the bills let alone something so frivolous and expensive as a silly old pink laced dress.

One day it was her birthday and her mother presented Barbara with a gift. It was a large package wrapped in lovely wrapping paper with a rose-colored bow. To her wonderment and delight, inside was the pink laced dress. She put it on and at once danced about the house in rapture. There were times when Barbara would earnestly beg her mother to allow her to wear the dress before bedtime. Relenting, her mother would rock in the old wooden rocker with Barbara perched on her knee. They sang foolish songs or read silly stories filled with charm and adventure.

Yet, there were times when Barbara would wake sobbing. She had dreamed of being alone in the dessert. Her mother had deserted her like her father. She would call for her mother, but nothing would come out. There was only silence. Barbara would try running home, but she could only move in slow motion and never got anywhere. The dream was real and frightening. But she could take heart while she sat on her mother's lap, dressed in pink lace, rocking to the lyrics of "Pony Boy." Reassured in the soothing comfort of her mother's arms, she would predictably fall asleep.

A horn honked and Barbara noticed that the light was green.

When they returned home Barbara opened the door and Jed raced through the kitchen and into the dining room. He paused momentarily in front of the bureau that held the collection of family portraits. Giggling, Jed howled at them "Piggy Market, Piggy Market" and then ran up the stairs and into the nursery. Unsurprising, the door closed with a loud bang.

Walking into the dining room Barbara set the car keys on the bureau and glanced at the picture of her mother amid the family photographs. She lifted the picture by its silver frame. The picture was taken years ago when her mother was young and first married to her father. Her mother was undeniably attractive.

That was before her bout with cancer which sapped her of her strength and snatched her of her natural beauty. Shortly thereafter, Barbara became pregnant, and her mother so looked forward to her first grandchild. Despite the suffering brought on by the malignancy, she became giddy with expected joy. As Barbara's due date came closer, all her mother wished was a little more time. But a little more time was not in the offering.

In the weeks and months that followed she fought and suffered but it was not to be. Her pendulum stopped and her chronometer ceased to tick. Wish as she might, there was no phantom and enigmatic power in the doctor's satchel that could protect her. The disease had finally taken its toll and that refined, elegant lady who Barbara came to know and love, ceased to be. That was just one week before her son Jed was born.

Holding the picture closer, her mother appeared life-like, so real. Her long red hair was drawn into a tight bun and rested at the nape of her neck.

Ringed about her throat were a string of white natural pearls and from each ear dangled a matching set of earrings.

Barbara recalled how she loved to watch her mother get prepared for a date night with her father. She would comb her long red hair to one side with a glossy turtle shell brush. It rippled like red silk in the light. She would then neatly curl it up and fasten it into a bun at the nape of her neck. Next, her mother would take out a white string of pearls from the jewelry box. Placing them around her neck, Barbara would help fasten them from behind. Next came the earrings. It was part of the ritual and always the same. She would first fasten a pearl earring to her left ear and then the other to her right.

There was the brief reading of a story, a song, a prayer, a hug and then a kiss good night. There was the oft repeated "Night, night, don't let the bugs bite. If they do, hit them with grandma's shoe until they are black and blue." It was followed by a giggle, a snicker, or a snort.

Her mother would always leave the bedroom door ajar; just enough to let a reassuring shaft of soft light enter the room. The lingering scent of sweet lavender perfume, her mother's favorite, was the last thing that Barbara remembered before she drifted off to sleep.

"Mother," she quietly grieved. "Why did you have to leave me ... so soon. So all alone." Barbara brushed away moisture from her cheeks.

~ ~ ~ ~ ~

Days passed when Barbara unexpectedly awoke. She had been drifting with the rise and fall of that warm distant tide resembling sleep. Coming from the neighboring room was the soft familiar voice of Jed.

"Piggy market ... piggy market."

Debating whether to rise, Barbara finally donned a robe, slipped on slippers, and wandered into the bathroom. The sudden rush of water signaled the dispatch of the nightly nuisance and she found herself standing in the dim light just outside Jed's bedroom. Faint laughter issued from within. Barbara peeked through a gap in the door and glimpsed Jed balanced on the corner rocking chair with one foot raised. He had one of his toes between his thumb and index finger. Shaking it with a continuous giggle he ordered, "This piggy to market." Then he touched each additional toe adding, "and this, and this and this piggy too."

In a fixed voice she summoned him, "Jed, why aren't you asleep?"

Barbara detected the hollow drumming of little feet on the hard wooden floor as Jed sprinted across the nursery to the safety of his bed. She opened the door and clicked on the light. She had ample time to study him as he leaped headlong into his wrinkled bedding and placed the pillow over his head.

"Piggy market," he squealed in a muffled voice. "Piggy market."

"It's too late for Piggy market," she remarked with feigned irritation. "It's very late and you must go to bed."

"Blankie. Blankie," he implored.

Barbara glanced around the room and discovered his "blankie" draped over the arm of the old wooden rocker in the corner. Retrieving it, she handed it to Jed who eagerly secured it in his outstretched hands. Immediately fingering each fold, Jed came to the one corner which was slightly wet and discolored. Thrusting one corner into his mouth, he began nibbling it and mumbling, "Piggy market. Piggy market."

"No piggy market tonight," Barbara replied.

Thus decreed, she then bent down and kissed Jed on the forehead. As she turned to leave, Barbara thought she could detect a slight trace of lavender. It was reminiscent of the variety of perfume her mother use to wear for special occasions. Ever since the clock episode Barbara was touched by random thoughts, and feelings. Of late, she was a troubled escapee from her past.

"Jed, could we talk about the songs you sing and games you play?" she asked. "Where did you learn them?"

Jed looked at his mother with a blank expression and slowly he grinned, "The lady."

"Lady? Which lady?"

"The night lady."

Before Barbara could make sense of it, Jed sprang from his bed and ran out the nursery door. Down the hallway he sprinted until he came to the staircase.

With one hand on the railing, Jeb planted one foot followed by the other. Quickly he rhythmically descended the stairs one stair at a time, thump-thump, thump-thump, thump-thump.

Barbara tried to keep up, but Jed was too nimble-footed for her. By the time she reached the hallway, Jed was halfway down the staircase. Quickly she snapped on a light just as Jed reached the bottom stair.

"Jed, where are you going?" she yelled as his little form disappeared downstairs into the obscurity of the dining room. When Barbara entered the dining room and turned on the lights, Jed had already slid a chair in front of the bureau and was climbing up.

"Jed," she implored, "What on earth are you doing?"

He squealed, "Night Lady," and then he pointed to a picture on the bureau. Drawing closer Barbara noticed that Jed was pointing to one of the pictures on the bureau. There was a sudden motionlessness, except for the steady tick-tocking of the Seth Thomas clock hanging on the wall. Barbara gently grasped the picture frame and pointed to the image of her mother.

"You mean this lady?" Barbara asked.

Jed nodded. "She plays with me at night."

Stunned, Barbara stood in silence. In her hand she held the picture of her dead mother. Tears formed in the lower rim of her eyes and once breached, they slid down her cheeks. A slow muted sobbing followed.

"Mother," she sighed. "I am so lonely since you went away." Hugging the picture, Barbara imagined she detected the scent of lavender.

From the darkness behind her came a voice, "Now don't cry, my dear. You see? ... I never really left, now did I?"

Then Barbara could hear the faint lyrics of a familiar song from long ago.

"Pony Boy. Pony Boy. Won't you be my pony boy..."

Barbara began to sing the lyrics softly to herself. Turning around Barbara caught a glimpse of a beautiful red-haired woman dressed in an evening gown, pearl necklace and matching earrings ascending the stairs. An amusing young boy was following her up the staircase one step at a time. Giggling he was saying,

"Piggy market, piggy market."

Barbara brushed the tears away and followed the two figures up the staircase.

The dining room clock tolled once and continued with a steady tick-tocking. Upstairs the tender voice of a young boy was heard singing softly. In the background his singing merged with the steady tempo of the click-clicking of an old wooden rocker.

"Pony boy, pony boy," a young boy sang. "Won't you be my pony boy?"

The voice from the older woman joined in, "Don't say no, cause here we go, riding down the lane. Giddy-up, giddy-up, pony boy."

In the nursery mirror, the reflection of a young girl wearing a pink laced dress appeared in the doorway. She looked to the old wooden rocker where sat a red-haired woman with the young boy on her lap. They rhythmically rocked back and forth.

Click-click. Click-click. Click-click

"Again," the young boy giggled to the red-haired woman. "Pony boy again!"

"Ok, let us sing pony boy again," she tenderly replied.

The girl in the pink laced dress whirled about and then begged earnestly, "Piggy Market too? Piggy Market too?"

"Yes," the night visitor smiled affectionately, "Piggy Market too."

Acknowledgements

I would like to thank my wife Susan for her insight, perspective and patience. I would also like to thank my editor Cindy Casey, who helpfully suggests and revises, guiding thoughts and language into the printed word. Finally, I would like to express my gratitude to Lenny Hall, a friend and skilled photographer, for the reproduction image for the cover and my author portrait.

ABOUT THE AUTHOR

Mark A. Clarke grew up in Upstate New York. Enlisting in the United States Army during the Vietnam War, he served in an Airborne Infantry Regiment in Europe.

Mark earned a bachelor's degree in English Education at SUNY Oswego, a master's degree at Saint Rose and post graduate studies in a PhD program at Syracuse University. Studying Anglo-American literature for a semester in London, he met and discussed the works of Kingsley Amis, Ruth Fainlight and Gordon M. Williams.

Mark taught for more than thirty years in a public school in Columbia County, where he met his wife. He is a member of the American Legion, 509th Parachute Infantry Association and the 82nd Airborne Association and has served with numerous civic organizations that pertain to veteran issues as a member, lector and in leadership positions.

His first book was *COLUMBIA: Those Who Honorably Served*, which recounted the lives and service of 200 veterans from Columbia County. His second book, *Harriet's Egg*, is an enchanting children's story about kindness, determination, and the power of motherly love. Mark's third book – his second children's book – is *Digger Digger Digger*, a delightfully crafted story in poetic verse that journeys into a child's world of make-believe.

Mark and his wife of 40 years have two children and make their home in Ghent, New York, while enjoying winters in Florida. He stays active in his community and in his spare time writes.

Mark loves to hear from his readers. If you want to chat about your time in the military, life in the Adirondacks or just to say, Hi! ... his email address is clarkemark509@gmail.com.